Colter, Cyrus

The rivers of Eros

The Rivers of Eros

Cyrus Colter

THE SWALLOW PRESS INC.
CHICAGO

First Edition
  First Printing

Published by
The Swallow Press Incorporated
1139 South Wabash Avenue
Chicago, Illinois 60605

This book is printed on 100% recycled paper

LIBRARY OF CONGRESS CATALOG NUMBER 73-189191
ISBN 0-8040-0563-X

To

Imogene

To

Mary Elizabeth

To

David Ray

The irrational, the human nostalgia, and the absurd that is born of their encounter—these are the three characters in the drama that must necessarily end with all the logic of which an existence is capable.

—CAMUS, *The Myth of Sisyphus*

When one is on the soil of one's ancestors, most anything can come to one. A black woman once saw the mother of Christ and drew her in charcoal on the courthouse wall.

—TOOMER, *Fern*

Chapter One

MAY 1971. After the coldest spring in memory, the shoots, the shrubs, and the flowers were burgeoning again at last. In the afternoon Clotilda had moved her new sewing machine out into the little sun room that jutted off the ground floor of her house and sat there in the sunlight surrounded by a thicket of plants—philodendrons, rose trees, ferns, rubber plants—doing trial runs on what the salesman had vowed to her was the "world's most versatile automatic zig-zag sewing machine." She discovered that practising eyelet buttonholes on the automatic buttonholer was fun, and she intended next to drop in one of the new discs and do some fancy piping or embroidered borders. Her face, fleshy, slack, a dark walnut-brown, showed by occasional, intent lip-biting frowns her zeal to master this new investment, for, except for the three roomers she kept, she made her living by sewing. And if people bragged on the work she turned out on the old needle-jabber she had just traded in, they would see something now for sure. Her roomers were vital to her, though, and for more reasons than one. True, in this big house their rents paid *her* rent; but, more importantly, they were the kind of people, if she must have roomers, she was proud to have—"educated" people.

She and her two grandchildren slept downstairs. Lester was eleven and had a bunk off the pantry, and Adeline (Addie), sixteen and a half now, shared with her the first-floor back bedroom. They were her dead daughter's—Ruby's—children, as prized by Clotilda as her own daughter had been although Ruby was her only child. Lester, rough and ready, was really no worry. But Addie—there was no describing her feelings toward Addie. They were agonized and ever-changing : there was love, pride, fear, pity, self-examination, furtive tenderness, bewilderment, guilt—always guilt.

Now, in the living room out of her view, Clotilda heard the front door open, then close.

"Ah, ha! I saw you sitting there—I saw you from the street." It was the low purring voice of Miss Letitia Dorsey, a roomer, as she stalked into the sun room. She was a giraffe-tall octoroon with saucer eyes, and wore a mound of artificial sprigs and lilies on her head for a hat.

"Tish, honey!" Clotilda's darksome features fragmented in smiles. "I was just tryin' out this new gadget, girl. Lord, it does everything."

Letitia—a stenographer—carried a package which she clamped under her arm in order to pull off her long white gloves. Though forlornly past fifty-one, she still kept her voice low and velvety. "D'you know what I've got here?" She patted the package. "Guess. Go on—guess. Seven yards of the most beautiful light wool you ever saw—for a suit."

"Ooooh!—let me see." Clotilda shifted her heavy bulk in the chair reaching for the proffered package. She took her scissors, snipped the twine, and peeled back the wrapping paper. "Oh, Tish! You got taste, girl. Wow." The fabric was lovely—sky-blue and soft. "My, ain't you fancy."

Letitia's face, pale and long, beamed through her white powder. "I'm going to be your very first customer, Clo!—on your new machine."

"No you ain't, either." Clotilda laughed and picked up a cigarette. "I'm startin' my baby a spring coat—tonight."

Letitia pouted. "Oh, Addie got the jump on me."

"No, she didn't—she don't know a thing about it. She needs a coat bad, though, poor kid." Clotilda ran her hand through her stiff, grey hair. "I sneaked the goods in here last week. It's yellow, bright yellow, for that child."

"Oh, that's sweet, Clo!" Letitia's long eyelashes fluttered wistfully.

"When she comes home from school, I'm gonna haul it out and surprise her," Clotilda snickered. "But I'll have to take her measurements again. Lord, is she fillin' out!—hips all round, and little bubbies swellin' out."

"Oh, Clo." Miss Letitia flushed.

"But she's still a baby to me—always will be."

Letitia sighed. "Yes, I know."

There was a silence now between them, as much history passed through their minds.

"Well, will I be next, then, Clo?" Letitia's long thin frame towered over the sewing machine.

"You'll be next, darlin'—indeed you will. Say, you're gettin' to be a regular fashion plate, you know it? No wonder Rev. Claiborne's always eyin' you." Clotilda guffawed, showing her stubby, yellow teeth.

"That old buzzard!" Letitia cried. "One foot in the grave and he's the freshest thing in Chicago."

"And can preach the loveliest sermon—makes 'em cry. Watch him, girl—watch him . . . he's a sly fox." Clotilda wrapped up the fabric.

"I'm dining *out* tonight, Clo!"

"Oh, no, now!—who with?"

"Doctor Wilson."

"Aw, honey. That poor old fella's old enough to be your daddy. He was married for almost fifty years. You ain't thinkin' about gettin' mixed up with somebody like that, are you? He ain't a doctor. He's one of them chiropodists—a corn trimmer. Probably broke besides."

There was a touchy pause. "Clo, who said anything about getting mixed up with him?"

"Now, don't get huffy and sensitive. Tish, honey, I want you to get a *nice* man. I was married for nearly thirty years myself. It ain't no joke, girl; and Eugene was a good provider—worked every day of his life, worked himself to death, in fact. So I know what I'm talkin' about. I don't want you to get mixed up with some old broken down——"

"Oh, Clo—I don't pay any attention to you." Letitia sighed and picked up her package.

Clotilda brightened. "What you going to wear?"

"I don't quite know yet—maybe my good black dress. We're going downtown."

"Well, whatever it is, sugar, you'll look good in it." Clotilda crushed out her cigarette and got up. "I gotta start gettin' some food together around here—the kids'll be comin' in pretty soon. Lord, this diet Dr. Weaver's got me on is killin' me. But I'm down to a hundred 'n seventy-two. Ain't bad, eh?" Her dark hands pressed her abdomen. "Streamlined, girl."

Letitia fluttered her lashes and tittered. "Oh, Clo!"

"But that Lester—Oh, that Lester. Can he eat! He oughta get tired just carryin' it around." They went into the living room, which was plain, but neat, and, like the sun room, contained a forest of plants. The furniture, though sturdy, was drab, and arranged around a massive old piano—a Knabe grand—given Clotilda years before by a wealthy white woman she had sewed for.

"But remember—Lester's growing, Clo." Letitia paused at the foot of the stairs.

"And how—up and out. He pushes outa his clothes as fast as I can put 'em on him. He's doing better in school this time, though—but still horses around a lot."

Letitia started upstairs. "I'll see you, Clo—I'm going to get in and get a bath before the Rover boys come." Both burst out laughing.

"Don't you dare talk about my roomers!" cried Clotilda.

"Clo, have you seen Hammer's new glasses?"

"Merciful Father! Saw him with 'em on last night. Did you *ever*?"

"How does he keep those things pinched on his big flat nose?"

"Lord only knows—there's a little chain attached to 'em. I guess so if they come *un*pinched, and fall off, that little chain'll catch 'em."

Letitia, a skinny five-feet-eleven on the stairs, tittered again. "Honest, he's a scream."

Clotilda stood at the foot of the stairs in bedroom slippers, her dark, dropsied legs without stockings. "And he's still at that dad-gum book, you know—been writin' it for nearly two years now. He's gonna give us the real lowdown on the Negro, honey—tracin' him back to Africa, back to a thousand-year civilization, he says. It's a good thing he got outa the Post Office when he did—retired. He couldn't do both—he stays down at the Library practically all day now."

"Mr. Neeley kids him about it every chance he gets," Letitia said.

"Oh, Neeley—he would. He's jealous of Hammer, that's all; *has* been—ever since he took that room next to Hammer and found out he was workin' on a book. And Neeley's a college graduate, girl. Admits it—Parks College, down in North Carolina. But he never got any further than the Post Office all these years. That's what's eatin' *him*. I don't think Hammer even graduated from college—do you?"

"I doubt it," Letitia said. "He probably had a year or two."

Clotilda paused in thought. "But on the other hand, how can he be writin' a history book if he didn't? Don't it take some college education to do that?"

Letitia smiled. "I would imagine. But getting a book published is something else again."

"Aw, I see." Clotilda's eyes opened. "I see—you don't always get it published. Lord, I know now what Neeley's hopin'. No wonder poor Hammer's slavin' so down at that Library—no wonder."

"You have to give him credit," Letitia laughed, continuing upstairs. "I'll see you later, Clo."

Clotilda went thoughtfully into the kitchen.

At four o'clock Lester came in from school. He was a chunky, brown boy with his hair in a modest Afro. He loped along the corridor, by-passing Clotilda in the kitchen, and went to his cubicle in the back. Suddenly, on entering his room, he broke into a wild dance, bleating out snatches of a bawdy song, as his knees gyrated and his elbows seesawed up and down:

"I wanta big-legged Mama!
Want her l-o-n-n-n-g and t-a-l-l-l-!
I wanta big-legged Mama! . . . . . "

Clotilda yelled from the kitchen. "Lester! . . . Lester! . . . You cut out all that old low-down carryin'-on in there. D'you hear me?—and come in here."

Lester went in the kitchen.

"Where'n the world did you learn *that*, now? Honest to Goodness, I never saw anything like you school kids now'days."

Lester was surveying the pans on the stove.

"Nice educated boys don't carry on like that, Lester, and sing those kinda songs. Now, do they? You wanta be an educated man when you grow up, don't you?"

"Yes'm." Lester walked over to the stove and peered into a pan. "Whut we gonna have, Grammaw?"

"Just listen—'whut we gonna have.' Don't you ever think about nothin' but stuffin' your gut?"

Lester looked at her. "Let's have some pot roast, Grammaw."

Clotilda threw her head back and laughed. "Boy, I'll 'pot-roast' you up side the head if you don't get outa my face. Say, I gotta job for you. When Miss Dorsey upstairs gets out of the bathroom, I want you to go up there and mop that bathroom floor good, and put new paper on the shelves in the medicine cabinet, and clean the mirror. Will you do that for me?"

"Yes'm—can I have a piece of cheese cake, and some milk?"

"All right—you go take off your school clothes, and I'll have you a nice piece of cheese cake and a big glass of milk here when you get back. *That* oughta hold you. Lord, boy."

Lester started out of the kitchen. Then he turned around. "You told Addie to do the mirror and shelves last Saturday," he said.

Clotilda stopped peeling a potato and looked at him—knowing he was right and that Addie had ignored her; it was the same old story, over and over again, having to make excuses for Addie, to lie for her again. "Oh," she said, "I had some other things for her to do—she couldn't get to it."

Lester clumped out.

Clotilda finished the potatoes and lifted her weight up onto a stool at the sink to string and snap the beans. She was uneasy, distressed—knowing she shouldn't have lied to Lester; that she couldn't get away with it much longer. He was smart, plenty smart. His grades might not be so good sometimes, but it was only because he played around so much. He wasn't dumb, not by a long sight. He knew Addie seldom did as she was told and that she never got bawled out about it, either—like he did sometimes. What in God's name could be done for Addie? Clotilda knew she had never been able to do, or even say, anything harsh to the girl—and probably never would. This failure frightened her; today you had to ride herd on a youngster coming up in Chicago—especially a girl. But she hadn't done it with Addie. Addie was so hard to understand, and harder to talk to; kept things to herself now that she had no mother. How Ruby had loved that child!—no more than Addie loved her, though. Ruby couldn't move for her; used to laugh and say Addie wouldn't even let her go to the bathroom; would start squalling and just raise Ned. God did some funny things in this world; you'd drive yourself batty trying to figure them out. Ruby gone nine years already! Could it be that long?—Addie was only seven and a half, and Lester just turned two. If Addie at the time had been nearer Lester's age, it wouldn't have hit so hard—Lester of course remembered nothing. But Addie was always smart for her age anyhow—so being seven and a half was really more like ten or eleven. Now at sixteen she wouldn't talk about her mother—about any and everything else, yes, but not about Ruby, kept it locked inside her. But it had made her bitter, headstrong and wild-acting; yet she laughed a lot—was real flighty sometimes. Jesus, have mercy on them all!

Lester was back now—for his cheese cake and milk, and was then sent off upstairs with a mop and pail.

Soon the telephone in the hallway rang. Clotilda climbed down from her stool and went in to answer it. It was Addie calling from Thelma Smith's; she was going to eat dinner there; Thelma had asked her. It was plain to Clotilda from Addie's manner that she had not phoned for permission, but only to inform.

Clotilda hesitated. " . . . Okay then, honey," she finally said. "But you oughta be home by dark. You'll have to leave right after you eat—and catch a cab. Have you got enough money? All right. All right, then, baby."

Frowning, she returned to the kitchen. Addie *would* be late, when she wanted to measure her for her coat. And her homework— as usual it was the last thing Addie thought about. And the boys would soon start calling—tying up the phone; if she acted so grown-up already, what would she be like in a couple of years?— when she was eighteen! Clotilda thought if she couldn't find it in her heart to be tighter on Addie, she at least ought to lighten up on Lester. One of these days he was going to get wise and maybe hate her. Lester was a good boy, so much easier to understand and handle than Addie. Should he be punished for it?

When Lester finished cleaning the bathroom he came down-stairs at the same moment Titus Neeley, the roomer, was coming in at the front door. Neeley was short, with a scrawny neck, and light-skinned. He put his head in at the kitchen and grinned at Clotilda and Lester. "Smells good! Good ole-fashioned boiled dinner. Good evening, Mrs. Pilgrim. Good evening, Lester." By habit Neeley spoke so fast his speech came in a spate of words loosed like a clip of automatic rifle fire. He was fifty-five years old, nervous and aggressive.

Clotilda had whirled around. "Why, Mr. Neeley—you here already?"

"Off at four this week—mail's light." The words flew and stopped. Then he looked at the stove again. "Hmmmmmmm-uh! Smells good. Green beans, ham hocks, potatoes, and corn on the cob. Smells good enough to eat. Hmmmmmmm-uh!" Lester viewed him gravely.

"Why don't you eat with me and Lester?" Clotilda said. "Addie's over to a girl friend of hers and Miss Dorsey's eating out."

"Just had dinner, Mrs. Pilgrim, but wish I hadn't—or lunch, or breakfast!" Little Neeley clipped off the words, thrust up his chin and, like a banty rooster, crowed a laugh at the ceiling.

"You're sure welcome," Clotilda insisted. Lester sighed.

"Is Mr. Hammer in yet?" asked Neeley, glancing at the stairs.

"No, he hasn't come in." Clotilda brought a pan back to the stove.

Little Neeley's eyes twinkled. "I got bad news for *him*." He laughed up again.

"How's that? Bad news? . . . "

"About his Negro history. Ha-ha-ha-ha! I bet him about a little item he's putting in it—that he was wrong. And he is!"

Clotilda studied him.

"He's claiming Haile Selassie for us." Neeley laughed straight up. "But it seems Haile's not claiming *us*! Haile says he and his people, Abyssinians, are some kind of dark Semites—descended in the Bible from *Shem,* not Ham! Ha-ha-ha-ha! I checked on it today down at the Library. Wait'll Hammer hears!"

Clotilda at the stove, her dark face and stiff grey hair damp from perspiration, was glum. "It's a wonder you didn't run into Mr. Hammer down at the Library," she said. "He practically lives there."

"I know it—I know it," Neeley shot back, still laughing. "Big deal!" Then he hurried upstairs.

Clotilda turned to Lester. "Did you study that in school?—about Haile Selassie?"

"No'm—not yet."

"I wonder if Neeley's right?"

"I don't know, Grammaw."

"You 'don't know'—boy, you ain't learnin' a thing. Poor Mr. Hammer," she sighed. "All right, come on, let's eat. I bet you 'know' *that.*" She laughed and kneaded Lester's head. "Did you wash those hands of yours?"

"Yes'm."

"Let me see—hold 'em out."

Lester put out his hands.

"Okay."

They sat down at the kitchen table, bowed their heads, and Clotilda mumbled a quick grace. As they were eating, Letitia came downstairs dressed for her dinner engagement. Despite her big, excited eyes and svelte attire she looked tired, wistful, standing in the kitchen door.

"Come on. Let me see you, Tish, honey," Clotilda said. Letitia, simpering, stepped into full view. "Ain't you a lovely sight!—My! What time's he coming?"

" . . . Oh"—Letitia's long lashes quivered—"Dr. Wilson had to see some patients coming in late. I called a cab—we'll save time if I go there."

"Why, sure—that's all right," Clotilda said, laughing.

Letitia smiled now at Lester. "Lester, you did a real nice job upstairs. Clo, the bathroom's shining."

Lester was busy with his corn on the cob. Clotilda smiled across the table at him. "Oh, Lester's my buddy. He knows Grandma's gettin' old, and gets tired easy—so he pitches in and helps her wherever he can."

Lester laid aside his ravaged cob and reached for a piece of corn bread.

Soon a horn sounded outside. "Oh, that's my cab, probably," Letitia said, swishing to the front door. "See you later! I won't be out late."

"Okay, honey—have a good time, now." Clotilda sighed and resumed eating.

"When's Addie coming home, Grammaw?" Lester said.

Clotilda started, then said with tense control, "Oh, before long, I guess. I told her to leave Thelma's before dark."

They finished dinner.

"Want me to help you with the dishes?" Lester asked.

"Why, sure, honey, if you want to—you can dry 'em."

"I bet Addie don't get home by dark," Lester said.

"Oh, yes, she will."—Clotilda spoke before she thought. "But maybe they had dinner late."

They had gotten up from the table when the telephone in the hallway rang. "Get it," Clotilda nodded. Lester went out to the phone.

"Hello . . ." she heard him say. "No—not yet—I don't know—Yeah—Okay." He hung up, and came back. "Jack Griffin," he said, yawning.

"Oh, Lord—Addie's so haughty with that boy she's about to drive him stone crazy. What'd you tell him?"

"—Didn't know when she'd be back."

Clotilda looked at him.

"Well, I didn't, Grammaw."

"Dear Jesus—that Addie! Well, that's all right, Lester." Clotilda began clearing the table.

Outside it was nearly dark.

They carried the dishes over to the sink, where Clotilda started the hot water. Lester, in blue denims and sweater, hung a clean dish towel over his arm and stood waiting, his round, brown face impassive. "Grammaw, what's wrong with Addie?" he soon said, taking up the plate Clotilda had just washed and scalded.

Clotilda spoke quietly. "What do you mean 'what's wrong' with her?—nothin's wrong with her."

"She don't mind you—don't do nothin' you say."

"Oh, Addie don't mean anything by that. She's just a young girl havin' her first dates, thinks she knows a little more'n she actually does. *You* won't ever be like that, because you're a boy. It's different with girls, Lester—they're headstrong sometimes. I was myself, when I was comin' along. Addie'll be all right."

Lester continued drying dishes. Finally he said, "Sometimes in the bedroom there she talks to herself—do you ever hear her? Talks about her fine new clothes, and her big swimming pool, and bosses her maids around."

Clotilda again threw her head back and laughed. "Oh—that! Why, that's nothin'. Any young girl daydreams like that—especially when she's gettin' to be a young lady. Some boys do, too—don't you?"

Lester shook his head emphatically. "No'm."

"Oh, Lester," Clotilda sighed. They finished the dishes in silence.

At almost eight o'clock Ambrose Hammer came in with a sheaf of newspapers under his arm and lugging a bulging brief case. He was a tall, black man—and wore long, spreading sideburns down his face. The tiny chain on his pince-nez dangled at his temple precariously as he closed the door and gazed around at Clotilda and Lester who were now watching television in the living room.

"Why, Mr. Hammer!" Clotilda laughed. "Say, you're loaded down there."

"Good evenin', friends." Hammer smiled gravely and looked down at the brief case. "Yes, the material accumulates."

"Well, how're you gettin' along with it?—Lord, you'll kill yourself on that book."

"Oh, it's goin' good—the worst's over." He gave a slight, satisfied lift of his shoulders and elevated his eyebrows twice, as the chain on his pince-nez shimmied.

"Goodness, don't your eyes get tired—doin' all that reading?"

"Not much—not much, Mrs. Pilgrim."

"I see you got some new glasses, there." Clotilda kept a straight face.

" . . . Yes." Hammer momentarily averted his gaze. "I thought maybe I ought to have an extra pair around . . . ." He turned to Lester. "How're you, young man?"

"All right," Lester said.

"Mr. Neeley was asking for you, earlier," Clotilda smiled.

"Was he?" Hammer was casual and glanced up the stairs.

"Yes—he's up there."

He looked at her quizzically. "Well, I gotta little more work to do tonight," he soon said, starting toward the stairs. He turned and smiled. "I'm into the nineteen twenties now, you know. The situation of the Negro is changing fast—after the first World War. There was the big exodus North—epoch-making. I want to make it dramatic, of course—make it stand out, Mrs. Pilgrim. I'm gettin' down to the pay-off now."

"You gonna put this book out, Mr. Hammer?—sell it?" Clotilda's face showed anxiety.

"That's the aim of scholarship . . . of research, Mrs. Pilgrim—to disseminate knowledge." He stood even taller.

"Oh," Clotilda said, gaping.

Hammer mounted the stairs.

When the television western was over, Clotilda turned abruptly to Lester. "Go call Addie," she said. "And tell her to come home right now. And I mean *now*."

Lester looked at her; then got up and went to the hallway telephone. He dialed, and soon she heard him talking: "Grammaw says for you t'come home." There was exasperation in his voice. "I don't care—she says *now*. No, not any 8:30. *Now*." He hung up and returned to the living room.

"What'd she say?"

"Wanted to stay till 8:30." Lester lay back in his chair. "I told her t'come now."

Clotilda gazed off in space. "Can you beat that!"

Lester watched her. "Grammaw, why're you scared of Addie?"

She caught her breath. "Lester, are you crazy?—'scared' of her. The idea." She reached for a cigarette. "When'd you start havin' brain storms?" Then she sighed.

Lester turned the television dial to another station, and they watched an inprogress drama. After that he went back to his room to do homework—leaving Clotilda immersed in thought.

It was nine o'clock when Addie arrived.

She burst in at the front door with an armload of books and wearing a red plastic shoulder purse. "Hi!" she cried, kicking the door shut with her heel. Her young face was very light-brown and freckled, her stiff red hair worn in a high Natural.

Clotilda sat under the floor lamp near the piano pretending to read the evening paper. She looked over her spectacles at Addie and said nothing.

Addie started through the living room to the back. "Oh, I'm so tired!" she wailed. "That Thelma!—she talks you crazy! Crazy!"

"—And what did you talk *her*?" Clotilda said.

Addie stopped and looked at her, then breathed wearily and continued into the hallway out of sight.

"Just a minute, Addie—I'm talkin' to you. Where're your manners?" Clotilda removed her glasses and transferred her weight forward in the chair.

Addie came back—she was wearing thick high heels—and, smiling, moaned, "*Now,* what've I done?—I'm a little bit late and you're mad at me!"

"No—I ain't, Addie. I'm sad. I'm sad because you don't mind me any more—don't do a thing I say. Even Lester notices it."

Addie dumped her books and purse in a chair and stood impatiently, her fists rammed in her jacket pockets.

"First of all," Clotilda said, "I don't like you goin' by Thelma's so much after school. You know half the time her mother ain't home from work yet. You get over there and never wanta come home. Why is it?"

Addie laughed, then sighed again. "Oh, Grandma—you wouldn't understand!" She searched for words. " . . . There's just so much going on with the kids all the time that—"

"—That I wouldn't understand, eh?"

"Well, maybe you'd understand . . . you just wouldn't be interested."

"Now, just think a minute—how do you know? Just how do you know that? Sit down there."—Clotilda pointed to the chair in front of Addie. "Sit down."

Addie, removing the books and purse to the floor, sat in the chair, scooted down, and shot her legs out straight, then kicked off her shoes.

Clotilda watched her—but began coolly. "Now, whatever got it into your head you oughtn't to talk to me?—that I wouldn't be interested? Where'd you get that—huh? Why, some nights when we're layin' back there in the bed, I'd *love* for you to talk t'me—and tell me all about what you have been doin' all day; about the other kids; the teachers; even the boys. But no—what do you do? You turn your back and go on to sleep. *Now* you say I wouldn't be interested." Clotilda leaned forward in her chair. "D'you know one thing, Addie? I'm inclined to believe there's some other reason. Maybe you don't tell me things simply because you don't want me to know 'em. Oh, I don't mean you're doin' anything wrong necessarily when you're out of my sight; but you just don't want me to know what you *are* doin'—even if it ain't wrong. Now, how do you think that makes me feel?—or can you imagine?" Clotilda bolted forward on the edge of her chair and pounded her breast. "I'm your *mother*!—the only one you got, anyhow. I tell you, a young girl oughta have some older person she can talk to. You may think you know ev'rything, but I'm here to tell you y'don't. And you can't say I'm hard on you, either—God'll never forgive me now for bein' so easy with you." Clotilda, all her distress in her face, gazed for a moment out the front window at the lighted street; then turned again to Addie. "Yes—it's true. You just don't tell me things because . . . " She stared.

Addie's finger tips were lightly tapping her lips, to screen a yawn. Finally she smiled, " . . . Maybe I don't want to worry you."

Clotilda's jaw sagged. "Worry me! Worry me about what?"

" . . . Oh, about anything." Addie stood up and uncoiled herself in a tiptoeing stretch. "Grandma, I got math to do yet tonight."

"Addie, you say things just to be mean and contrary. What makes you like that?"

"Oh, Grandma." In exasperation Addie bent to collect her books and purse from the floor. "Can't we talk some other time? I'm beat. Honest, I am!" She looked once at her shoes lying on the floor, then went off down the hallway in her stocking feet.

🌀　　🌀　　🌀　　🌀　　🌀　　🌀

It was after midnight that same night when Clotilda said her brief perfunctory prayers and climbed into bed beside Addie, who had been asleep for almost an hour. They were in their bedroom behind the kitchen; the house was dark and silent—except that through the partly-opened window, and faraway, could be heard an occasional faint roll of thunder and the usual night noises of the city. Lying in bed in the dark seemed always to spur Clotilda's brain to action, gathering up thoughts that the bustle of the day had shooed aside. She would think of yesterday's work unfinished and of tomorrow's which somehow must be done—there was always a deadline.

Hattie Maple had called that morning about the alterations on her dress—a cheap dress, Clotilda thought—and had even sent a beautiful *Vogue* ad for her to copy. On the other hand, she had finished Irene Jones' suit a week ago, but still no word from Irene, and of course no pay. Speaking of pay, the rent had gone up another fifteen dollars—to $225 a month now—and she would have liked in turn to suggest a small raise to Messrs. Neeley and Hammer. But she knew little Neeley would pause and frown, laugh uneasily at the ceiling, then shoot a lot of questions. He might even ask for a new mattress. Better let well-enough alone.

Neeley sometimes wasn't as nice as Hammer, even if Hammer was a little pompous-acting. Hammer didn't mean anything by it; it was that book he was working on that made him feel so important. She heard walking overhead—yes, probably Hammer up there now, she thought; the man couldn't sleep for beating his brains out about that book—Lord! She turned over in bed toward Addie who was sleeping with her face to the wall. In the dark she could hear Addie's breathing, soft and regular, and could feel the slight swelling and falling motion in the blankets over them.

Somewhere, far off, a fire engine siren's caterwauling came through the night, wailing unendingly before finally dying away. Letitia had come in an hour before, saying little about her date, and Clotilda gathered old man Wilson had bored her. But poor Tish didn't get asked out much—unless by that trifling Maceo Sims, ten years younger and always out of work. Sure—he'd be tickled to death to get *any* woman with a steady job. Clotilda felt good that she had talked Tish into giving him the gate. Tish was like a member of the family—even took her meals with them. It was beginning to rain now, not hard, but Clotilda could hear the big solitary drops hitting the window panes. She wondered if she'd have to get up and close the windows; she hoped not, for she loved the fresh wet smell of the grass and shrubs behind her house.

She felt Addie shudder in the bed. For a moment nothing more. Clotilda lay still. Suddenly there was a violent lurch toward the center as Addie lunged up from the pillow. Then it came—a shrieking, piercing scream. Clotilda pitched over, groping for the little chain on the night stand lamp. She jerked it on, flooding the room with yellow light. Addie sat bolt upright in bed, her stiff red Afro hair awry and her eyes in a wild, popping stare. She was mumbling something in a fierce whisper. Clotilda dove for her and smothered her in her arms.

"Baby! baby! baby!" With all her weight she bear-hugged Addie to her and rocked her back and forth. "Now, now—it's all right, it's all right! Grandma won't let anything get you! My baby musta ate too much, that's all—had a nightmare. Now, now— there—there." She tried to stroke Addie's frenzied hair as she rocked her to and fro. "Be quiet, now—be quiet! Poor baby!" Addie, finally realizing where she was, tried to wriggle free. Clotilda held her. Addie panicked and began to fight. Clotilda turned her loose. Addie immediately collected herself and began to smooth down her hair. There was misty perspiration on her forehead, and soon she put both hands to the sides of her face as tears welled in her eyes. But she did not cry. She only sat shuddering.

Clotilda looked stricken. "Aw, come on, honey," she begged. "Let's get up and go in the kitchen. We'll make some cocoa— that'll quiet your nerves and make you sleepy again." Now Clotilda heard much walking overhead and knew upstairs they had all been awakened. It was not the first time.

Addie slowly got out of bed and put on her robe, then went into the little first-floor bathroom. Clotilda, in a flowing kimono, hurried into the kitchen and turned the stove on to heat milk for the cocoa. Soon Addie came in the kitchen; she had washed her face and brushed her hair, and was quiet. She sat on the high stool, her hands limp in her lap, and stared at the floor. Soon she raised her hands to her face again as tears glistened in her eyes. Clotilda went over and stood beside her, then put her arm around her. "Bless your heart," she said without looking at Addie. Both stared ahead and said nothing. Finally Addie glanced up at her with a faint smile; but then almost at once her face was musing, cold.

"Aw, baby." Clotilda hugged and shook her. "Bless your heart. The milk'll be hot in a minute—you'll feel a whole lot better, I'll tell you, when you get some of that hot cocoa down you."

Addie only gazed at the floor.

When the milk was hot, Clotilda, at the kitchen table, poured Addie a cupful over the instant cocoa; then poured herself a cup. Addie got down from the stool now and came over to the table. They both sat and sipped the cocoa in silence.

Soon they heard the floor creak. It was Lester standing in the kitchen door.

"Oh, no!" cried Clotilda, laughing.

Lester, his pajamas buttoned to the throat, stood blinking and rubbing his eyes.

Clotilda's laugh was excessive. "We mighta known it, Addie! —We mighta known it. That boy was 'sleep and dreamt he heard some plates rattlin'. Honest to God—Lester." She continued laughing.

Lester was still blinking and rubbing his eyes. Addie smiled briefly at him.

"Go on, get you a cup, Lester, baby," Clotilda said, "—so you can have some cocoa too. There ain't no pot roast around here, though. Lester, you're a mess. That boy can smell vittles a mile off!" Clotilda kept up her jittery laughter.

Lester brought a cup and saucer back to the table. "Addie woke me up," he said.

Immediately Addie's eyes flashed. There was silence. But soon she laughed. "I did, did I?"

"Yes," Lester said. "— Again."

Clotilda intervened. "Here, Lester—let me fix your cocoa. Now, you kids—we ain't gonna sit up here all night and chit-chat. You gotta go to school in the mornin' and I got two days' work t'do."

Lester stirred his cocoa.

"Oh!—Miss Addie!" Clotilda cried—it had suddenly struck her. "I got somethin' to show *you*!" She jumped up from the table, held her kimono around her, and bustled out of the kitchen. Soon she was back with a big flat paper box. She placed it on a chair, lifted off the lid, and took out the coat fabric—bright yellow. From the table Lester and Addie craned to see.

Addie gave a wan smile. "It's pretty."

Clotilda stood for a moment admiring the fabric herself. Finally she placed it back in the box and turned to them again, her dark face a riot of smiles. "D'you know what I'm gonna do with it?—on my new machine?"

They looked at her.

"I'm gonna make my granddaughter a *bea-y-o-o-o-tiful* spring coat!"

"Oh, Grandma!" Addie jumped up and ran to the box. She put her hand under the fabric and lifted it out. "Oh!—it *is* beautiful! Oh!—Gee!" She whirled around to Clotilda. "When're you going to make it?"

Clotilda grinned and put her fists on her hips, then narrowed her eyes to slits. "I was goin' to get started on it earlier this evenin'. But no—you had to stay practically all night at Thelma's. When you got home I was so put out with you I felt like forgettin' the whole thing—honest t'goodness, I did." She laughed again, as Lester watched her.

"Grandma, we can do the measurements tomorrow night!" Addie cried. "I'll come right home!—*Can't* we?"

"Why, sure we can—if you'll just get here like you say . . . and start mindin' me once in awhile." Clotilda winked at Lester and sat down at the table again to sip her cocoa. Lester had finished his, and sat watching Addie.

"What're you looking at me for like that?" Addie said, suddenly angry.

Lester looked at his grandmother in protest, then again at Addie.

"You've just been sitting there staring at me!" Addie said.

"Aw, no, he hasn't, honey," Clotilda said. "Lester don't look at nobody long." She laughed. "I wish he did—look and listen more at *me*. Ain't that right, Lester? But he's a good boy—I ain't gonna let anybody talk about Lester. No, sir-e-e-e!" She gave another boisterous, nervous laugh.

Addie looked distraught. Tears shone in her eyes again.

Now Clotilda was decisive. "Look, you two—both of you clear outa here. Right now—and get back to bed. We ain't gonna be sittin' up here till the crack of dawn, gabbin'. Okay—vamoose!" She stood up.

Addie and Lester got up; Lester stretched. Finally both went back to their rooms.

Clotilda sat down at the kitchen table again; her hands dropped helplessly in her lap. Once more the house was quiet. She stared at the floor in bleak concentration, then slowly shook her head in a baffled dismay that quickly turned to gloom as old, tenacious memories and fears returned; it seemed she had lived with them an incredibly long, long lifetime. Lord, oh, Lord, she thought. Is there no grace at all for me? I have tried to atone a hundred . . . a thousand times. *Still* is there no grace? And once more, for the thousandth time, her mind stumbled back over the history that had spawned her present wretchedness. It was for this history she had so long sought to atone. For years—from her daily self-communing, her desperation for deliverance—its lurid details had burnt themselves into her brain. She sat awed, fascinated, bewildered, obsessed, by events now thirty-five years in the past.

Chapter Two

IN THE summer of 1935 young Clotilda and her husband, Eugene Pilgrim, had come to Chicago from her home town of Paducah, Kentucky. Eugene, seventeen years older than Clotilda —who then was twenty-five and skinny—was at first not keen on making the move. But they were childless; and, too, he thought he might land a good job. As for Clotilda, she was eager to join her younger sister, Pearl. Pearl had come north as maid with a white family, but she soon married a Chicago boy, Chester Jackson, and started a family. To Clotilda this was progress. So once in Chicago, Eugene took what odd jobs he could find until at last, after much looking, he got steadier work as a sand cutter at the International Harvester foundry. They soon left the rooming house where they had first stayed and rented a drab three-room apartment, furnishing it out of a second-hand furniture store. And it was then Clotilda's boredom set in.

Moreover she came down with the flu during their first winter. Pearl, pregnant again, and leading daughter Irma by the hand and lugging her little Jimmie up in her arm, came every day, despite bad weather, to do house chores and maybe bake a meat loaf or make beef stew for Eugene's dinner later. During these wintry afternoons, while the children slept, the sisters would sit talking in the front room until time for Pearl to go home and get Chester's dinner. The room was small and boxy, with steam on the windows. There were three chairs, a sofa and a radio; and the curtains, dingy white and heavy-hanging, framed windows that needed washing.

Clotilda and Pearl always talked about "home" back in Paducah, and about their Aunt Clem, who had reared them; about the high rents in Chicago, hopes for some new furniture, their pastor, and their husbands. Most of all Clotilda wanted a nice place to live in when Eugene could afford it; a good stove to cook on, and some pretty rugs. Pearl wanted Chester to get a job with hours that would let him go to night school.

"Ches's got a good head on him all right, but he didn't finish high school," she complained. She sat in a straight-back chair at Clotilda's, her ponderous stomach in her lap—yet she was small and gnome-like, with darting eyes and a quick smile. "We didn't finish high school, either," she said to Clotilda, "but it's the *man* that needs the education. Ches could get a better job, maybe. He sure don't like porterin' . . . pushin' a broom. He needs somethin' to give him more confidence in himself."

"You think so?" Clotilda said.

"Yes. If he could go to night school—he ain't but twenty-four —and get his high school diploma, he might get somethin' better. But we ain't got the money right now—with this little one comin'. I told him we oughtn't to have no more kids for awhile." She gave her shrill little laugh. "He's bashful as all get out, but still he won't leave me be when he comes home. Always pattin' me and carryin' on. I call him 'old tomcat!' "

Clotilda cried out laughing. "Oh, no!—not Ches! That ain't Ches!" Convalescent, she was sitting on the sofa in a bathrobe worn over her nightgown. "But it's you," she reproved. "You oughta be more careful if you don't want no more children right now."

Pearl rolled her eyes in playful spite. "Like you, huh? *You* sure must be mighty careful."

Clotilda laughed. "Well, I know how to be all right, if I have to. It sure seems like *you* don't, though." Both laughed and went on to other talk.

Soon Pearl was studying Clotilda's face. "You look better," she said. "—a whole lot better. But you was sure mopin' around here this time last week. That's why I put you to bed."

"Ha! You put me to bed. Ain't that something. Remember— I'm the one that used to change your diapers."

Little Pearl squealed a laugh. "Yeah, and last Sunday, when you was stretched out there in the bedroom, moanin' and goin' on, I thought I was goin' to have to change yours."

Clotilda, laughing, watched Pearl out of the corner of her eye. "All right, Miss Smarty!"

Through the second-story window they could see the snow flakes falling onto the street below and on the moving cars and hear the clatter of the El trains back of Wabash Avenue. The little front room was warm. "My!" Pearl said, "they sure give you good heat here. Wish I could take some of it home—our place's cold half the time. Ches told old man Tate, the janitor, I was goin' to have a baby and couldn't be sittin' up in a cold place. Ches got kinda nasty with him; I was surprised—Ches is generally so easy-goin'. He's awful nice about my condition—brings me ice cream all the time, and bananas. But he always was good to me."

"Yes," Clotilda sighed. "That's sweet, real sweet."

In the bedroom little Jimmie awoke and started crying.

Clotilda stood up. "You better be gettin' on back home, and fix Ches's dinner," she said.

Pearl smiled. "First I'm gonna fix yours, and Eugene's."

"I feel all right now, Pearlie—my legs ain't weak like they were. You go on home. I gotta piece of ham back there in the kitchen that I'm goin' to throw in a pot of navy beans. You run on, now."

"Clo, you ain't got no business cooking yet. Why don't you wait a couple of days, till you get your strength back? Come on."—

Pearl pulled herself up from the chair and started into the kitchen —"I'll put the beans on and make a pan of corn bread; it won't take but a jiffy. You're gettin' ready for a set-back if you ain't careful."

Clotilda followed her into the kitchen. "No foolin', I'm feelin' okay," she said. "I can tell, 'cause I'm hungry as a bear."

"I don't care 'bout that," Pearl said. "I'm gonna fix this food today, and tomorrow I'll stay home. Then you can take over. Give me your apron."

Clotilda laughed, then sighed. "Oh, Lordy. Come here, then." She took an apron off the nail beneath the window sill and tied it around Pearl's bulging belly. "Girl, this thing won't hardly go 'round you. You're gonna throw twins, looks like." She pointed to the cupboard. "The beans're on the second shelf there; and that piece of ham's in the bottom of the ice box."

Pearl's pregnancy was in the eighth month, but she moved agilely around the kitchen. Clotilda's little ice box stood four feet high and held only twenty-five pounds of ice. All eating was done on a card table that stood in the middle of the kitchen floor and was covered with a clean piece of bed sheet. A three-burner gas stove, coated with scales of blackened porcelain, its oven door propped shut with a chair, did the cooking. Pearl took the little piece of ham from the ice box and held it up in her left hand. "Merciful Father," she said "You're gonna starve Eugene to death. Ches knows a place down on 31st Street where you can get pretty good little hams for a dollar and a quarter. He'll pick up a couple, and I'll send him by here with one tomorrow."

"We ain't on charity, you know," grinned Clotilda.

"Don't I know that? Eugene makes more'n Ches. We'll let you pay us, all right. Just the same, he'll bring it tomorrow when he gets off. You can bake it for your dinner, and slice off it and fry it for your breakfast."

Clotilda laughed. "Pearlie, what would I do if it wasn't for you? Tell me the truth, now—are you sorry I come trailin' up here after you?—pesterin' you; gettin' sick on your hands."

"You talk crazy. I was tickled to death and you know it."

"But Paducah—it was so dead down there! I was dyin' to leave. And Eugene couldn't get a job that paid anything. Still, I had to keep after him all the time to get him up here—jawed at him night and day. He's 'fraid of a big place like Chicago, I think."

"Well, he come up here and got a pretty good job," Pearl said. "Pays mor'n Ches gets porterin'."

"Foundry work is so hard, though. Sometimes he's so tired when he gets home he goes to sleep at the dinner table."

"Ah, ha!—now it comes out!" whooped Pearl. "That's why you don't have to worry about gettin' kids. Don't hand me all that stuff about you 'being so careful!'" She leaned against the wall and laughed.

"You can act real bughouse sometimes," Clotilda grinned. "Hurry up and get on outa here!"

Later, around five o'clock, that evening—it was snowing and already dark outside—Clotilda sat alone near the lamp in her front room reading a paperback novel, entitled *The Rivers of Eros.* Pearl had cooked the beans and corn bread and gone home by three-thirty, leaving Clotilda idle and glum. Pearl was so light-hearted, Clotilda thought, and with cause; for Chester, in his way, appreciated her. Pearl knew it. How in God's name could Eugene be so blind to the ways of a woman!

Yet Clotilda was convinced he didn't aim to do wrong; he was honest, she thought, and only acted according to his nature. So maybe he'd soon improve; catch on better. But still it was the biggest mismatch ever made. And how her Aunt Clem had pushed it!—saying what if Eugene *was* older; he'd just make a better husband, that was all; wasn't he a hard worker?—why everybody in Paducah knew it. "There ain't a lazy bone in that man's body," Aunt Clem said. "—He's settled, and won't be throwin' his money away; but'll bring it home." Clotilda had had a case on young Mitchell Watkins at that time. They had been sweethearts since the sixth grade. But Mitchell's family moved away, to Chattanooga, and that was the end of that. The last she heard, Mitchell was going to Talladega College in Alabama. She couldn't forget how miserable she was the day they said goodbye at the Sunday School picnic. Mitchell left the next day. They exchanged letters for a few weeks, until Mitchell's letters fell off and finally stopped. So she married Eugene; and Aunt Clem was happy. They kept house— if it could be called that—for three years in Paducah.

But Eugene had come from an illiterate family and wasn't too eager for a nice home. His passion was hunting and fishing when not working. Clotilda loved to "make" things; her Aunt Clem had taught her to sew, and soon she was making her own clothes, and Pearl's too. But when Pearl, with the family she worked for, left Paducah to come to Chicago, Clotilda was wretched. She and Pearl—as orphans reared by Aunt Clem, their mother's sister—had been inseparable. Clotilda begrudged Pearl her escape, and when Pearl married a Chicago boy, Clotilda felt deserted.

Once, during this time, she had been unfaithful to Eugene— with a dining car waiter called "Happy," in town for twenty-four hours. But she felt no remorse, and remembered that hot afternoon, in the dingy rented room, with gusto and good humor. "Happy" had raised her spirits for a day and she was grateful.

But now, in Chicago, she was in a rut again—drab house, dull husband, few friends. She couldn't shake the mood off. How was it she could envy Pearl so and love her too? She wondered.

At six o'clock Eugene came home. Clotilda had bathed— curiously viewing her dark, thin body in the mirror—and dressed. She was in the kitchen putting the plates on the card table when Eugene came in and set his lunch kit down. At forty-two he too was thin, and of average height, with rough, very dark skin; he wore a mackinaw and a cap with ear flaps.

He grinned and rubbed his hands—"Whew—cold out there, Clo. How'ya feel?—y'look better."

"I'm okay, Gene, honey. How d'you feel?"

"Pretty good. I'm gettin' used to that damn work, I guess—my muscles ain't so sore." He looked at the stove. "What you got? —beans?"

"Yeah—Pearl was here and fixed 'em with the rest of that ham. Tomorrow she's gonna send over a ham. Chester knows some place where he gets 'em cheaper."

"Cheaper." Eugene laughed. "I bet."

"Well, cheap or not, I ain't got enough money in the house to pay for it—dollar and a quarter."

"I'll give you the money all right."

"Go wash up." Clotilda smiled and cut her eyes at Eugene.

When they sat down to eat they were mostly silent. Eugene, half-dozing from fatigue, ate from a big plate of navy beans into which he often dashed catsup; simultaneously he broke off and devoured huge chunks of corn bread.

At last Clotilda looked at him. "I was thinkin'—I oughta go out and try to get a job somewhere," she said.

"Why's that?"

"We need so many things—furniture, and sheets, and things for the kitchen."

"I'll pick up some more furniture . . . Saturday afternoon, when I get paid. They got some whoppin' good buys over at that place on———"

"Oh, Gene, I don't mean second-hand. I want some new stuff. If I found a job, we could get some things—on time, maybe. We wouldn't have to be eatin' on a card table."

Eugene looked at her. "It's a table, ain't it?" he grinned. "—four legs and a top; and holds all th' food *we* can eat."

Clotilda's eyes went up to the ceiling—"Dear Jesus."

"Clo, you cain't work and keep house at the same time. What's the use throwin' money away on a lotta high-toned furniture, with you out on some little chinchy job that won't pay nothin' nohow? We'll get some furniture before long—soon as we can get squared away. But right now you oughta be home takin' care of what you have got."

Clotilda's gaze went into her plate. She said nothing.

"You get down in the dumps so easy," Eugene frowned. "Poutin' all the time. Why is it? That's how you got sick, probably. You mustn't be like that. We'll get outa the barrel pretty soon. You see if we don't."

" . . . All right," Clotilda sighed. She pushed her plate away.

Eugene laughed. "You was the one that wanted to come up here, you know. Remember? I'm ready to go back any time—tonight—an' take some of that high-toned furniture money and buy me the bes' coon hound in Kentucky—an' just take life easy. Any time, baby."

Clotilda smiled. "Oh, shut up, Gene."

When Eugene finished his dinner, he wiped his mouth with the back of his hand, stretched, and pushed back from the table. "Whew, I'm beat. I'm gonna turn in early, Clo. Set the clock for five-thirty, will you?"

The next afternoon, shortly after three o'clock, Clotilda sat alone again in the front room reading her paperback. It was only ten days until her first Christmas in Chicago, and from the window where she sat she could see the wet snow coming down onto the rooftops across the street and the pavement below. The sky was slate grey and threatening; and on the sidewalk black children romped home from school. She sat watching them; children hadn't meant much in her life; she had never imagined herself a mother, certainly not of Eugene's children. She hadn't necessarily shunned the idea, but whenever it came it never seemed just fit or right, somehow. She kept watching the street now. The snow was changing to a thin, cold rain, but later the cars and buildings would be glazed with ice. Then she saw the tall fellow hurrying across the street, toward the entrance of her building, carrying a round package up in his left arm as he would a baby. She knew it was Chester, with the ham. Soon she heard him coming up the stairs. But she did not hurry to the door when he knocked; she just strolled.

"Who is it?" she called innocently through the door.

"Me—Chester."

"Oh." She opened the door. "Ches! Come in." She was laughing now.

Chester, grinning, sidled in with his package, his overcoat damp from the chilling rain. He was out of breath. "How'ya doin'?" he said. He was lean and smooth brown-skinned, but with large, wide eyes, and wore a little mustache that thinned out to a shoe string when he smiled and showed his perfect teeth. He gave the parcel to her.

"Oh, my ham, I bet," she said. "Pearlie said she was gonna send it. Thanks. Sit down—I'll get your money."

"I didn't ask for no money," Chester grinned. "—Pearlie just told me to bring the ham. How you feeling?"

"Oh, I'm all right, Ches." She smiled at him.

"Gene okay?"

"He's fine. He don't get home till around six—he's got so far to come. Sit down a minute—while I put the ham in the ice box." She started into the kitchen. "Take your coat off and sit down," she repeated.

Chester got out of his overcoat and put it and his hat on a chair—he wore a jacket and necktie, but his shoes were thin and wet. He sat down on the sofa and surveyed the room. Soon Clotilda came back, laughing. "Don't you look at this room so hard," she said. "It won't take it. I ain't got it fixed up like I want it yet."

Chester smiled, looking lost. "It's good as ours," he said. He darted glances at her as he stirred on the sofa. She went over and took his coat and hat from the chair and hung them in the closet; then came back and sat in the chair.

"What you been doing with yourself, Ches?"

"Oh, just workin' every day."

"Gets wearisome, don't it?"

"Kinda." Chester sat idly. He crossed his long legs now and let his eyes wander around the room again. Soon they came to rest on Clotilda, who was smiling at him; and they flew away.

"Doin' *any*thing too steady gets wearisome," Clotilda said. "—like settin' up in this house all day long."

"Yeah, you're right, I guess. But Pearlie don't seem to mind settin', somehow."

Clotilda laughed. "She wouldn't—she don't have time to mind—always full of babies."

Chester grinned, then laughed.

"*Now* you're fixin' to be a daddy again."

" . . . Yeah." He glanced at her out of the corner of his eye.

"You're a busy boy, Ches." She threw her head back and laughed.

Chester was faintly rueful, "I ain't been busy lately, though." He grinned.

Clotilda squealed. "Ches! Shame on you!"

He laughed awkwardly and picked up the novel Clotilda had been reading. "Well, I ain't been," he said.

"Cross your heart and hope to die?"

"Cross my heart and hope to die." He started leafing through the book's pages. "You like to read?" he said.

"That's all I got to do—or listen to the radio. I read late last night—while Gene, he slept."

He continued leafing. "This a pretty good tale, is it?"

"Yeah—real good. I found it on the street car a couple of weeks ago. Somebody forgot and left it on the seat. It's real good."

Chester inspected the cover. "The Rivers of Eee-ross—that right?"

"I guess that's the way you say it—or Air-ross, maybe."

"About rivers, eh?"

"No, not necessarily about rivers. Well, I *guess* not—it's kinda hard to understand, some parts of it. It's really mostly about lovin'."

Chester's glance faltered; then he smiled. "Lovin'? . . . What kind of lovin'?"

"Ches!" Clotilda giggled. "Lovin' between a man and a woman!"

"Oh." Chester's mustache thinned in a grin.

"There's more to that book than just that, though, I think," Clotilda said. "It's a funny kinda story, in a way. Strange."

"What's rivers got to do with it?" Chester said.

"I still ain't sure—and I'm about finished with it." She sat reflecting.

"I don't care nothin' about a story I can't understand," Chester said.

"Oh, you can understand what's *happenin'*, all right—all the time. There's a lot of lovin' goin' on." Clotilda laughed again. "It's plain as your nose what's happenin'."

"I thought you said——"

"But it's the *meanin'* of what's happenin' that I don't get. There's a 'forward' in the book that tries to tell you all about what it means; but it's lousy. You can't make head or tail of it. It says the rivers are to wash the guilt away in."

"Yeah?"

"You see, this woman, Mary Zampa—she was crazy at the time—was always wantin' to go into these rivers, to wash herself. But actually there is only one river in the book." Clotilda laughed. "And it's a creek—on the back of their farm. But she was always thinkin' it was a different river every time she waded into this creek. But most of the book—the best part—is about when she was a young gal. Was she a rounder!—a real slut. Went with first one man and then another; and caused trouble for a lot of people; grief to her family and all; finally got her brother killed, fighting defending her reputation. She was a real hussy. Ah, but when she got older, her chickens started comin' home to roost—at least she thought so. Then she started duckin' and dodgin'—feeling guilty, and low-down; tryin' to make amends, by doing some of the weirdest, craziest, things you ever heard of—like baking bread for the crows that her husband was tryin' to keep from eatin' up all the crops; making rhubarb pies for the prisoners in the little county jail; and finally, tryin' to take a bath every day, with Castile soap, mind you, summer and winter, in this little creek on the back of their farm. Of course she was stone crazy then—loony as a broom. But she always thought she was goin' into a different river every time. Even had a different name for each one—she was very particular. Then one morning—it was in November—they caught her in the creek buck naked. That's as far as I got—but there's only a few pages left. They were gettin' ready to put her in the insane asylum then. The 'forward' talks for three solid pages about guilt, guilt, guilt. I don't know yet what happens to her when they get her in the asylum. I guess about the only thing she can do is die—and the book's runnin' out of pages. But the best part was about the *good* times she had, when she was a young gal. The happy times. I don't care much for the very last part."

Chester took his big eyes off Clotilda and looked down again at the book in his hands.

"You wanta read it when I get through, Ches?"

"Well . . . okay," he finally said. "But maybe I oughtn't to take it home. Pearlie's kinda funny about——"

Clotilda laughed. "You don't have to say where you got it, do you! Or you can take it where you work, and read it on your lunch hour."

" . . . Okay." Chester gave his slow grin—"Yeah, I can."

"Here—I'll turn down the pages where the *real good* parts are," Clotilda laughed, getting up. She came over to the sofa and sat down beside Chester. As their shoulders touched, he could smell her talcum powder. She reached over and took the book from his trembling hand and, still giggling, started going through the pages.

Suddenly she turned on him and laughed. "What you tremblin' about, Ches?"

He grinned. "Clo, you crazy."

"Want some blackberry wine?"

He looked at her. Then, seeming to ponder for a moment, he drew up his long legs in embarrassment. His painful groin was swollen. Finally, again his mustache thinned in a grin. "Sure," he said, his voice quaking.

Clotilda got up and went into the kitchen. Soon she returned with a half full bottle of wine and two glasses, and Chester loosened his necktie.

🔯 🔯 🔯 🔯 🔯 🔯

The following afternoon, Pearl was back—pulling her pregnant weight and dragging her two children up Clotilda's stairs. She entered the living room, and, panting, sank into a chair. "I got the kids outa the house for a little fresh air," she said, "—and to come by here a minute to see how you're gettin' along."

Clotilda smiled. "Oh, I'm doin' okay, Pearlie. There's nothin' wrong with me—and you oughtn't to be climbin' stairs in your fix."

Pearl laughed. " 'Fix' is right—I'm clumsy as an ox. Well, it won't be much longer now. I'll sure be glad, if only cause of Chester. He's nervous as a cat now'days; eats like a bird and rolls and tosses mosta the night. Last evenin' he just picked at his supper; and later on he couldn't sleep. He musta stopped off some place too, after he left here—there was whiskey or wine or somethin' on his breath. Ches almost never drinks. So I better hurry up and have this baby—before maybe I start losin' my husband." Pearl gave her squealing little giggle.

Clotilda looked away. "Oh, Pearlie," she laughed, "you're a mess. You sure are a mess, Pearlie."

Chapter Three

JULY 1962. Clotilda's daughter, Ruby, had developed into a sightly girl by the time she reached her teens, with a smooth coffee complexion, slender waist, and pretty teeth. Yet, though her character inclined toward the serious, she showed little interest in an education beyond high school; this, despite Clotilda's hints that if she wanted to go on to college, or to secretarial school maybe, the wherewithal would be scraped together somehow. Ruby would not commit herself; she got her high school diploma at seventeen and worked for a year as a wardrobe girl in a downtown dress shop. Then just before her nineteenth birthday she married.

Zack Parker, her husband, a strapping fellow with sorrel-tan skin, red hair, and a heavy, Negroid nose, was an auto mechanic. Clotilda, to Ruby's surprise, was pleased with the marriage, adjudging Zack likeable and ambitious; she was entertained by his bluff, laughing, sometimes hilarious ways, his wit. She already knew his mother had died early and that his father, a part-time barber out of Memphis, and a tin horn gambler, had reared him, doing a passable job at that, everything considered. The boy finished high school before entering the army and afterwards went to an auto mechanic's school under the G.I. Bill; then he got a job in a big westside repair shop. He had been twenty-seven when he married Ruby, and was now thirty-five. And Ruby now was twenty-seven.

After the first year of their marriage little Addie arrived. But over five years elapsed before Lester's Caesarean birth. By the time Lester was a year old, Zack had saved, and borrowed, enough money to go into the car repair business for himself on the south-side, and moved his family into a modern five-room apartment on Eberhart Avenue. They were an average, happy family; Ruby doted on her two children and wished for more, but the doctor advised against it. So she looked after the two she had and kept a clean, bright house. Clotilda was a widow now; Eugene had died three years before, leaving her saddled with the big rented house in which they kept roomers. Pearl and Chester, years before, had moved to Cleveland, where they reared a family of seven.

One hot afternoon in early July, 1962, Clotilda dropped by Ruby's apartment to see the two grandchildren. She was heavy now; her dark face was jowly, and her hair past grey. She rang Ruby's bell in the vestibule and started the wearisome climb to the third floor. As Ruby opened the door to Clotilda, Addie, now seven and a half, stood peering out from behind her mother.

"Hi, sweetheart," Clotilda, perspiring and out of breath, said to Addie and put her arm down around the child's shoulder. "She's growin' like a weed, ain't she?" she said to Ruby.

"She sure is, Mama." Ruby, smiling, wore pink slacks, a white blouse, and costume bracelets. "Mama, those stairs get you, don't they? Here, sit down and rest." Ruby removed a small magazine from the armchair to the floor.

"Where's the little one?" Clotilda settled her bulk in the chair.

"He's asleep." Ruby laughed, showing her pretty teeth. "— Lester's about to sleep his life away. But it's okay by us; when he's awake he's a rough customer. Want a coke or something, Mama?— or can of beer?"

"Yes, beer, honey." Clotilda shook her head. "I oughta be drinkin' water, though, and not all those calories." She looked up at the windows. "My, my, look at the pretty drapes; they're pretty, even if I did make 'em myself." She laughed. The draperies were orange and mint-green, against beige walls. But the furniture was not expensive, yet modern in design, and new.

Ruby went back to the kitchen for the beer, leaving Clotilda with Addie. "Come here, baby," Clotilda said, "and talk to Grandma." Addie came and stood beside her chair and smiled. Clotilda leaned forward and stroked Addie's stiff red hair. "I guess your hair's always gonna be red," she said. "We thought there for awhile it might change, but it won't now—it's just like your daddy's."

"Mama likes my hair," Addie said, in mild reproach.

"Well, we all do, honey. It'll be pretty. And you're always gonna have those few freckles across your nose." She touched the bridge of Addie's nose; then lifted the chin in the palm of her hand. Addie gazed up into her face. "You might even be good-lookin' someday," Clotilda laughed.

She talked to Addie about her school vacation, her play-mates in the neighborhood, about Lester's sleeping, and the recent street carnival; but soon Addie's interest waned. Clotilda noticed her watching the door leading to the kitchen where Ruby had gone.

"What's the matter with you, honey?"

Addie looked at her but did not answer.

"You wanta go in there and see what's takin' your mama so long, don't you?" Clotilda laughed.

Addie looked off and finally nodded her head.

"Well, go ahead, then. I can see you ain't interested in a lot of gossip, like most women. Go on back there if you want to." She patted at Addie's little buttocks as the child skipped out of the room.

Clotilda sat back in her chair and fanned her face with the magazine she had retrieved from the floor. Her eyes roamed the room. Ruby had learned the knack of keeping house, all right, she thought. And Zack apparently encouraged her—something Eugene had never done; over the years she had made the effort alone, furnishing the many places they had lived in piece by piece until she was at least reasonably satisfied. Eugene hadn't even liked the big piano—and it a gift. He said it took up too much room and that nobody in the house could play it anyhow—which was true, until Letitia came to room with them. Still, shortly before he died, Eugene would sit in the living room and listen while Letitia played and sang hymns.

As a laborer all his life he hadn't made much money, leaving Clotilda only three thousand dollars in insurance and four hundred dollars in savings. In her heart she hadn't grieved at his death; she hadn't loved him, nor had she hated him; she just knew him. He seemed to sense this, and reacted by lavishing his affection on Ruby —without ever a dream of suspicion. Clotilda had watched it all with a fearful awe—Ruby not only had Chester's big eyes and his perfect teeth, but his wide, slow smile as well. Clotilda marveled at it, and reflected that this shameful history was locked inside her breast, and hers alone.

Now Ruby and Addie came back into the living room. "Sorry, Mama, the phone rang," Ruby said, and handed Clotilda a cold can of beer. "Mama, don't you want a sandwich or something with it?"

"No, honey. I'm tryin' to cut down on my eating. I'm way too heavy, and shouldn't be swillin' this beer."

"Zack drinks a lot of beer, too," Ruby said, sitting down. "He weighs almost two hundred now."

"Yeah, but he's tall with it; big-boned. I ain't seen Zack in over a month. How is he?"

"He's okay, I guess." But Ruby's smooth brown face sobered. "He's got problems at the shop, though—business could be better. And sometimes he takes cars in for repairs on credit, and don't always get his money right away. It's a headache when you got a big overhead."

"Lord," Clotilda said, "as if I don't know—with that big white elephant of a house I got."

Addie came over now and stood in front of Ruby. She was gravely silent, watching her mother. Ruby had done the child's red hair in four stiff little braids that would not lie down; she turned her around now, still trying to arrange the braids. Addie gazed back over her shoulder at her mother and seemed appeased. When Ruby had finished, Addie turned around and faced her.

"*Now* whatta you want, lover?" Ruby smiled, relaxing in the chair.

". . . Nothin'," Addie finally said.

"Then, why don't you go play?—and let me talk to Grandma awhile." Ruby smiled Chester's wide smile.

Addie looked at her, then suddenly laughed, but said nothing.

"Lord," Clotilda said to Ruby, "she's your shadow, ain't she? Come over here, baby," she said to Addie. "You don't have to go off nowhere. You can talk to Grandma, too. Come on."

Addie looked instead at Ruby, and did not move.

Clotilda turned on Ruby with a troubled laugh. "Why, I never saw anything like it—in all my born days."

There was pride in Ruby's smile. "She won't hardly let me go to the bathroom."

Addie hugged the arm of Ruby's chair and giggled.

Soon Ruby said, "Oh, Mama—I don't think I told you—I got a letter from Aunt Pearlie the other day."

Clotilda froze, then nervously smiled: "That right? She writes you more'n she does me." She sipped the can of beer.

"She says you owe her two letters already. I think she really wrote me to find out how *you* are. Why don't you write her?"

"I will. I'll write her tomorrow for sure. They all gettin' along okay?"

"Well, guess what," Ruby laughed. "Little Noreen ran off

and got married. That is, ran off from home. She got married right there in Cleveland."

Clotilda laughed. "Poor Pearlie. I bet she had a fit. Noreen was the baby. Now all Pearlie's children're gone from under her. My, my."

"Uncle Chester hasn't been well, she says. He's got arthritis—real bad; is in bed most of the time now; suffers somethin' awful—moans and goes on all the time, she says. The doctors can't seem to do a thing."

Clotilda at first strained forward, then eased back and looked away. ". . . Well, well . . . ," she finally said. "Is that a fact." A lurking, retributive fear had come into her face. "My God," she thought.

"But Aunt Pearlie herself's as chipper as ever," Ruby laughed. She looked at Clotilda. "What's the matter, Mama?—that beer too cold for you?"

Clotilda sat up. "Oh, no . . . I'm okay."

Meanwhile Addie had taken a seat on the floor at Ruby's feet.

🌀　　🌀　　🌀　　🌀　　🌀　　🌀

Zack Parker's repairshop-garage was located on 51st Street, and fronted under a big sign—"Acme Auto Service." The place was dingy and poorly lighted, but large and structurally sound, resembling inside, with its high rainbow-arched ceiling and steel girders, an airplane hangar. Zack was not the owner; he rented. There were four employees: "Pinkie" Williams, skinny and black, janitored and operated the tow truck; little Herman washed cars; and the other two, Dave Flood and Sonny Greenlee, were mechanics.

Sonny, although younger, twenty-eight, was a better mechanic than Flood, but he was vain and temperamental. They called him "Sonny" because of his adolescent face, which could be serenely faunlike, or distant, sulky, according to his mood. His skin, a satin-mahogany black, was a foil for his glistening—passé—"processed" hair, impelling the waitresses along 51st Street, discussing his amatory prowess, to cry with joy: "Oh, girl!—that Sonny Green-lee! He's the coolest thing! How can he stand that old nasty car grease on his hands! Tell me, tell me!"

Sonny had been married and divorced and had a little daughter who now lived with her mother. He gave Zack Parker a full day's work and was a great engine trouble-shooter and ignition man, but he could not take orders. He worked on the cars *he* wanted to work on, and did what *he* decided was necessary to make them run—even to installing parts not bargained for by the owner, and making a bigger bill. But big Zack, though hot-tempered, had poise and patience too—up to a point—and was a good mechanic himself.

So he joked with Sonny and kidded him along, but there wre times when he could not hide his smoldering anger and made snappish, cutting remarks. Sonny seldom talked back, but he was sure to sulk for a week. This always made Zack angrier, and, unable to solve the situation, he would go home silent, morose, his light coppery face a mask for his edginess. Or when in addition Dave Flood, the other mechanic—who drank—failed to show for work, Zack, after the trying day was over, might go to the "Oasis," a restaurant-bar down the street from the garage, and drink too many bourbons and water. Then he would become a different man. What he might do could never be predicted. Sometimes he playfully cursed "Sudsie," the bartender, threatening to buy the "Oasis" and fire him; or he might sit at the bar in silence, sullen and mean, his arms thrust forward around his drink, glowering into the mirror. On such occasions no one meddled with him. But next day he was at the garage by 8:30 as usual, alert and courteous to customers.

One afternoon, in mid-July, Ruby and the children came to the garage. She had offered to clean out the files in Zack's "office" and put his records in some semblance of order. Five minutes after she arrived little Lester was asleep and Zack had to put him on the back seat of a car. The office consisted of a dirty, unswept, little glass-enclosed corner of the garage, where Ruby, sitting at the desk on newspapers, went to work sorting out the files. Everything she touched was coated with grease or dust and her hands were soon grimy. Zack stayed in the office long enough to show her where all his helter-skelter papers were kept and then went back to help Dave Flood hoist out a truck motor. As Ruby sat working, Addie leaned against her leg and talked without letup—Addie's chattering when alone with her mother and her silence around others averaged out normally.

Soon Addie said, "Mama, look at your hands."

Ruby laughed. "And look at yours. They're just as dirty—and you're not doin' a thing but interferin' with me."

"I don't like to come here," Addie said.

"Why? This is Daddy's place of business—where he makes the money to feed us!"

"It's dirty."

"Sure it's dirty, honey. But you can't fix cars and have things clean."

Addie had finally disengaged herself from Ruby and was playing with a pile of invoices when she saw the corner of a large photograph protruding. She pulled it out. " . . . Oh," she said, "Here's Daddy." The picture was soiled but recent; Zack in shirt sleeves, was standing beside a new Buick, and flanked by two girls, both brown, shapely, and mascara-eyed; all three were laughing. "Who are these ladies, Mama?" Addie thrust the picture before Ruby. Ruby took it, looked once, and frowned. She studied it. Addie leaned over her knee, craning to see again. "Who *are* they, Mama?"

"Oh, I don't know," Ruby finally said, her face cold, drawn. "Maybe some of Daddy's relatives; maybe his cousins—in Detroit. He's got lots of them." Her face set, knowing Zack would return, she spitefully laid the picture face up on Zack's desk. Then she continued sorting files.

Soon they heard Lester fretting. "Go bring him in here," Ruby said. Addie went and got little Lester out and led him waddling back into the office. She and Ruby were looking at him, when someone said :

"Hi, guy."

They turned to see Sonny Greenlee standing in the door smiling down at Lester. "*Hi*, guy," he repeated. Then he turned to Ruby and Addie. "Hello, there," he smiled. He wore clean grey coveralls and was freshly shaved, his hair processed and gleaming, and held his arms down close at his sides in a way that hid his grimy hands.

"Hello," Ruby smiled, flustered—in a reflex action she tugged her skirt down over her knees. Addie stood and gaped at Sonny.

He appeared oblivious. "Well, I see we got plenty help today," he grinned.

"Don't you need it?" Ruby finally laughed. "Just try and make sense out of some of these files, and see." She waved her soiled hand at a sheaf of dirty bills.

"Ah, that ain't me," Sonny said, vainly touching his shining, anachronistic hair. "That's the boss's department. I don't even come in this office. Had to today, though." He smiled the cozy, cryptic smile the waitresses loved.

Ruby felt her face stinging. Then her spunk came up. "Now, why would *that* be?" she said, looking straight at him.

Sonny laughed, but hesitated; then said, "Well, when I saw you a minute ago, I said to myself back there in the garage, 'Hey now! Who's that fine-lookin' queen up in Zack's office?—I gotta go check this out.' So I came on up here."

Ruby, still seated, reached down and picked up Lester and set him in a chair on newspapers. "Well, you see now who it was," she said, intently wiping Lester's mouth with a piece of Kleenex. Addie cut deeply hostile eyes at Sonny.

"I sure do see," he grinned. There was an awkward silence. "But that don't make me have to change my opinion, does it?" He laughed again.

"No," Ruby said with a brazen smile. "Your opinion is your opinion." She turned to her work.

Now Sonny looked at Addie. "I know what *your* name is," he said. Addie looked at Ruby. "It's Adeline—Addie," he said.

Addie ignored him.

"Tell him that's right, honey," Ruby said offhandedly—she appeared very busy now.

Addie looked out the window and said nothing.

Sonny's gaze strayed for a moment—and he saw the photograph on Zack's desk. He did a double-take; then looked at Ruby and smiled. "Oooh, la, la," he murmured, picking up the picture; he studied it.

Addie spoke up now, possessively. "That's my Daddy."

Sonny whistled and touched his black, pomaded hair. "Is that who that is, sugar?" he said, mock wide-eyed. "Well, it sure is, ain't it?—sure enough."

Ruby looked at him and curled her lip.

"Those're his cousins from Detroit," Addie said, now standing beside Sonny and looking over his wrist at the picture.

"Is that right?" said Sonny, gaping at her in simulated wonder. "Well, whadda you know. Why, I saw *this* cousin just the other night in the Oasis—that's a restaurant down the street, honey. And I think I've seen this other cousin somewhere too—it just don't come to me right now."

"Okay, wise guy," Ruby said; she wore a brassy smile. "You win. Now, how about lettin' me finish this work for my husband?"

Sonny's face assumed the wistful, faunlike expression that so enraptured his women. He tossed the photograph back on the desk and gazed out the window, far away. "You know," he mused aloud, "I can't seem to understand Zack, can't understand him at all." Now he turned the full force of his serene, animal gaze on Ruby. "You make both of those 'cousins' look like old hags," he said; then he went moody.

Ruby guffawed. "You oughta be on television," she said. "Honest to God—you'd make a million dollars."

Addie's face went from one to the other as if watching a tennis match.

Sonny looked at the floor and pondered Ruby's remark, then sighed. "Yes, yes—old hags," he repeated. "Sure is a pity. You know, I'd like to talk to you sometime."

Ruby laughed again. "Sure—I'll talk to you. I'll have Zack invite you out to dinner. We can talk all you want—right there at the table. Is it okay for me to tell him you wanta talk to me?"

Sonny's face showed his resentment; he was silent. Suddenly he turned on his heel and walked out. "I don't care what you tell him," he said over his shoulder.

Tense and upset, Ruby began alphabetizing the files now. But Lester was drooling and nodding again, and Addie was too tired to talk. "Come on, you two," Ruby said; and took them out into the garage to the car where Lester had slept before and put them in. "Now, get some shut-eye, both of you—so Mama can finish her work." She went back into the office. The first thing she saw was the photograph on Zack's desk where Sonny had tossed it.

She picked it up and studied it again. What were they so damned tickled about? she thought. What was so funny? She'd just bought Zack that monogrammed shirt in May—two months; old lover boy, personality kid—look at him *cyaw-cyaw* and show his ivories. And the two chicks—who were they? Sonny had seen them somewhere—he would; the new Buick must have belonged to one of them; or maybe to the guy that took the picture and had it blown up for Zack, in memory of the grand occasion. It looked like they were somewhere out in the country she thought—a cozy foursome maybe. It must have been a foursome; Zack couldn't handle two women; that she knew. Maybe it was some roadhouse, with rooms upstairs, or a motel—the chicks looked like the type, all right; the chippie bitches. She ought to throw the picture in his face.

Instead Ruby slipped the photo back in among some grimy vouchers and filed them; then went on to finish her work.

᧚ ᧚ ᧚ ᧚ ᧚ ᧚

Three days later, around eleven o'clock in the morning, Ruby, her smooth brown arms bare in a skimpy house dress, was busy waxing her kitchen floor. The kitchen was bright and modern with a small electric range and a new white porcelain sink. Addie and Lester sat in the kitchen doorway on the same chair, chattering at each other and watching their mother. Ruby said to Addie, "Don't you let Lester come near this floor till it's dry, honey." For three days, no matter what house chores she did, Ruby's mind was preoccupied, distressed; and she was cross with the children, which was unusual. Lester was not old enough to notice or care, but Addie saw and felt the change. With Zack, however, Ruby was deadpan, non-committal, yet, friendly enough. Now as she waxed the floor she tried to reassure herself that a photograph with some girls didn't mean her husband was tired of her; or even that he was getting wild.

Still, she hated to think of herself as dumb, a "square"; there was nothing worse, she thought; many a wife, good women, had sat by and let their husbands get away with almost anything only because the wives didn't know the score; or else acted like they didn't—buried their heads in the sand. She would never do it, but would watch and wait. Besides she had nothing yet to confront Zack with—a photograph, yes, if she could find it again; but the photograph by itself proved nothing. Yet she was furious with him, but resolved to hide it.

When she had finished the kitchen and the floor was dry, she prepared lunch for herself and the children, with Addie close on her heels. Ruby had only to take the dishes down from the cupboard; Addie set the table, took the milk from the refrigerator, and poured it in the glasses; then shepherded Lester to his high chair and somehow got him up and eating. Throughout she kept up an incessant prattle with her mother, asking questions so outlandish Ruby, despite everything, wanted to laugh—questions which a week before she, Ruby, could hardly have waited privately to tell Zack about and which he would have laughed at before thinking up some funny, crazy answer that was smutty or wrong or both.

She and Addie now sat down at the kitchen table for their lunch. Lester, there too in his high chair, was wide awake and noisy, and Addie, talking fast, ticked off the dishes she claimed she could cook: spaghetti, pancakes, rice, meat loaf, biscuits, bacon, oatmeal, and eggs—all were parts of her fancy.

In the middle of the meal the telephone rang. Ruby got up and went into the little passageway leading to the living room to answer it.

"Hello," she said.

"Hello . . . Ruby?" It was a man's soft, hesitant voice.

"Yes—who's this?"

"Sonny—this is Sonny."

"Sonny . . . ?"

"Sonny Greenlee."

"Oh . . . Well? . . . " Ruby's voice turned to ice.

"I wanted to apologize for acting so bad when you was down here at the garage the other day," Sonny said.

"You don't have to apologize . . . and I don't have time to talk."

"I'm sorry you don't," Sonny said. "I had something I wanted to tell you. Well. . . maybe some other time."

"No, not some other time, either!"

"Ruby, don't be that way," he soothed. "I had something I wanted to show you—that I think you'd like to see; and if you wanted to, you could keep it. Why're you so dog-gone haughty and uppity with me? I don't think you're really that way—I sure don't. You're really a very nice person, if you want to be, and . . . "

"Listen," Ruby cut in, her voice husky and strange, "why

don't you leave me alone? I ain't thinking about seeing you. I didn't tell my husband yet about you botherin' me, but, so help me God, another peep outa you and I will. He'll mop up that garage with you—and then fire you."

Sonny paused. "Well, to tell you the truth, I ain't afraid of neither one of those things happening. But if *you* want me to leave you alone, I will. I'm just sorry I got you mad at me, that's all— I didn't mean any harm callin' you up. Okay, then. So long. I'm sorry—honest, I am." His voice was limpid, silken, corny.

Ruby hung up. When she turned around she almost stepped on Addie standing behind her listening. Addie, eyes wide with curiosity, went ahead of her into the kitchen. "Who was that, Mama?"

Ruby glowered at her. "Shut up and quit askin' so many questions! You wouldn't know anyhow. Eat your lunch."

Addie sat down again with a long face. Both ate in silence as Lester drooled his food and beat his big spoon on the high chair tray. Ruby soon forgot about Addie's snooping in thinking about herself. What was Sonny up to?—that bastard. The brass. The nerve. Zack would kill him if he knew. What was it Sonny wanted to tell her?—to give her?—something she'd like to see, he'd said. Well, it couldn't be anything *he* had. Surely he didn't think she'd see him for some measly trinket. No, he had something else in mind.

Maybe . . . it could be . . . he had something on Zack. They had no love for each other; that was certain. Yes, that was no doubt it—he wanted to see her to deliver the goods on Zack. But what was in it for Sonny?—surely more than just getting back at Zack. Could he really think she'd go out with him for pleasure? . . . ah, but maybe for revenge. He wanted to nail Zack to the cross, too—get him dead to rights. Something to tell her, he said; something to show her; she could keep it if she wanted to. Not another photograph—God forbid. Maybe something worse.

Better to forget the whole thing. Men would be men—sometimes dogs. Better not to know everything they did, certainly not go out of your way looking for it. You'd sure find it. Better to shut your eyes and plug your ears. She'd done right to get rid of Sonny; he'd have only stirred her up with a lot of tattling crap she shouldn't know about anyway.

So that's what love did to a wife, she thought. It was a damn curse. You wouldn't care *what* a man did if you didn't love him. But men had no conscience. She remembered when she'd had Lester by Caesarean operation. Zack, at the hospital that afternoon, had cried like a baby. She was doped up and groggy, but so happy. That night he came back, drunk, and cried again. And again she was so happy. But later that same night he might have gone out with some chick, for all she knew. It was a man's damn world. Women had no rights in it.

Sitting at the kitchen table, Ruby felt the hot tears slipping down her face. Addie watched her, and soon she too began to cry. Ruby collected herself at once and got up, drying her face with her paper napkin.

"What's the *matter*, Mama?" yammered Addie. "What's the matter with you? That man made you cry."

Ruby started; then looked at her. "Are you crazy? What man?"

"It wasn't a woman," whined Addie. "I could hear. It *wasn't* a woman!"

Ruby glared at her; then sighed. "Honest to God, Addie, you're the limit."

Now Lester started beating with his spoon again for attention; then he gurgled a laugh. Ruby looked at him, and soon her wet face gave way to a sad smile. She lifted him out of his high chair, as he belched in her face and thrust his palm into her flattening nose; then he laughed again. She let him down and stood him on the floor. "Come on, big boy," she said, snuffling. "Let's all go up front and play awhile—come on, Addie. We'll do the dishes later." The three walked up the little passageway to the living room.

The following Monday, Dave Flood, Zack's second mechanic, failed to show for work till noon. Changing into his work clothes he was red-eyed and wobbly from a week-end of drinking. Though not boon friends, he and Sonny worked well together; they knew each other's faults and joked about them. But Flood did not share Sonny's dislike for Zack, perhaps because Zack, who liked liquor himself, had permitted Flood a leeway in the shop that, in Sonny's view, was warranted neither by Flood's skill as a mechanic nor his steadiness.

Sonny was also tolerant of Flood, especially whenever Flood expressed admiration of Sonny's winning ways with women. Having been something of a skirt chaser himself in his younger days, Flood, now fifty, claimed he was "over the hill." So in the shop when they were working together, he loved to hear of Sonny's exploits and savor all the piquant, lurid, reminiscent details.

But this Monday noon Flood was barely dragging, from his hang-over and the loss of sleep; he needed Sonny's help on work Zack wanted out that day.

"Hey, now," Sonny, in clean coveralls, grinned at him. "Didn't think you was gonna make it today. You look pale, man."

Flood, thin and ebony-hued, grinned back, his eyelids drooping. "Yeah, I'm beat. You gotta help me put a new head gasket on that thing." He nodded at an old Chevrolet he had worked on the past Saturday. "Then I gotta put a new voltage regulator on it. The guy that owns it oughta push it over a cliff."

Sonny, touching his glistening hairdo, thought for a moment. "I don't know, man. Zack wants that Buick outa here today, too." He pointed to a new tan Buick over on the grease rack. "You know who's *that* is, don't you?"

Flood looked and grinned. "Yeah—his chick's . . . Mabel's. You gotta get that one out, all right."

"Plugged air vent," Sonny said, "and a carburetor adjustment. Won't take too long. Maybe I can give you a hand then."

Flood fumbled in his tool kit for a wrench. "Zack's wife's gonna ketch up with him one of these days," he said. "She was in here last week. I saw you up there in the office gunnin' her, you sonofabitch."

Sonny grinned. "I wasn't gunnin' her. She's a fine lookin' heifer though, ain't she . . . man, oh man. All I can say is, Zack needs his head examined. But I ain't botherin' her."

Flood cut his weary eyes at Sonny and laughed. "Don't hand me that. I know you, you horny bastard."

"No foolin', man. I just went up there to the office that day to see what she was doin' around here; she had the kids with her. Say, she was cleanin' out Zack's files and flushed a big picture of him and his chick, Mabel—with some other gal—standing in front of Mabel's Buick. She had the picture layin' right out on top of Zack's desk when I saw it."

"Did she say anything about it?"

Sonny shook his head. "No—but she smells a rat, I'll bet. She ain't nobody's fool."

"You better leave her alone, then," Flood laughed.

"Man, I told you; I ain't studyin' that woman."

Flood waved him off. "You figure she's mad at Zack now, and ripe for the pluckin'. I know you."

"Aw, go to hell," Sonny grinned, and walked off.

The following Wednesday noon Zack drove home from the garage for lunch. This was rare, but he had been out late the night before, sporting, and was used-up, tired. After lunch with Ruby and the children he sought out the shade of the back porch and stretched out on the old settee of springs for a short nap. Ruby had been waiting for some such chance, her decision made before. She hurried into the bedroom, put on a better dress and some street shoes and, holding Addie back inside the front door, left the apartment.

A cab took her down to 51st Street to the garage where she thought Sonny would be; she rejected enduring any longer the doubt about Zack; she'd know the truth, she told herself getting out of the cab in front of the garage; better to know it than to go on reliving the last few days. She entered the garage through the big front door used for vehicles and walked back toward the rear. But she saw no one, no activity. Then she heard sounds over near the wash rack; it was little Herman, the pygmy-like car washer, in his wet rubber apron and boots. But she saw no one else. Herman's back was to her as she went over; she smiled and spoke—"Hello, Herman."

Herman turned around gaping. "Howdy-do," he finally said, and grinned. " . . . Why, Ruby . . . "

She looked over at the other cars. "Is Sonny around anywhere?" She seemed shaky.

Herman was hosing off the top of a Cadillac. "No'm," he said. "Him and Flood just went out to get something to eat. They oughta be back 'fore long, though."

Ruby stood for a moment. " . . . Okay," she finally said, sidling away. "I'll see him later." She smiled at Herman, then went back the way she had come. As she went out the big front door, "Pinkie" Williams, the tow truck man, was towing in a steaming Dodge. They glanced at each other as she went on up the street and flagged a cab for home.

Twenty minutes later Sonny and Flood strolled back from lunch. As they passed the wash rack, little Herman, dragging on a cigarette, looked at Sonny and hesitated. But soon he said, "Sonny, Zack's wife was just in here lookin' for you."

Sonny stopped still and looked at him; then a slow, preening smile came over his face. He looked at Flood, who was grinning and shaking his head.

Nodding toward Sonny, Flood said to Herman, "We're gonna be missin' this bird around here, Herman. You watch. He'll be out at Dan Taylor's Funeral Parlor."

Herman grinned nervously, but said nothing.

"Where's she now?" asked Sonny.

"Gone."—Herman seemed glad.

Sonny walked up and stood over Herman. "What'd she say?" he grinned.

"Said she'd see you later."

Flood snickered, and whispered to them, "Was she carryin' her drawers in her hand?"

Herman grinned and, embarrassed, looked at the floor.

"Come on—let's get to work." Sonny strode away.

Zack returned to the garage at two-thirty. When Sonny saw him up front in the office, he, Sonny, ducked out the back way and went up to the corner delicatessen, where he shut himself in a sweltering phone booth and dialed Ruby.

Addie answered.

"Is your mama there?" Sonny's voice was cool velvet.

"Who is this?"

"Don't you worry 'bout that, sugar. Come on, let me speak to your mama."

"Hello." Ruby had grabbed the phone.

"This is Sonny."

"Yes . . . ?"—Her voice trailed off.

"I'm sorry I wasn't there. Can I see you?"

"You cannot. I've changed my mind—and don't call me up no more." She slammed the phone down.

Sonny, jerking his ear away, replaced his phone on the hook. His lips moved in soft, obscene curses—"that God-damned hinkty bitch." As he walked back to the garage, he filched a little packet from under his coveralls breast pocket flap and carried it in his hand. When he entered the rear of the garage, he went to the toilet, locked the door, and undoing the packet, took out a cheap little gold-filled locket on a tiny chain—the gift he had asked Ruby to see. Tossing the box in the waste can among the greasy paper towels, he stood and held the tiny locket dangling over the toilet. Then he let it drop, spat viciously in behind it, and flushed the toilet. For the rest of the afternoon he spoke to no one.

Later that afternoon, about four o'clock, Pinkie, the tow truck man, came in the office to ask Zack about getting off early; he said he wanted to go to the ball game, a twi-night double-header.

Zack was seated at the desk. "Okay, Pinkie—but watch that hootch," he warned, grinning. "I don't want you showin' up here in the morning half stiff, like Flood—because you gotta start scraping and scrubbing that garage floor. Hear?"

"Sure—okay." Pinkie's stygian face broke into multiple, unctuous smiles. "I'll be here, all right—I'll be here, Zack. Say, could I lift ten bucks offa you till Saturday? I gotta get my laundry out and . . . "

" . . . get some gin," Zack laughed.

"No, no, Zack. Oh, I might drink me a coupla beers at the game. That's all. Aw, no."

"Okay. Say, I'm plannin' on going out to that game myself— if nothin' turns up to stop me." Zack took a ten-dollar bill from his wallet and handed the bill to Pinkie.

"Thanks—thank'ya," Pinkie grinned, folding the bill and sticking it down in his watch pocket. "We'll settle up Saturday, hear?"

Zack laughed. "Yeah, and that'll take the auditors. You'll probably owe me."

Pinkie hollered a laugh and started out. Suddenly he stopped, thought a minute, and said, "Did your wife find you, Zack?"

Zack had picked up a pencil to start figuring some bills on his desk; he only half-heard. Finally, not looking up, he said, "When?"

"Today—around noontime."

"Noontime?" He looked at Pinkie.

"I guess you was out to lunch."

"Hell, I went home for lunch—she fixed my lunch. What's wrong with you?" He went back to figuring the bills.

"No foolin', Zack. She was leavin' as I was comin' in."

Zack tossed the pencil on the bills and leaned back with a nettled laugh. "Pinkie—Christ! Who else saw her?—nobody."

Pinkie paused and thought. "Let's see, I was towin' in that Dodge . . . "

"Who else was here," Zack grinned.

"Herman was back there at the wash rack."

Zack laughed. "Okay—Pinkie, you better lay off that wine. It's softenin' your brain."

Pinkie's grin was slight. "Ask Herman—see if I ain't right."

Zack turned to him with a wistful smile, then shook his head as Pinkie went out.

He resumed figuring the bills. But his mind strayed off, requiring him to re-add the column. Pinkie was so damn sure about it. Strange. And Pinkie knew her when he saw her, all right. It didn't figure. He tossed the pencil on the desk again and got up, but then sat back down and stared at the naked walls. What the hell would she want down there at the garage? he thought. She'd already fixed up the files the day she came with the kids. Pinkie was crazy; she couldn't be two places at once. How long had he slept at noon on the back porch?—about an hour maybe. Zack got up again. Herman could settle it; Herman knew her too. He went out into the garage; he wouldn't ask Herman, he'd *tell* him.

When he got back to the wash rack little Herman had finished washing cars and was cleaning out the drains with a broom. He grinned at Zack, who was casual.

"About what time was my wife in here, Herman?"

Herman looked at him and went immobile; then finally put his horny, midget hand into his breast pocket for a cigarette. When he got the cigarette in his mouth, he started patting himself for a match.

Zack stood and waited on him. And when Herman could not find a match Zack made no move to give him one.

At last Herman removed the cigarette from his lax lips and said, "What time was she in here? . . . Let's see—I reckon . . . Well, I don't hardly know, Zack. Let's see . . . "

Zack swallowed; but recovered at once. He squinted at Herman. "Well, it must've been after I left, wasn't it?"

" . . . I reckon so—I wasn't payin' much attention."

"What'd she want?"

" . . . I don't know, Zack, what she wanted."

"Who'd she talk to?—Sonny, Flood?"

"Oh, no—they was gone, too."

"Then she only talked to you."

" . . . Well . . . she didn't say much."

"What *did* she say?" Zack put his foot up on a crate and reached in his shirt pocket for a cigarette.

"Oh, she was just lookin' around, I guess—I think I told her you was gone to get somethin' to eat. She said okay; and pretty soon she left."

Zack studied Herman. He put the cigarette in his mouth, lit it, and, ignoring Herman's cigarette, tossed the match on the wet cement floor. "Okay, Herman," he finally said, and went back up to the office.

He sat down at his desk again and finished the cigarette; then picked up the telephone and started to dial Ruby. But he put the phone back, got up, and started out to where Flood and Sonny were working on adjacent cars in the rear. It was then he saw the huddle breaking up—Herman was leaving Flood and Sonny and going back to the wash rack. Zack strolled up to Flood and Sonny, who were suddenly busy.

"Soon be goin'-home time, boys," he said. "I'm gonna try and get out to that second game tonight if I can."

Sonny kept his head in the motor he was working on; but Flood looked at Zack and grinned. "Yeah, I'd like to get out there myself."

Zack was composed. "Herman says my wife was in here today, around noontime."

Flood looked at him. "Yeah?"

"Yeah. You guys were out, huh?"

"We went out right after you did, Zack." Flood seemed relieved.

Then Zack said, "You knew she was here, though."

" . . . Oh . . . " Flood, a sluggish thinker, looked around for Sonny. But Sonny's head was still in the motor, with only his buttocks pointing at them. " . . . Well," Flood said, "I didn't exactly know. . . ."

Zack laughed. "Well, if you didn't *exactly* know, how did you know?"

Sonny straightened up now. "Well, *I* didn't see her," he said with a dreamy calmness, "and didn't know she was here."

"—Neither did I," echoed Flood.

Zack laughed, and turned the matter off. "I guess she was lookin' for some shoppin' money or somethin'." He pointed at Flood's car. "You gonna finish that today?"

"Sure am," Flood said, and got busy.

Dead-pan, Sonny watched Zack walk away.

About six forty-five that evening, long after the men had gone, Zack locked up the garage, went out to his car parked at the curb, and drove over to the Oasis. He needed a drink and—before going home—time to think. He entered the restaurant-bar, walked back and climbed onto a stool, grinning at Sudsie, the bartender. Sudsie reached for a bottle of sour mash bourbon and set it on the bar before Zack; then placed up a glass of ice water and a shot glass and poured the shot glass full of whiskey.

"Howya doin', boss?" Zack said.

"Okay—if I could only be out to that ball park tonight," Sudsie sighed and departed down the bar to other patrons.

Zack tossed off the first shot glass, poured another, and dumped it into the glass of ice water. Then he sat looking at himself in the mirror. What the hell was Ruby up to? he wondered. Was she checking up on him?—snooping? He didn't get it; it was weird, weird as hell; it didn't look good at all. She knew something; he wondered how much. The guys at the shop—lying bunch of bastards, all of them, except Pinkie on the tow truck; Pinkie had told the truth today; he had seen her, no question; the proof was those lying, dodging, clowns—Herman, Flood, and Sonny. Old Sonny; so cool and calculated; ladies' man; great bed fellow; a "whiz," the waitresses called him—so much staying power, they said.

But Flood, that dumb sonofabitch, had gone all to pieces—stuttering, back-pedaling. Poor little Herman was scared. And he didn't tell everything. What could Ruby have asked him? It was sure something he didn't want to tell. Maybe she had asked who came around, or maybe she had seen him in Mabel's Buick—with Mabel in it. Well, *he* hadn't bought it for her; it was hers; she had even offered to lend him money in a pinch; Mabel wasn't a bad girl, but just a playgirl. How much did Ruby really know? She had been so quiet lately, so solemn, slow to smile, and cross with the kids. She had something on her mind, all right; you didn't have to be at all slick to tell that.

What a husband, and father, he'd turned out to be, Zack thought. What man ever had a better wife than Ruby?—or two finer kids? Funny how a man got such a kick out of chasing around—and still love his wife so. In that respect women were supposed to be different; at least good women. Why were men different? Well, how should he handle Ruby now? If he only knew what she knew. At any rate he could start being nicer to her now; there was always room for that; but the change mustn't be too sudden; it would give things away; convict him. He reached for the bottle of bourbon on the bar and started to pour a third drink, but thought better of it; there was too much facing him at home. He pushed his glass away, paid Sudsie, and left.

When he got home around 7:30, Ruby and the children had already eaten their dinner. "You didn't call," Ruby said. She was sitting on the sofa with the newspaper in her lap and Addie leaning against her. "We didn't know when to expect you." She spoke with a cool sobriety.

"Sorry, Babe. I should've called. I got tied up at the last minute."

Ruby flashed her eyes at him. "You didn't get tied up at the garage. I phoned there; nobody answered."

"Yeah, I had left there—I had to go by and dun some money out of a guy," he lied, then smiled at Addie; then looked around the room. "Where's the young'un?"

"Lester's asleep." Addie spoke with her mother's coldness.

Ruby got up to go in the kitchen, and Addie jumped to follow her. "I don't want you back there," Ruby said to her. Then sighing—"I've got to put Daddy's dinner on the table. You talk to *him* awhile." She went out.

Addie stood with down-looking, joyless countenance. Zack, smiling at her, sat down on the sofa and glanced at the newspaper. "Come on over here and sit down," he said.

Addie studied him, then went over and sat on the sofa.

Zack turned and watched her, amused. "What you been doing with yourself this afternoon?" he said. "Did you draw some more pictures?"

Addie, looking off, shook her head.

They were silent; and Zack, yawning, picked up the newspaper and scanned the headlines. But soon he turned to her again. "I see the cat's got your tongue."

Addie was in deep thought. Then she looked up at him and said: "Daddy, where are your cousins now?—in Detroit?"

He smiled at her. "What, honey?"

"Are your cousins in Detroit?"

"I haven't got any cousins in Detroit, sweetie. Where'd you get that?"

"We saw them."

" . . . You saw them? . . . Where?"

"At the garage. We saw a picture of you and them."

Zack folded his hands on the newspaper. " . . . a picture of me and my cousins. Who saw it?"

"Me and Mama and a man did."

Zack took in her whole little tan, freckled face in his gaze. Then he smiled again. "Now, let's see, honey—who was in the picture?"

"You and two ladies."

"You and Mama saw it—and a man. What man, Addie?"

"The man that works at the garage—the black, pretty man with the shiny hair."

Zack's facial muscles loosened; he stared at her. The photograph he had misplaced, and Sonny Greenlee, came in on his mind like a meteor. Sonny!—that sneaking bastard. Zack sat very still now. "Why was the man in there looking at it, Addie?"

"He came in there to see Mama."

"He came in there to see Mama. Well, well . . . . Was Mama there today, too?"

Addie was slow to answer. Finally, she shrugged. " . . . After lunch . . . you were 'sleep on the back porch . . . she left."

"Has that man ever been here, honey?"

" . . . No. He hasn't *been* here . . . he has . . . ." Addie paused.

Now Zack realized he was talking too fast, failing to hide his urgency, and that Addie had sensed some faint significance; she was hesitating. "Well, that's all right, honey. He's a nice man. Has he called Mama on the telephone?"

Addie looked off and took her time. "Today," she said.

Zack's cunning smile made his coppery pug face cruel. "Well, what's wrong with that?" he said.

Addie turned on him and glared. "He makes her cry."

"Cry, honey? When did he make her cry?"

"The other day."

"Well, go on—what happened?"

"We were eating. He called up and they talked. Mama came back to the table and was eating again. Then she started crying."

Zack felt flaccid, enfeebled. He lay back against the sofa, not trying to think, his head pirouetting. Finally he felt himself getting up; he went to the front door. "I'll be right back, honey," he turned and said. "I forgot something." He opened the door and went out.

Soon Ruby came back in the living room. Addie lay on her stomach on the sofa doing a garish, cubistic, crayon drawing. "Where's Daddy?" Ruby said. "In the bathroom?"

Addie, sullen from her banishment, spoke in revenge. "He had to go back. He forgot something."

"Forgot something! Well, my God, I wish he'd make up his mind. I'm in there slavin' over a hot stove in July, fixing his dinner, and he forgets something." Muttering, she flung herself back into the kitchen.

There was a wild screeching of tires. The car careened around the corner and came alongside the curb in a hurtling, quivering halt. Zack leapt out and ran up the street the short distance to the entrance of the building where Sonny Greenlee roomed. When, taking three steps at a time, he reached the third floor, he started beating on the door. Soon a withered old black woman, her bottom lip a pouch of snuff, opened the door and peered up into his face.

"I wanta see Sonny!" It was a menacing demand.

"Well, tryin' to break my doh down ain't gonna get him fuh you. He ain't here."

"Where is he?" Zack was trembling.

"Only Jesus in heaven knows that." She slammed the door.

Zack went back down to the car. He sat under the steering wheel awhile. The night was hot and people were sitting in kitchenette windows or lolling on their front steps; swarms of large and small insects made swirling chandeliers of the hot street lights, while the little bell on the ice cream vendor's cart tinkled above all the gabble and laughter. He could wait for Sonny, he thought, but the black bastard might not come home at all, might be shacked up with some gal all night long.

In that instant Ruby's brown, pretty, now smiling, now sad, face swam into this thoughts, while Sonny's image would not leave; the two were lodged there together, and the vision sickened him; his mouth was dry as dust and his eyes stung. He started the car and drove south toward 51st Street and the Oasis; but after pulling up in front he could not bring himself to go in for fear his face would announce his catastrophe.

He turned the car around and headed back to South Parkway then south again to 55th Street where he went in a tavern strange to him called "Trent's," and ordered a double bourbon and water. The drink was soon gone and he ordered another; he had forgotten about food in trying to find Sonny; but he could raise no clues. He thought of Flood; but finding him would be useless; he would merely stutter and lie again. There was left only little Herman; it was Herman she had gone back to the wash rack to talk to; he admitted it; but he lied when he tried to infer she had asked for him, Zack; no, she wasn't looking for Zack, and only a simple-minded sonofabitch like himself would want further proof of it.

He ordered his third double bourbon from the bartender. Herman was a good little guy, he thought, but had dodged his questions, then lied; but he was scared. Well, if he could be found tonight, he wouldn't lie again and live. Zack downed the drink, paid the bartender, and left. When he got in the car he realized he didn't know where Herman lived. He'd have to go to the garage and check the records. He drove back down to 51st Street to the garage, unlocked the big door and went into his office.

The place was suffocating. He pulled the string, lighting the greasy bulb over his desk and sat down. He seldom came there at night; the place seemed so different; how he slaved there in the daytime, though, trying to wring a living out of it—putting up with sloppy help; unreasonable, late-paying customers; creditors; a garage landlord every month looking over his shoulder to see if receipts would support another rent boost. All this to provide for his family—make possible a nice home, a car, good clothes, wholesome food, a respectable neighborhood—and that slut puling over a cheap conk-haired pimp; making her husband the laughing stock of every tavern and pool room on the Southside.

His tortured thoughts, and the burning whiskey in his empty stomach, made him hotter; blind from pouring sweat and rage. He yanked out his handkerchief and mopped his face and short stubborn red hair; he felt his wet shirt sticking to his back as he pawed through the files for Herman's address, which he finally found to be far out near 95th and State. He got up and pulled the string overhead and the place went dark; he locked the doors and returned to the car, driving west to State and then straight south.

Little Herman, who must have been sixty, and his wife lived in three rooms over a grocery. Zack found them in the kitchen putting up fruit. Herman was calm, on seeing him, seeming almost to have expected him, and offered a chair; Zack declined and asked if he would come out and sit in the car. So they went out.

When they were seated in the car Zack turned to Herman, whose tiny dark face looked scorched, shriveled, under the street light. Zack said: "Herman, you didn't tell me the truth today—about my wife comin' to the garage."

Herman, composed, looked straight ahead through the windshield at the noisy children on the sidewalk. "My daddy always told me," he said, "that I'd stay outa trouble longer by not talkin' when I should be listenin'."

"Yeah, but I asked you."

"Yeah." Herman's voice was low, ineffectual.

"Who all was there when she came?" Zack said.

"Just me."

"She came back to the wash rack?"

"Yeah."

"What'd she say?"

"Asked if Sonny was around anywhere. I told her no—that he went out to get somethin' to eat."

Zack was quiet; then he sighed, exhaling a reeking whiskey breath. "What'd she say, Herman?"

"Said okay; she'd see him later." Herman shrugged—"Then she left."

Twenty minutes later Zack was home. When he entered Ruby and Addie were watching television in the living room. Ruby did not speak and refused to look at him. He kept on through to the kitchen, opened the stove, and took out his dinner—chuck roast and potatoes. He had not sat long, eating, when Ruby and Addie came in.

"Do you want me to fix you some lemonade?" Ruby spoke with cold exasperation.

"No." Zack's voice was feathery light.

"*I* want some, Mama," Addie said.

Ruby ignored her and went to the sink to run hot water for the dishes.

Zack kept his head in his plate and spoke in the same light tone: "Did you ever find Sonny today?"

Ruby froze. Then turned around and faced him. "What?"

"Did you ever find your pimpin' boy-friend today?" He went on cutting a piece of meat on his plate with a steak knife and forked it into his mouth, never looking up.

Ruby turned back around to the dishes in the sink. "I don't know what you're talkin' about." Her smooth brown face was ashen now and her voice skipped. Addie stood across the table from Zack, watching him.

Zack, still chewing his food and not looking up, said: "Did you love-birds talk on the telephone today?"

Ruby turned around and faced him again; she was backed up against the sink now with both hands behind her back on the rim of the sink. Her voice was hollow; yet her lip curled in a daring smile. "Well, if I *was* doin' anything, I'd just be playin' catch-up—you can bet on that."

Zack stopped chewing and glanced at her. "You whore," he said, and continued eating.

Ruby's face went slack. She dropped her hands, and her buttocks bumped back against the sink. Then her bravado smile returned. "Well, look who's talking. You, runnin' after every little chippie you lay your eyes on—and coming in here abusing me with all that filthy language right in front of your own child. Yes! I went lookin' for him! Yes! he calls me up! And what're *you* gonna do about it!"

Zack was half standing now, bent forward, but with the table cloth still covering his crouched legs. His yellow face had turned almost black, and his head and eyes seemed swollen to bursting. "You street-walkin' whore," he said, and picked up the knife.

Addie screamed and circled the table to him. He swept around at Addie with his left arm, catching her in the middle of her body, and hurled her halfway up the wall, shattering her arm at the elbow.

Ruby's eyes were dilated; speech hung in her lungs. Zack advanced on her. Then her voice came: 'Oh Zack! You *know* I was lyin'! You *know* it! I was lyin' to you because I loved you. Zack! Zack! You *know* I——"

He drove the knife six inches into her throat, just over the collarbone. The blood spurted sideways onto the white enameled sink, but Ruby, her eyes back in her head, groped and fought for the knife. But soon, her legs jutting straight out, she began to slip down in front of the sink, her dress sliding up her thighs to the waist, showing twisted stockings, garter belt, and panties. Zack, knife in hand, stood breathing over her.

Addie was screaming at the top of her lungs as she threshed and rolled on the floor in the corner. Now someone was pounding on the front door. Addie crawled over to where her mother lay doubled up on her side. Ruby was clutching at her gory throat and gasping for air. Addie went wild with screaming. Her shattered arm dangling, she threw herself across Ruby, covering herself with blood—it was soaked in her dress and smeared on her face and red hair. 'Mama! Mama! Mama!" she screamed, wallowing and kicking on the floor. "Mama! Mama! Mama! Mama!" Zack stood over them in a convulsive daze. There was loud, incessant beating on the front door now, and soon sharp knocking at the back. Then the doorbell started ringing.

Ruby rolled over on her back now, her hands falling away from her bloody throat. Addie had lost her voice from screaming. She lay moaning and sobbing; then in a wild fit she tried to crawl into Ruby's arms. "Oh, Mama! Mama!" she whimpered. "Oh, Mama! Please, Mama!" Her voice throttled in whining sobs. Then the wails of approaching police sirens came in through the screened windows.

Ruby on her back lay still now. At last she seemed able to breathe, for she took a deep, deep breath, her great eyes staring at the ceiling. Soon she looked sideways at Addie, as if to speak; instead a tear ran off her cheekbone. Then her jaw dropped and she was gone.

Chapter Four

JUNE 1971. Clotilda's roomer, Ambrose Hammer, now labored fourteen hours a day on his "History of the Negro Race." He could not type and, therefore, had to write out all the drafts in his slow, awkward longhand, but he persevered. Night after night, since his somewhat early retirement from the Post Office, he sat in his room and wrote into a big loose-leaf binder, and in this way converted the downtown Library notes he had taken that day into the text of his book. He set a strict regimen for himself: every morning except Sunday, up, shaved, and out of the house by eight; breakfast downtown, and then to the Library reference room by nine. He would return to the Southside by late afternoon for dinner in some neighborhood restaurant before coming home for an hour's nap, after which he worked in his room till midnight. This last was the part of his day—or night—he fancied most; partly for the bookish atmosphere his room afforded him, and for his chance, as he worked, to engage in Negrophilic reverie.

Many items of the room's furnishings were his own; the thick rug and the three good chairs were relics of his broken marriage; and the desk, the shaded desk lamp, all the books, the small television, the little replica of Michelangelo's statue of David, and three large portraits—Mrs. Eleanor Roosevelt, black scientist, George Washington Carver, and, largest of all, directly over the desk, Martin Luther King delivering his famous "I Have a Dream" speech at the 1963 March on Washington—were later acquisitions. The large bed was Clotilda's property.

One evening in early June, Hammer, in shirt sleeves and house slippers, sat at his desk, writing. Above the desk lamp's cone of light his face, dark, massive, sober, its tree-trunk sideburns like grizzled shadows down both his cheeks, hovered over the manuscript; and high on his broad nose perched the pince-nez, from which the tiny gold chain shimmied at his temple.

After a while he heard the doorbell ring downstairs. Soon Clotilda came to the foot of the stairs and called him. He withdrew his long legs from beneath the desk and went out to the head of the stairs where, looking down, he saw Clotilda—heavy, her stiff hair very grey—standing below with a man at her side.

"It's Mr. Turner, Mr. Hammer," she called up.

"Hello, Lord Nelson," Hammer said in his deep voice; then, sighing, waited for the man to come up the stairs.

"Ambrose, how you, boy?" grinned Lord Nelson Turner as he reached the top. He was small and dark-skinned with a misshapen, tallish head—but sprightly, though in his sixties. They shook hands and he followed Hammer into the room.

"I'm pretty good, Lord Nelson," Hammer said with his solemn smile. "—and busy."

"I shoulda phoned you. I was drivin' by, though—so I just rung your bell. I won't keep you."

"Sit down." Hammer waved him toward a chair.

Lord Nelson sat down. He wore a conservative suit, but loud red bow tie and white socks. "Ambrose, what I wanted to talk to you about was . . . well, we want you to speak at our lodge next month. You got the unanimous vote of the committee."

Hammer smiled and sat back down at his desk. "Now, Lord Nelson. Watch your step." He was pleased.

"No, no—we want you. They want you to talk on Black history."

"Ho, ho! We, or they?"

"The committee."

"Lord Nelson, who else on the committee but you knows I'm interested in the subject?"

Lord Nelson looked at Hammer and thought for a moment. He and Hammer had worked thirty years together in the Post Office before their near-simultaneous retirement; he had been a mail sack handler and Hammer a clerk. "Well," he finally said, blinking, "they know you read a lot, Ambrose. They know that."

Hammer gave his deep chuckle. "You were in there sellin' them a bill of goods, Lord Nelson." He lifted off his pince-nez and holding them in his huge hand, smiled at Lord Nelson. "Come clean, now, Lord Nelson."

" . . . Well, they was up against it, kinda." Lord Nelson's fingers puttered at his bow tie. "Then my wife thought of you. She had heard me talk of your book, y'see."

"Now we're gettin' to the truth of the thing," Hammer said.

Lord Nelson tittered. "Well, it was a good idea, wasn't it, Ambrose?"

"I don't know . . . I don't know," Hammer reflected aloud. "What could I say of interest to the estimable gentlemen of your lodge? Huh?" He smiled again.

"You could speak on 'progress.' That's what your book's about, ain't it?"

"My book is about history. History has not always meant progress."

At that moment Miss Letitia Dorsey passed the bedroom door on her way to her room at the end of the hall. She glanced in. "Hello," she smiled in passing.

"Good evenin', Miss Dorsey." Hammer stood up. "Oh, Miss Dorsey."

Letitia came back.

"I was meanin' to see you," he said, putting on his pince-nez.

" . . . Yes?" Letitia's long eyelashes fluttered. Then she remembered to speak to Lord Nelson.

"I was wonderin'," Hammer said to her, "if you had any spare time . . . to do a little typing for me, now and then?"

Letitia, as tall as Hammer, hesitated; her eyes went wide and startled; finally she smiled again. " . . . Oh, Mr. Hammer . . . I don't know—I don't know whether I could do *your* work." She gave her nervous little, self-effacing snicker. "It might be too difficult for me, really."

"Ho, ho!" came Hammer's deep laugh. "Now, Miss Dorsey, Miss Dorsey. The only trouble you would have would be decipherin' my hieroglyphics."

Lord Nelson, gaping at Hammer, blinked again.

" . . . Well, we can talk about it," Letitia finally said. "We'll talk about it, Mr. Hammer."

"Very well. Later on I'll show you some of my stuff, and see if you feel like tacklin' it."

" . . . Okay." Letitia at last smiled, and fled.

Lord Nelson whispered to Hammer, "She goes to Root Street Baptist now—I see her there on Sunday mornin's sometimes."

Hammer reflected. "Is that so?" he said.

"She comes sometimes with Mrs. Pilgrim's granddaughter."

Hammer lifted off his pince-nez and sighed. "Yes—Addie. Poor Addie. Miss Dorsey spends some time with her. The child's unhappy. . . . Lord Nelson, you'd better have your lodge committee write me a letter. That will make it official—although I do not charge an honorarium. Meanwhile I will be turnin' over in my mind two or three stimulatin' subjects that might be of some interest to your members for an evening."

Lord Nelson was pleased, and soon left.

Hammer now sat down at the desk again to collect his thoughts and resume writing. He had flicked off the brighter ceiling light, transforming the room into a deep gloaming save for the hooded light cast down by the green-shaded desk lamp. Sheets of notes were spread out before him as, with dark, earnest face, he consulted first one loose page and then another. He had been thus working for fifteen minutes when the stairs creaked under Clotilda's slow, heavy ascent. Soon she stood at his door. Her dark, sagging face was lined and her hair beyond grey.

"Mr. Hammer, I hope I didn't do wrong by tellin' Mr. Turner you was up here."

Hammer's ceremonious countenance loomed indistinct back of his little shaft of light. "No, that was all right, Mrs. Pilgrim."

"I was afraid it might be somethin' important."

"He just wanted me to make a talk at his lodge."

" . . . Oh . . . Yes, I see . . . " Clotilda's words dragged out as, preoccupied, she lingered in the doorway. "Mr. Turner's nice, ain't he?"

"He is." Hammer studied her from the dark recesses of his station.

"Do you know *Mrs.* Turner pretty well, Mr. Hammer?"

" . . . Yes, I think so."

Clotilda smiled. "They say she's a wonderful tea reader—spiritualist."

Hammer's face could not be clearly discerned, and he was silent. Finally he said, "Yes, they do say that, Mrs. Pilgrim."

"Have you ever been to her?"

"No, I haven't." He moved in his chair and the momentary light showed the trace of a smile in his eyes.

Clotilda said nothing for a moment.

"Were you thinking about goin' to her?" Hammer said.

Clotilda smiled. "Oh, I don't know. But they do say she's a wonderful adviser, and can see things way, way before they happen."

"Do you have to be a tea reader to do that, Mrs. Pilgrim? Throughout history wise men and women have seen things before they happened."

Clotilda sighed. "I guess so." She sidled back from the doorway into the hall. "But everybody don't know where to find people like that, Mr. Hammer. And they wouldn't take up any time with you if you did, probably."

Hammer leaned forward into the light, his dark face grave, patient. "Sometimes, though," he said, "people that *will* take up time with you don't really see much—no matter what they claim."

Clotilda reflected on this. "But they say Mrs. Turner told Mr. Turner he was goin' to get hurt in an automobile accident, two months before he got his leg broke. And everybody figures she kept Emmy Webb from goin' crazy, after Emmy's youngest boy got in that trouble and went to the pen. Emmy would just go and talk to her, for a whole hour or two sometimes, and after awhile— it did take months—she about got all right."

Hammer was silent, inscrutable, in the semi-darkness. Finally he said: "Hyacinth Turner—psychoanalyst. Ha! Mrs. Pilgrim, Mrs. Pilgrim, get ahold of yourself." He stood up. "You've got to let me do some work, now."

"Oh, excuse me, excuse me." Clotilda retreated toward the stairs. "I forgot you was workin', Mr. Hammer—I forgot."

Hammer, contrite, said, "Oh, I didn't mean to run you off like that. I *have* had interruptions, though, haven't I? And Mr. Neeley will be comin' in soon, no doubt."

Clotilda had started down the stairs. "Oh, don't pay me no mind, Mr. Hammer. All this time I shoulda been at my sewing machine, workin'. All this time—my, my. Yes, Mr. Neeley will be comin' in, laughin' and tellin' you how to write your book." She gave a high, empty little laugh.

Hammer was gentle as he closed his door.

Later that night in the living room—it was after midnight and the household was asleep—Clotilda pushed back from her sewing machine and stopped work. She got up and went back to the kitchen for a can of beer before bed, thinking the beer might at last bring sleep. She remembered how her sister Pearlie, dead five long years now, used to laugh and say beer was the only sleeping pill she, Pearlie, would ever need. Now poor Pearlie was in her everlasting sleep; likewise her husband Chester, with his torturing arthritis, less than a year later—how the millstone of time ground on. Clotilda, her eyes and temples aching, opened the refrigerator. When she sat down at the kitchen table to sip the beer, she watched her hand trembling on the frosty can. She was not surprised, nor alarmed, only stoical—after two days of the crisis inside her, her feelings were narcotized, benumbed; now her mind sought only a detour of realities.

It had happened two afternoons before—on Tuesday—while, during the last week of the semester, Addie and Lester were still at school. Clotilda had been alone in the big house and had decided finally to clean out some closets, especially the closet and dresser in the first-floor bedroom she shared with Addie. Tying a scarf around her head, she had entered the bedroom and started to work. The bed was high and old-fashioned; and the dresser was a cumbersome old mahogany chiffonier with five big drawers, the top three of which she had assigned to herself and the bottom two to Addie. The large closet took her almost an hour to clean and rearrange. Then she began on the dresser drawers, going from the top one down to the bottom, a drawer at a time, removing everything, including the brown, brittle newspaper lining. She turned each drawer upside down, dusted it inside and out, and folded in fresh newspaper; then neatly put the clothing back.

She had finished her own three drawers and one of Addie's. Now she pulled out the very bottom drawer. She took out Addie's blouses, underwear, and two T-shirts and laid them on the bed. When she pulled out the yellowing newspaper that lined the bottom of the drawer, Addie's little red change purse, from her red plastic bag, lay pushed back into the far corner of the drawer. Clotilda grinned: "That little rascal . . . hoarding what little change I give her . . . so afraid somebody'll find it—stashing it away." She picked up the change purse and opened it. In it was a little tin box, thin and flat, only slightly larger than a tin box of aspirin. Her chewed-down fingernails gave her difficulty in opening it. Finally it came open. There staring at her like a pair of translucent eyes were two compactly-rolled, rubber contraceptives.

Clotilda barely let her eyes land on them before she glanced away, half-recognizing, half-unbelieving. Then her eyes flew back and photographed them, as she swallowed and retreated to the bed. She did not sit down at once, but stood gaping at the two little rubber sheaths so neatly rolled and powdered—the small tin box had been made to hold three, but only two now remained. Then she sank down on the edge of the bed and shut her eyes so tight the creases and crevices in her face made an African tribal mask, agonized and frenzied. Finally she gave a guttural, muffled, half-shriek, and, clutching the little tin box in her fist, lurched on her face across the bed in frantic sobs.

Now, past midnight, as she sat at the kitchen table with the can of beer in her twitching hand, she realized she must talk to someone, or go crazy. Although a perfunctory church member, she had never been devout; she believed in God, but not necessarily in His goodness. She sensed Him more as an angry God. Why else, she had for years asked herself, did He let things happen as they did sometimes? The preachers and the church people were always saying it was to test you, to try your faith. Well, try your faith in what?

She stared now across the kitchen at the opposite wall and for minutes reflected on her life; then mournfully turned up the can of beer to her mouth, drained it, and set it down. Addie, Addie, Addie. The child would never have been born into the world if it hadn't been for her, Clotilda—for there would have been no Ruby. Poor, poor Ruby—if there was a heaven, she was surely there. And Zack—almost surely doomed to wear away the empty balance of his life inside high, grey penitentiary walls. But Addie . . . Addie. A mere child—not yet seventeen. Gone to the devil in hell already. Could it be that one life, one sad, sinful life, hers, Clotilda's own, had brought on all this misery? Confused, she could not be sure; and there was no one to talk to about it, no one to answer the jagged questions, no one to unburden to. Her mind was fogged now with murky riddles, disorder—guilt.

🌀   🌀   🌀   🌀   🌀   🌀

Friday noon of that week school let out for the summer. Lester expected later to go to camp for two weeks, and Addie had a two months job as a file clerk in the black insurance office where Letitia worked. Clotilda weeks before had asked Letitia to get the job for Addie. It was not so much a matter of money as one of keeping the girl's active mind and body occupied. Late Friday afternoon Addie was in the kitchen. She had just finished ironing a slip and now sat bent over the ironing board doing her nails, in preparation for a high school friend's party that night.

Clotilda stood at the kitchen sink preparing dinner. Although her back was turned to Addie she often managed to watch her out of the tail of her eye as Addie touched silver lacquer to her nails. Since Tuesday Clotilda had lived in a torment of indecision about her. She dare not confront Addie with the evidence, for, knowing Addie's desperate nature, she was uncertain, fearful, of the consequences. On the other hand, it lacerated her soul to sit by and see her continue on this sordid, self-destructive course.

After her siege of tears in the bedroom Tuesday afternoon, Clotilda, frightened, had decided to leave Addie's two dresser drawers as she had found them. She placed the old newspapers back and, as nearly as she could, laid in the clothing as it previously was. Then, blinking her wet eyes and snuffling, she had shoved the little red change purse containing the tin box back up under the paper to the remote corner where it had been before. But ever since then she could hardly remain in the same room with Addie without fighting off welling tears, and being shifty and evasive when they talked. And at some time during every single day, in

Addie's absence, she would steal into the bedroom and take out the little tin box—each time with her heart in her gullet for fear the cache might be missing or one of the little latex objects inside gone.

"Grandma," Addie laughed, sitting over the ironing board, "you're not expecting me in by any eleven o'clock *tonight,* are you?" She was applying the lacquer to her thumbnail.

Clotilda, still at the sink, did not turn around. "No, I ain't expectin' you in by eleven. But what time *do* you expect to get in?"

"I don't know—but it won't be late. Jack's dad won't let him stay out after midnight, you know." Addie laughed again, extending her arm full-length to appraise the self-manicure—her coppery Afro hairdo was thick and dramatic, neatly rounded in oversized yet perfect proportion to her light-brown face, which was made more attractive by the slight spray of freckles across her nose. Her eyes were quick, nervous, desperate.

"Nothin' funny about that," Clotilda said, finally turning around. "It shows Jack Griffin's father's got sense." She was certain little Jack was not the culprit—he was too nice a boy.

"Jack sure thinks so. He's always talking about him—Dad this, Dad that, Dad the other." Addie sighed and lifted her eyes to the ceiling in comic resignation.

Clotilda was making beef stew and went to the refrigerator to take out the meat. "Well, I don't know his father at all," she said, "but that sounds to me mighty like he's all right—to have his boy talk about him like that."

Addie laughed a little hysterically. "He's probably dull—just like Jack."

Clotilda, before thinking, spun around and faced her. But Addie was again busy inspecting her nails. Clotilda stood glaring at her.

Suddenly Addie looked up. "Oh, Grandma," she cried, "didn't you like to have a good time when you were young?—didn't you? Didn't people that just plodded and plodded along, no life in 'em, no fun, just bore you till you wanted to scream? Didn't they? They do me. Maybe what I'm thinking about's only in the movies or on television, I don't know. In the movies and on television things're so different, exciting; people're doing things, things they never did before and probably'll never do again; not just getting up in the morning, going to work, coming home, eating supper, going to bed again. Don't real happy people do more than just that? *Don't* they?" The passion in her freckled tan face had darkened it and distended the veins in her forehead. "Just staying on one *same, same, same* old level all the time is awful! . . . It's an awful, horrible, drag! It's really wasting your life, that's what it is!"

Clotilda stood gaping. Finally she returned to the sink. Addie talked on:

"Jack just talks about his father all the time, and about school, his own different jobs, his stamp collection—oh, the dullest things in the world. It's awful, I tell you. He never talks about wanting to do anything to show he's an unusual person, a person trying to get something out of life, something exceptional, exciting, that makes the time go so fast it's not dragging and horrible all the time——"

Clotilda threw up her hand. "Lord, have mercy! You sound like a broke phonograph record. What got you wound up like that?" Then suddenly her mind took in the total past, and her tone changed, softened. "Addie, honey, where'd you learn things like that? Huh? You ain't yet seventeen. It wasn't in *this* house. Where was it, honey?—where'd you get ideas like that?" Her voice, no longer angry, was imploring. "Come on, honey, tell me."

"I didn't learn it from anybody. I just know it, that's all. Grandma, didn't you ever want to do anything but work, work, work every day at your sewing machine—then stand all evening over that hot stove?—and then go to bed, and get up, and do the whole, same, thing all over again? . . . Didn't you ever want to do things that got you away from all that for a little while? Away from things on your mind; and do something that made you happy and excited for a little while at least. Didn't you?"

Clotilda opened her mouth to speak but no words came.

Suddenly Addie laughed. "Come on, now, Grandma; didn't you have a good time—back in your young days?" She laughed hysterically again.

Clotilda's face had gone blank from disbelief. " . . . Addie, I swear you're losin' your mind—I swear before God, honey. What ever got you on this subject anyhow, of havin' a good time?—*I* didn't bring it up. *You* did—all of a sudden, just like a thunder clap. Is that on your mind *all* the time?" Suddenly Clotilda remembered to smile; then she forced a laugh. "Girl, that brain of yours is workin' night and day. If it only worked like that in school, you'd be at the head of the class. Now, wouldn't you?" Clotilda laughed haplessly again.

At that moment Lester walked into the kitchen.

"Aw-aw, look out," Clotilda grinned—so glad to see him. "Lester, where you been, sweetheart?"

"Baseball practice." Lester, wearing blue denims and a T-shirt, was laconic, dour. His Afro was short and neat and the sun had deepened the buff-brown color of his face. Also his left eye was faintly discolored—bruised.

Clotilda looked at him hard. "Lester, come here—what's wrong with your eye?"

"Nothin'." Lester was sullen; he cast down his gaze and started on through to his little room.

"Now, you just wait a minute, young man. What happened to your eye?"

Lester at the door turned around. "Nothin'—I got run into at home plate." He left the kitchen.

Addie stood up now. She had finished her nails.

"What're you wearing tonight, honey?" Clotilda said, poker-faced.

"My green dress."

"Oh, that's nice. D'you like that dress?"

"Yes, it's pretty," Addie smiled. "You made it, Grandma—it's got to be pretty. Everybody likes it."

Clotilda was cutting up the carrots and green peppers to go into the stew. She smiled, then sighed: "But sometimes, honey, you act like you don't care about what I try to do for you. I always like to do things that'll make you happy, but looks like you never care about things that'll make *me* happy."

Addie stood looking at her and was silent. Finally she said, "Oh, Grandma, that's not so—but what could I do? You're so busy all the time; and you've got the house . . . "

"Honey, why, we could be a *lot* closer. We could do more things together—go to the movies . . . that is, nice movies, and go to church; you could have a party for your friends right here in the house if you wanted to."

Addie looked away. " . . . Okay," she finally said.

"Ain't that right, now?" Clotilda watched her.

" . . . Okay." Addie was sidling toward the kitchen door.

Clotilda grinned. "From now on, you and me're goin' to be pals. How about that?" Then she laughed nervously. "Why, grandma and granddaughter can be pals; nothin' wrong with that, is there? Of course not."

Addie stood at the door. "Okay, Grandma . . . okay." She went on back to their bedroom.

Clotilda, deep in thought, put the beef stew on the slow burner. Then she sat down at the kitchen table and stared out the window.

🌀   🌀   🌀   🌀   🌀   🌀

That evening when young Jack Griffin left Clotilda's house with Addie—to go to the party—it was still daylight, although the summer sky was fading in pale hues of lilac and salmon pink. Lester had gone a few doors down the street to Norman Simpson's, a school friend; and Clotilda, alone in the house save for Hammer upstairs, worked at her sewing machine. Somehow, despite everything, she had felt a little less heavy-hearted since her talk that afternoon with Addie. She was determined now to force herself on Addie, if that was necessary to bring them closer together. The child needed help, Clotilda reflected, and companionship, love— a hugging, showy kind of love, at that. Clotilda believed now that she had been too hesitant, unsure, even afraid, had let Addie awe her, hadn't pried enough into her personal affairs, her thoughts. Addie could still be helped, must be helped—saved. She would work harder with the child; be more aggressive; make up for lost time—before it was too late.

It was after eight-thirty, and just dark—Clotilda was still at her sewing machine—when the doorbell rang. She started, then looked up, but kept her seat. At last she got up. Before she reached the door the bell rang again—a long, grating ring. Finally she opened the door to a woman and boy standing on her lighted front porch. The boy was black, and larger than Lester, although perhaps the same age. He wore a gauze spot bandage on the top of his bare head where an area the size of a silver dollar had been shaved clean. The woman, about thirty-five, was also dark, but skinny.

Clotilda stared at them. "Yes?"

The woman frowned, then looked her up and down. "Are you Lester Parker's grandmutha?" she said.

"Yes—I am."

The woman shoved the big boy forward. "Well, looka here at what he done to James today." She raised her hand to the boy's head and pushed his head down forward. "See? He got him down and beat him with a sharp rock. It took six stitches—*six*."

Clotilda gaped, then turned around to her living room, but remembered Lester was down the street. "I don't know a thing about it," she said. "Lester didn't mention it. Are you sure it was him?" There was faint defiance in her voice.

The woman took in a swift angry breath. "Am I sure it was

him!" She turned on her son, who wore a hang-dog look. "Tell her!"

The boy glumly nodded his head. "It was him, all right—Lester."

"Is your boy here?" the woman said.

"No—he's out," Clotilda said.

"Well, my husband's goin' to have him arrested if you don't pay for our doctor's bill and the prescription. It was eighteen dollars!"

Clotilda studied the woman, "Well, I'm gonna look into this thing first. Lester'll be home pretty soon; I'll ask him about it. Why would he want to do a thing like that? Sounds kinda fishy to me."

"Well, it ain't fishy!" the woman said. "Your boy accused James of sayin' something about his sister—and it's a lie!"

Clotilda's mouth hung open now—she remembered Lester's bruised eye. Finally she said: "Well, Lester musta had *some* reason —if he did do it. You let me talk to him first. What's your name?" she asked the woman.

"Mrs. Lights. We live 'round on Evans Avenue. Jefferson Lights—it's in the phone book. My husband's goin' to swear out a warrant for him sure as he's livin', if you don't pay."

Clotilda's voice rose. "Well! Do you think I'm simple enough to reach in my pocket and give you eighteen dollars and never saw either one of you before in my life? I'm gonna look into this thing first. I'll call you—tomorrow."

The woman glared at her as they left.

Clotilda closed the door, went to the telephone, and called down the street to Norman Simpson's, where Lester was. Lester was home in five minutes. Clotilda let him in. Following her into the living room, he was glum, uncommunicative. Clotilda calmly walked over and sat in the big armchair beside the piano, pointing Lester to a straight-back chair. "Sit down," she said.

Lester sat down.

"Some Mrs. Lights was just here—with her boy," she began. "She says you cut him on the head with a rock today."

Lester pouted at the floor and said nothing.

"Well, did you, Lester?"

" . . . We got in a fight . . . yes'm." He would not look at Clotilda.

"What happened?—tell me about it."

"We got in a fight, that's all. Anything can start a fight."

"Well, what started this one, Lester?"

Lester sat up straight, then glanced at Clotilda, but said nothing.

"I want to know, Lester. Why don't you want to tell me?"

He finally looked away again.

"They're gonna put you in jail."

"I don't care."

"Well, how d'you like that! Listen, Lester, there ain't a thing on earth you can't tell me. You know that. Nothin'. Now, what happened?"

Lester turned to her, but spoke almost inaudibly. "He said somethin' about Addie."

Already Clotilda's face showed impending distress. " . . . What did he say?"

Lester looked past her. "Said she was goin' with a married man."

"Goin' with a married man!"

"He didn't say 'goin with'; he said a bad word."

Clotilda filled her lungs with air, then exhaled almost in a moan: "What married man?"

"Dunreith Smith—Thelma's brother."

"*Oh!*" A spasm of wild, shocked rage hit Clotilda. Everything was clear to her now. She blurted out before she thought—"Why, *sure*! Sure! Don't she go by that little bitch's almost every evening after school?—and don't get home sometimes till nine? Why, sure! No wonder people're talkin'!"

Lester looked straight at her. "Well, you let her do it, Grammaw. We call her up all the time, but she never comes home from Thelma's till late. But you never say nothin'—act like you're scared of her."

"Lester, you're crazy! Plain crazy, that's all. I ain't scared of her . . . That's so silly." But Clotilda's voice had weakened.

Lester only looked at her.

She too was silent now. She had known little Jack Griffin was not the offender—he was too nice a boy, she thought. So it was that trifling—some said handsome!—Dunreith Smith; rotten scum. He was at least twenty-eight, with a wife and two small children; and though with a family of his own, he had never left home, but lived with them cramped up in his mother's house with Thelma and two other, younger sisters. Poor, poor Addie—one minute Clotilda was wretched with pity for her, and in the next could have screamed at her in rage. Yes, Addie was guilty all right, she told herself; it was too awful to think about—guilty of giving herself away to a notorious, alcoholic, pot-smoking, married lecher. But now, at all costs, Clotilda was determined to keep the truth from Lester.

"Lester, you know that boy was lyin', don't you?"

Lester did not answer at once. "Yes'm," he finally said.

"So I'm not blamin' you one bit for what you did. You did right—for what he said about your sister. You did absolutely right. And they can't do a thing to you."

But the next day Clotilda went over to the Lights' and paid the eighteen dollars. And Lester refused to go to camp.

Almost a week later, on a Thursday afternoon, Lord Nelson Turner's wife, Hyacinth—a ponderous, sweating, yellow woman of sixty—was bustling about in the little room off her dining room she called her "study." She had just placed two comfortable straight-back chairs on opposite sides of a tiny table—her "transmission" table—and lighted a small incense taper fixed in a black dish on the radiator cover. She was alone; a "client" was expected in fifteen minutes. This was not to be a tea reading today, but merely a consultation—she sometimes started her people out with what she called "consultative readings," and maybe later, for a modest increase in fee, found it possible to declare them ready for a "definitive reading." This latter could mean reading tea leaves, bay leaves, parsley flakes possibly, or, in extreme situations —"dire cases," as Hyacinth with grave alarm sometimes referred to them—cinnamon granules. At one time she had had numerous clients, a following of sorts—at least a scheduled interview each day—but in recent years her vogue had waned, so that now each new interview filled her with a fresh, an intense, zeal to be of service. For she was no charlatan in the sense of any lack of dedication to her calling and had spent a lifetime—within the limitations of a stunted education—in trying to probe, to explore, the murky, submerged mysteries of human misery.

She had never met Clotilda Pilgrim, but she knew who she was—through her own husband and her husband's friend, Ambrose Hammer. Clotilda had telephoned for the appointment only the day before; Hyacinth was struck by the calmness, the repose, of Clotilda's voice, and said to herself, "This woman has no big problems—or else awful, terrible, ones. I can't make out which." So now she hurried about the little room, making it comfortable, neat, for the "interview."

The faint aroma of incense curling up from the taper was somehow redolent of a hushed funeral parlor, and the room was heavily carpeted, with two curtained windows in one wall and small, cheap, oriental-looking statuary in three niches on the opposite wall. On the smaller wall, hehind and above Hyacinth's chair, hung a large framed picture of herself when young, standing on what appeared to be a latticed porch with an aged white man who wore a Prince Albert coat and long white beard that entirely hid his cravat—Ben Candler Pigott, famed spiritualist, with whom

Hyacinth had "studied" down in her native New Orleans almost forty years before.

Twenty minutes later, at five minutes past three o'clock, her front doorbell rang. She walked through the living room and opened the door to Clotilda. Clotilda was dressed up. She wore a pale blue and white summer dress with short sleeves and white accessories, including a little white hat that sat up askew on her stiff grey hair—all of which somehow made her look broader, heavier; and a darker walnut-brown. She stepped inside, smiling.

Hyacinth's greeting was effusive. "Why, how do you do, Mrs. Pilgrim?" She was larger than Clotilda, and taller; and wore a plain black dress and sandal-type shoes. The house was not hot, but tiny beads of sweat stood out on Hyacinth's yellow forehead and glinted through the short hair at her temples.

Clotilda smiled at her. "I'm a little late, Mrs. Turner."

"Oh, not at all, not at all—I hope you didn't rush. I was goin' to set aside the balance of the afternoon for you anyway. For our purposes, you know, we must never feel rushed, or pushed—oh, never. Here, why don't you let me put your hat—oh, how cute it is!—on the mantle here." Clotilda lifted off her hat and handed it over; then removed her white lace gloves and put them in her purse.

"Would you like to come on back in the study?" Hyacinth said, already leading the way. Clotilda followed. They entered the little room and Hyacinth pointed out Clotilda's chair at the tiny "transmission" table. "I fixed a pitcher of iced coffee for us," Hyacinth beamed. "Would you take a glass with me?"

"Why . . . yes," Clotilda said nervously, sitting down. As Hyacinth went into the kitchen, Clotilda's big eyes took in the room—the faded, caught-back draperies; the picture; the little statuettes in their niches; the garish wallpaper. Although the little incense taper had burnt out, its aroma hung in her nostrils like a heavily-perfumed mist, giving a sense of the sought-for strangeness, the oddity, of the room.

Soon Hyacinth returned with two glasses of iced coffee on a tray. She handed one glass to Clotilda, took the other herself, then placed the tray on the radiator cover. Her activity had induced a wheezy breathing; she retreated, sat heavily in a chair against the wall, and smiled. "Now, we'll just relax a minute—quietly," she said, her damp, mountainous breasts swelling and falling. Both sipped the iced coffee in silence.

When their glasses were at last empty, Hyacinth got up and put them on the tray on the radiator cover. Then she returned and this time sat in the chair across the little table from Clotilda and shifted her bulk tentatively about in the chair as if on the verge of some great gymnastic feat. She smiled again at Clotilda. "Let us hold hands," she said. Clotilda, her heart pounding, placed her dark, dishpan hands up on the table. Hyacinth took them gently at first; but gradually applied the pressure; and soon she had them grasped and smothered in her own huge, moist hands.

"Be quiet, now, Mrs. Pilgrim," she said, "—and try to clear your mind. Our minds are tryin' to touch, you see—tryin' to communicate. It helps *me* to close my eyes; it might be different with you. Wanta try?"

Clotilda closed her eyes, but felt uncomfortable. Soon she opened them and looked across at Hyacinth, whose eyes were squinched shut and face a study in fierce fervor as she clutched Clotilda's hands in a fanatic's grip. Clotilda, watching her, felt strange—closed in, caught. Her mind, as if to escape, took a quick wide exposure of her total life, but this brought sudden self-pity. Now her emotion began to build, making her breathing choke and flutter, her eyes smart. Soon she could stifle the tears no longer; gently they slid down her face onto her little white lace collar. But almost as quickly, her embarrassment sobered her thoughts and staunched her tears. Now she wanted to use her handkerchief, but her hands were manacled.

After a few moments Hyacinth's vehement self-communion seemed to have reached its crest and subsided. She slowly relaxed her grip and opened her eyes, smiling now with grave pride at Clotilda's tears. Clotilda withdrew her hands and went in her purse for a handkerchief; then blew her nose. Soon, in a low assuaging voice, Hyacinth said: "Our beings have communicated—beautifully." Then there was a pause, as she sighed—"Why did you come?"

Clotilda first snuffled. "I had to talk to somebody," she said.

"What seems to be troublin' you?" For the question Hyacinth's face sought a false, beatific smile.

Clotilda sat looking at her as if she had not heard; but finally she answered: " . . . It's my grandbaby—my grand-daughter. I can't do anything with her. Now I think she's goin' with a married man."

Hyacinth's stare showed her only partially comprehending.

Clotilda said, "She's in high school yet—not seventeen."

"Oh, my." Hyacinth's face puckered in pain. "Have any steps been taken to stop it?"

"Nothin' yet—I can't seem to make up my mind what to do. I thought maybe you could see things in it I can't—then I'd know better what I could do."

"We first got to go to the causes of this thing," Hyacinth said. "I always go to causes; otherwise it's no good; I can't help."

A sudden quick ache of dread went through Clotilda. She sat looking past Hyacinth.

"The child lives with you, does she?"

"Yes," Clotilda said.

"What kind is she?—tell me about her."

"Well . . . Addie's a nervous child, headstrong sometimes. I've had her and her brother since they were small, since my daughter died. Addie's always been like that, I guess—flighty, hard to handle."

Hyacinth nodded her chin up and down with authority. "Yes —after her mother's death. It happens."

" . . . Yes," conceded Clotilda.

"Go on, Mrs. Pilgrim. You must tell me."

"Well, Addie won't mind me, won't do anything I say. She ain't sassy or anything like that, but it seems whatever I try to tell her for her own good just goes in one ear and out the other. And she don't seem to like to talk to me much about her little private things—boys and girls at school, teachers, puppy loves, and things like that—like a young girl ordinarily would. She keeps 'em to herself so far as I can see. She's got a school friend, Thelma Smith; she might talk to her, I don't know. This fella's Thelma's brother. He's rotten, and a grown man with a wife and two children. I've always tried to be good to Addie—kind, never struck her or whipped her in her life."

Hyacinth watched Clotilda. "It's strange you didn't, Mrs. Pilgrim—strange. All children need correction, at some time or other. Don't you think maybe you was too easy? And why, I wonder?—Why?" Hyacinth peered up the far wall in thought; then shook her head and thrust both hands up on the table. "Here, give me your hands again," she said, "—we're losing contact, seems like."

Clotilda surrendered her hands again, but this time Hyacinth only covered them with her own and closed her eyes in a deep fixation. They sat in silence for over two minutes. Finally Hyacinth opened her eyes and gazed at Clotilda. "Tell me how you feel about Addie *now*."

Clotilda looked at her and thought for a moment; then finally said: " . . . I feel sorry for her, I guess—mostly. I don't want her to ruin her life. That would be awful." She looked away.

"It would, of course," Hyacinth reflected aloud, frowning. "But I'm not tuned in right yet—we're not relating. Well, let's go on to another side of it, and tackle this angle again in a minute. Tell me, how do you know she's interested in this man?"

"Even the kids in the neighborhood are talkin' about it—my grandson got in a bad fight about it only a week ago."

"Oh, kids' talk—there may be nothin' to it."

"But then——" Clotilda faltered. "Well, I accidentally found some . . . some rubbers in her purse the other day."

"Oh!" Hyacinth sat up straight. "This *is* serious." She lapsed into frowning thought.

Clotilda was quiet now. She felt easier already, seeming to have rid herself of this awful fact and sloughed it off onto someone else. For a moment she felt as if it were solely Hyacinth's problem now. The feeling must have communicated itself to Hyacinth, for she sat with knitted brow; but then came back strong:

"Mrs. Pilgrim, you gotta go after this thing like killin' a snake. Don't wait. Do it now. Face her with the evidence. Put the law on that dog. Don't dilly-dally around with 'em any longer."

Clotilda was appalled—and the stricken look on her face seemed to exasperate Hyacinth.

"This brings us right back where we started," Hyacinth said. "Mrs. Pilgrim, why're you so afraid of this child?—afraid to take the steps you ought've taken long time ago? My intuition does not reveal it—I don't know why. But it keeps *askin'* it. There is some road block between us, Mrs. Pilgrim." Hyacinth, watching Clotilda, sat back in fretful judgment.

Clotilda writhed in confusion, dismay. " . . . But I don't know what she'd *do*," she cried. "—I don't know at all. She's a reckless, desperate child—I don't want to make it worse. I ain't sure *what* she'd do. I don't want any more blood on my hands!" Clotilda realized too late what she had said. Her hand started to her mouth; then stopped; but her lips remained parted.

Hyacinth bent forward and stared. "Ah-h-h," she breathed aloud, nodding her head in self-affirmation. "This thing has . . . ah . . . a long history—I can see that. There is an 'involution' of causes here—ah, yes, a 'concatenation,' as it were." She was using old Ben Candler Pigott's language.

Clotilda, anguish crinkling her face, stood up now. She shook her head. "I don't think you can help me today, Mrs. Turner. I'm kinda mixed up . . . confused. When I get myself together, maybe I can come back and you can help me."

Hyacinth remained seated. "You're only runnin' away from yourself," she sighed. "Addie's not your real trouble—yes, she may be your trouble today, this afternoon, but not yesterday and not tomorrow." Hyacinth finally stood up. "If you'd just face up to somethin'—and that somethin' has not quite appeared to me as yet, but it will—you might could be helped."

They stood facing each other across the little table. Clotilda went in her purse and dabbed her handkerchief once to her nose. "We'll see," she said. " . . . I'll try."

Hyacinth suddenly smiled on her. "Y'see, you're just runnin'—don't you see?"

Clotilda, handkerchief in hand, nodded. "I gotta get myself together first."

Hyacinth came around the table now and put her arm around Clotilda's shoulder. "Well, I'll be right here," she said, "—right here on call. Just don't do anything—nothin'—till you come to yourself a little. I see now I was wrong, tellin' you to take action now—maybe my vision at the time was blurred. Just do nothin'—and wait. Now, will you?" She patted Clotilda's shoulder. "Let things kinda come around. And then if you make up your mind—and only you can do it—that you want to clear whatever that road block is away, you come on back. Hear? I can help you."

Clotilda smiled weakly. "Thank you . . . thank you." She opened her purse. " . . . How much do I owe you, now?"

Hyacinth was awkward. " . . . Oh, that'll be fifteen dollars, I guess."

Clotilda went in her purse and gave her a five and a ten. "I know," she sniveled, "you won't tell nobody about my interview."

Hyacinth's set smile vanished. "Listen—it's written—the moment I speak to another, that moment my powers are stripped from me and my psychic eyes struck blind. Oh, you must know that, Mrs. Pilgrim."

"Well, I thank you—thank you."

Then Clotilda followed her into the living room, got her hat, and soon left.

When she arrived home, Lester had just finished washing the kitchen windows. Addie had not come home yet from her new job. Clotilda went into the kitchen and, dutifully smiling at Lester, took a can of beer from the refrigerator. She opened the beer and sat down at the kitchen table. "Come here, baby," she said to Lester between sips.

He came over docilely and stood beside her chair.

She looked up at him. Then she put her arm up around his waist. "Oh, you're such a good boy, Lester, honey—*such* a good boy." She bit her lip to control herself.

Lester looked quizzically at her.

"Lester, you must forgive Grandma when she snaps you up sometimes. She don't mean anything by it. You're the only one close to her in her whole life that never caused her any trouble— the only one. You're such a good boy, Lester, baby."

"Where you been, Grammaw?" Lester said, staring at her.

Clotilda only looked at him.

"What's wrong with you, Grammaw?"

She squeezed his hand and looked away, then slowly shook her head. "Does anybody know that?" she mused aloud. "Does anybody?" Then she got up. "Oh, don't pay me no mind, Lester." She laughed now. "Your old grandma's gettin' batty—real batty. Now, how about you and me throwin' us together some dinner, huh? How about *that*?"

Lester was still studying her. " . . . Okay," he said.

Clotilda reached for an apron and tied it around him.

Chapter Five

A WEEK later, about eleven-thirty one night, tall, august Ambrose Hammer, wearing slippers and red-and-white striped silk pajamas, sat on the edge of his bed. He yawned. He had just finished work for the night and was tired from four solid hours at his writing desk. Still, he was thinking of the talk he would make at Lord Nelson Turner's lodge. Only nine days remained and as yet he had no subject. He prized this invitation more than his composed, immobile face, his undisturbed behavior, indicated. He had never been asked to speak anywhere before. Yet so far there was no nervousness, no fear; he was confident. At first he mentioned the invitation to no one—except to Clotilda, by chance, in response to some remark of hers. Yet his self-esteem had been titillated, and the more he mulled over in his mind the available subjects for the talk, the more importance the event assumed. He regarded it as an opportunity, an event, and speculated on how large the audience that evening might be and even whether a hint ought not be dropped in favor of throwing the meeting open to the families and friends of the lodge members; he wanted it made something special; memorable.

Although the lodge, The Sons of Ezra, had on its roster more than one hundred members, Hammer, if anything, a realist, knew this number could not be counted on to crowd the hall to hear an unknown, unaccredited, lecturer ply them with their racial history. The thought made him unhappy; for, whatever the subject he might at last hit upon, he meant to say something important, edifying—something worthy of more than a mere handful of the more faithful members. He felt he must communicate—in a delicate way, of course—his concern to Lord Nelson Turner and through him to the program committee.

The problem of a suitable subject had plagued him for days. Wearily, he got up from the bed again and went over to his desk— the long red stripes in his silk pajamas made him look taller still. As he sat down at the desk, he reached over into a large cardboard box on a chair and rummaged for a blue notebook in which he kept the long, growing, table of contents of his book. Here he might find suggestions for a subject. He adjusted his pince-nez, opened the notebook on the desk before him, and began slowly turning the pages.

Soon there was a knock at his door.

Grudgingly he raised his head— " . . . Yes?"

"Ambrose . . . you gone to bed yet?" It was Titus Neeley's high, whispering, nervous voice.

Hammer sighed and removed his pince-nez. "—Come on in, Neeley."

Little Neeley opened the door and entered grinning. "Saw the light under your door, Ambrose. Thought you'd still be up, all right—working on your magnum opus, eh? Ha-ha-ha-ha!" Neeley hilariously shot up his chin at the ceiling, yet his face was grey and drawn.

Hammer nudged his pince-nez an inch or two forward on the desk and smiled; then closed the notebook. "No, I'd just about closed down for the night," he said. "What've *you* been up to?— out on the prowl?"

"Prowl, my eye," snorted Neeley, standing in the middle of

the floor. "I've been over to see a guy I know that works with me in the Post Office; he's sick, and in the process he touched me up for twenty bucks."

"He knows you're loaded," Hammer said.

"Hummph!—I'm loaded, all right; just trying to learn how to live on my pension, that's all—when I get it." Neeley, a bachelor, was sensitive about his height—five feet, one—and now stood forward on his toes to look taller. He was gaunt besides, with a little abdomen that suddenly protruded as if it contained a basketball. His Negro blood was negligible—he more resembled a consumptive Arab. Now, in confidence, he stepped closer to Hammer—"Say," he whispered, "what's wrong with old lady Pilgrim?"

" . . . Wrong with her? I don't know."

Neeley kept his voice low. "When I came in just now, she was sitting down in the kitchen, by herself. Just staring at the wall. Looked to me like she'd been crying."

Hammer seemed embarrassed. "Well . . . maybe she's got her problems, too, like everybody else." He got up from the desk.

"Can't imagine what could be wrong with her," speculated Neeley, " . . . unless it's money. Maybe it's money—how's she fixed?"

"How would I know?" Hammer yawned and looked at his wrist watch.

"Maybe she's still grieving about her sister," Neeley said. "Pearlie . . . that was her name. But, Lord, she was dead when I came here. That couldn't be it. It's probably money, all right."

Hammer yawned once more, and Neeley soon stepped toward the door. Then suddenly nodding at Hammer's littered desk, he gave his high, mirthless laugh, "How's the treatise coming? Ha-ha-ha-ha! Will there be one or *two* volumes of it? Huh? . . . Ha-ha-ha-ha!"

Hammer chuckled. "Only one, I guess."

"You haven't goofed any more, have you?—like you did about Haile Selassie. Ha-ha-ha-ha!"

"I try to goof as little as possible," said Hammer.

Neeley, still laughing softly, left and went to his own room.

Hammer closed the door and immediately started dressing. He put on his trousers, shoes, and shirt open at the throat, then eased his door open and started downstairs. The stairs creaked, and when he appeared at the kitchen door, Clotilda, who had heard, sat facing him with a curious, expectant stare.

"Why, Mr. Hammer!" She half rose from the kitchen table. Her eyelashes were wet.

"Good evenin', good evenin'," Hammer smiled.

"Come in—what'n the world're you doing roamin' 'round the house this time of night?—just like a cat." Clotilda, furtively brushing a tear off her cheek, laughed and sat down again. She wore a house dress and bedroom slippers.

Hammer at first said nothing but pulled out a chair at the table and sat down opposite her. "Can't I roam the house if I want to?" he finally said, giving his deep, soft laugh. "It's my home—the only one I got, anyhow." He put his big hands up on the table and laced his fingers.

"Well, I *hope* you feel that way about it, Mr. Hammer."

They sat self-consciously looking at, then away from each other. Hammer at the moment was stumped; though ignorant of Clotilda's immediate troubles, he at least knew a part of her unhappiness was Addie. At different times, from various sources—but not from Clotilda—he had learned the circumstances of Addie's childhood and had by then on three occasions heard the nerve-chilling night screams that came up from the first-floor bedroom, and the commotion that always followed. But now he sensed some fresh, uncommon calamity, and his feelings groped out to Clotilda. Yet he abhorred officiousness and though wanting to help, could not bring himself to ask unbidden questions. He shilly-shallied. Maybe if careful, he thought, he might draw her out, give her a chance to volunteer.

"Don't let me keep you up, Mrs. Pilgrim," he said. "I was

just goin' to *borrow* a glass of milk from the refrigerator—and got caught in the act." He laughed and felt uneasy lying.

"Oh—why, of course." Clotilda, urging her weight up from the chair, hurried to the refrigerator. "Why didn't you say so, Mr. Hammer?" She took out a carton of milk and reached up for a glass.

"Well, first of all, I didn't expect to find you in the kitchen at midnight," Hammer laughed, "—sittin' down here all by yourself like this—all wrapped up in your thoughts."

Clotilda placed the glass on the table before him and poured the milk. She would not look at him; and returned the carton to the refrigerator. But soon she smiled and sat down at the table again.

He thanked her and was silent.

"Oh, I was on my way to bed, all right," she finally said. "I was just sittin' here a minute, goin' over in my mind all the things I got to do tomorrow." She laughed and sighed.

Hammer, sipping the milk, watched her over his hoisted glass. When he put the glass down, he looked away and said offhandedly, "Haven't you and I been pretty good friends since I've been here in your house?—almost six years now." He turned back and watched her.

Clotilda at first looked quizzical; then sighed again. "Yes—yes, we have, Mr. Hammer."

"Well, friends talk to each other—confide—share each other's . . . well, aches and pains, so to speak." He chortled. "Don't they?"

Clotilda was instantly alert. Slowly she sat erect with a frozen sparkling smile. "Sure, Mr. Hammer—sure they do. . . . Why, have you got somethin' you wanted to tell me?—you in any trouble?" She gave him a bland stare.

Hammer sighed. Then smiled. It was no use, he knew. He finished his milk. "Okay, Mrs. Pilgrim, okay." He finally got up, went to the sink, and rinsed out the glass. "I guess I'll go on back up and turn in. Thanks for the milk—thank you."

"Oh, you're welcome any time; you know that." She smiled and stood up, "I'm goin' to turn in, myself." The strain now showed in her face.

Hammer said good night and went upstairs.

Clotilda had been crying because that afternoon, on her daily check of Addie's dresser drawer, she had found the little red change purse empty.

🌀   🌀   🌀   🌀   🌀   🌀

Four days later, on Monday, Titus Neeley learned from one of the lodge members—who, like Neeley, worked at the Post Office—of Hammer's pending speaking engagement. Neeley was at first flabbergasted, then he felt the needle of envy and told himself the invitation could only swell Hammer's head even more. Wasn't he smug enough already? Or else why hadn't he mentioned the speech, instead of keeping it such a luscious secret. When Neeley got home that afternoon he went straight upstairs, but Hammer was not in yet. Neeley returned downstairs to the living room, where Miss Letitia Dorsey, wearing glasses, sat reading a fashion magazine, her long stilt legs scissored priggishly together. The June sun, warm, mellow, was low in the west now and sent its flat bright rays through Clotilda's curtains onto the piano keyboard. Neeley could not remember seeing Letitia wear glasses before—as soon as he greeted her, she eased them off and slipped them in her purse.

Little Neeley sat down, affecting his gayest, jauntiest mood—"Miss Dorsey, wish we could *all* go hear Hammer Thursday night. Ha-ha-ha-ha!" He clipped off the words as his chin went up in a harsh, dry laugh.

Letitia, eyelashes fluttering, beamed proudly—"Yes . . . yes . . . but Mr. Hammer said we *could* go if we wanted to. The meeting's open to the public now, you know, and it's been changed from Thursday to Friday night." Letitia's long, smiling octoroon, face wore its usual mask of white powder, and her lips were made-up scarlet.

Neeley sat bolt upright with joy. " . . . Oh—so we *can* go! Great—oh, that's great! Now I'll go and give old Hammer some moral support. Ha-ha-ha-ha! He'll need it, too—he'll need it!"

Letitia slowly brought her bean-pole body erect in the chair as she gave him a sober, almost disapproving look; but finally she smiled again.

"You going?" Neeley inquired.

"Yes—Mr. Hammer's asked me to type his talk for him when he's finished work on it. I certainly want to go hear him."

"What'll he talk about? . . . the glory of the black race, I guess. Ha-ha-ha-ha!" Neeley swatted his knee.

Letitia's set smile faded. Although it momentarily reappeared, she soon got up, excused herself, and went upstairs.

Neeley, now alone, sat fidgeting. He picked up and scanned the evening paper, but felt jumpy, uneasy, irked; he sensed Letitia's displeasure at what he had said. Furthermore he detected her pride in her current collaboration with Hammer, for he knew she had also agreed now to type the manuscript of his book. Neeley had had no one take an interest in him since his mother died four years before. He was an only child; deserted early by his father, he was reared by his mother; the two had lived alone together throughout the years. Now since her death he was lost, irresolute—bitter. For he considered himself more than adequate to the demands of daily living, superior even, yet unappreciated. He knew Hammer was his only friend; still he envied him, felt himself more clever— wasn't he a college graduate? he thought. Hammer was not. And he was younger—fifty-five; Hammer was fifty-nine. Still people thought Hammer had achieved, had pushed beyond the range of a Post Office clerk. Neeley knew he himself had not.

Soon he heard Addie and Lester talking in the kitchen. Then

shortly Addie entered the living room, and, crossing in front of him, went over to the television.

"Hey there, Addie!" Neeley, laughing, shot forward in his chair.

"Hi," Addie smiled faintly, as she flicked the television on.

"How's the job?—how d'you like punching the old time clock for a change? The rest of us've been doing it for years, you know. Ha-ha-ha-ha!"

"Oh, it's okay." Addie was inattentive and stood aside waiting for the TV screen to light up. She wore a skirt, blouse, and high-heeled shoes. When the TV picture came on, pale in the sunlight, she sat down across the room from Neeley to watch.

Suddenly Neeley snapped his fingers in recollection. "Say . . . I saw you the other day—in a car on 58th Street—Wednesday . . . or Thursday, I think it was."

Addie tensed but kept cool and continued watching the TV screen. Finally she turned to Neeley, "Pardon me . . . ?"

"I said I saw you the other day . . . on 58th Street . . . in a car . . . in a piece of car, that is! Ha-ha-ha-ha!"

Addie was casual. "Not me . . . I don't think it was me."

Neeley studied her. "Are you sure? . . . Oh, yes it was you, too—don't tell *me*. Ha-ha-ha!"

Addie smiled and shook her head. "No, you got me mixed up with somebody else, Mr. Neeley." She kept her eyes on the TV screen.

Neeley's face wore a puzzled frown. " . . . Well . . . maybe so. I was standing there on Indiana Avenue waiting for a bus about six o'clock in the evening. I thought it was *you* sitting there in that old jalopey, and just as I was goin' to holler at you, a fellow . . . skinny fellow, real skinny, with a thick, bushy mustache, came out of a two-flat building and climbed under the wheel and drove off with you. I thought sure it was you."

Addie gave her hysterical little laugh. "It wasn't me." Dismissing the subject, she turned again to the television.

They sat and watched a variety show. Soon Addie cried out
in anguish, "Oh, I wish we had color television!—we could see
those beautiful costumes. I know they're beautiful!"

Neeley laughed. "You don't know how much color television
costs, do you? Some of them cost five hundred dollars, about. Five
hundred bucks!"

Addie smiled, then laughed, "It's only money." Then she
lapsed into a petulant silence.

When the TV program was over, she got up, left Neeley sitting
in the living room, and went to her bedroom off the kitchen. Earlier,
Clotilda had pulled down the bedroom blinds to keep out the sun;
still the room was warm, stuffy. Addie stood viewing herself in the
dresser mirror; her freckles, now smoothed over with brown face
powder, were now hard to detect. She was restless, sulky, angry
with prying Neeley. So he had seen her with Dunreith Smith; he
would!—the snooping little fool. Well, it only made her want to
see Dunreith more and to get out of that house for awhile that evening, but she knew asking permission would only create a crisis. In
the mirror she admired the new peach blouse she was wearing; she
had bought it downtown at Sears with her own money. She wished
Dunreith could see it; sometimes he gave a low whistle when she
looked extra nice.

Dunreith, Dunreith—she thought of little else these days, but
thinking of him always gave her a crick in the heart; it was a
brand new experience for her, yet one seeming at times to ease,
console her when she was unhappy at home, as she was now most
of the time. Wasn't her grandmother acting strange lately!—
moping around the house all day, getting angry with her one minute,
pampering her the next. She was silent for hours, but sneakily eyed
Addie every minute. It was awful to be watched so. Why did her
grandmother act so queer? She whispered to herself as she sewed,
rolled and tossed in the bed at night; in the kitchen she stopped
peeling potatoes to stare at the wall, also now chewed gum a lot,
like any kid in the street. And Lester!—was he snotty! What was

wrong with him, too? It sure was a wacky house. She sat down unhappily on the side of the bed, her hands in her lap. She wanted still to think of Dunreith, as she always did whenever she was worried. It made her feel better, at least for a little while.

All that day at the office Addie had been daydreaming, mooning, about Dunreith. She telephoned him each noon on her lunch hour, for she could reach him then—at the little shop where he painted signs. Dunreith fancied himself a commercial artist and considered this job only temporary. But Addie knew that liquor, pot, and other bad habits, blocked his progress. She naively felt it was only because the world was against him, as it had been against her, and that he had surrendered to it, stopped fighting—that is, until they had met. Now she believed he had changed; she had turned him around, she thought; he was trying now; he said so himself. They had unburdened themselves to each other. It didn't seem to her he was twelve years older than herself, for they talked on the same level, with freedom and ease, man to woman, woman to man. It flattered her. She felt she'd been right in telling him her whole life's story; she had given it to him, as she had given him her young body. Now he knew the secret that racked her daily existence—her mother. Mama, Mama, Mama. He didn't know what to say when she told him—just sat like a stone; finally he lit a cigarette and shook his head. No one before had heard it—Dunreith had now, though. No one ever would again; re-telling was re-living. Yet she had felt her story would make him see his troubles were nothing. If so, it was worth it.

Dunreith was her first and only man; she had been willing, eager, and remembered now the cheap room where he took her, the sleazy lavender bedspread, the old floor lamp with the long tassels. But she had not been afraid and now recalled with distaste only the rotten whiskey on his breath. He knew it was her first time and laughed and called himself 'old Dunreith, the cherry picker." Yet he'd been gentle, so gentle—almost unconcerned, she had thought. Afterwards he kept her well supplied with condoms, said he was afraid to carry them around in his wallet, for his wife often rifled his pockets for money.

There were many sides to this man, she thought; you never knew what to expect from him; when he was drinking, he laughed and kidded around a lot; he was happiest then. Liquor didn't make him mean as she'd heard it did some men. The one time he'd bawled her out he was cold sober—it was the afternoon she talked about her grandmother. She told him how wonderful her grandmother had been to her and Lester over the years; how awful, terrible, it would be if she ever found out about him. It made him angry. He called her a baby, a God-damn crybaby, and used obscene language. He scared her when he was like this.

But the times he swigged from the little half-pints of bourbon he carried around in the glove compartment of his car, he got so funny and romantic; he might also rant about civil rights and Black Power and, laughing all the while, curse all white people. But she could always handle him when he drank; this made her feel good, and older—a real woman. He also taught *her* how to drink—bourbon and Coca Cola in a paper cup, as they rode around in his ancient Dodge. She'd hated liquor at first, but gradually came to like it, with its fine little tingles in the pit of the stomach and the glow that came after. Then each time before she went home he'd make her chew coffee grounds to kill her breath. It was all so exciting.

Addie stood up from her bed now and, gazing again in the dresser mirror, studied herself. She thought she looked very neat, nice—but to what purpose? It would soon be dinnertime, and after that what?—another paperback or the same old weekly TV shows. She could leave the house, though, if she went right now—her grandmother had been out all afternoon and was not home yet, although it was after six o'clock—but even if she left, it was too late to phone Dunreith at his job; and if she called his house his wife might answer, or his mother, or even Thelma. Thelma probably suspected something anyway, though—she was no fool. Addie finally left the bedroom and went in the kitchen—where Lester sat on a box intently brushing a shoe in his hand.

"Grandma'll get after you," Addie said, "shining your shoes in the kitchen like that."

Lester glanced up at her, then continued brushing.

"Where *is* Grandma?" Addie frowned.

"How would *I* know?" Lester said.

They heard the front door shut. Hammer had arrived—his brief case bulging—and had paused in the living room patiently to listen to Neeley. Addie turned her back on them and glared at Lester, who ignored her. She paced to the kitchen window, then back to the table again. "Oh—this house!—this hotel! Sometimes it almost drives you nuts!" She started out of the kitchen.

Lester slowly raised his head and looked at her, then muttered something under his breath and went on brushing the shoe.

She turned, glared at him again, and started to speak, but instead wheeled and left the kitchen. Then he heard her slam her bedroom door.

Little Neeley was following Hammer upstairs now. "Yeah!—top secret!—classified!" he heckled and laughed. "Won't even tell your friends, your best friends. Ha-ha-ha-ha! Waiting for Friday night to knock us out, lay us low. Well, I'll be there to hear it—I'll be there!" Up went his chin as he brayed at the ceiling.

All the while Hammer's long legs were slowly climbing the stairs. He grinned. "You're welcome to come, my friend—welcome. Be glad to have you . . . right up on the front row."

"Got your subject all set, Ambrose?" Now Neeley was serious.

"I have indeed—wrapped th' whole thing up today. Just got to get it typed, that's all."

They reached the second floor and Hammer stopped in front of his own bedroom door, but so did Neeley.

"What're you gonna talk on, Ambrose?"

"Why don't you come Friday night and find out? If I told you, you might lose interest." Hammer, his hand on the door-knob, grinned again. "The committee's even set up a question-and-answer period after my talk." He opened the door, but Neeley lingered. Finally Hammer invited him in.

Although the windows were up, the bedroom was warm; and smelled of dank wash cloths and toilet soap. "Have a sit-down," Hammer said, then laughed, "—or a sit-*in*." He set his brief case on the floor at the foot of the bed, as Neeley sat down. Hammer took off his own coat and tie and hung them in the closet. "How 'bout a glass of sherry?" he said, and reached a carafe of sherry, with two glasses, off the closet shelf, then, carafe and glasses in hand, went over and slumped into the chair at his desk. "Whew, I'm a little 'toilworn,' as my mother used to say." He poured sherry into the glasses and reached one across to Neeley who sat back from the open door.

Neeley was pensive as he sipped the wine. Suddenly his drawn, chalky face lit up. "Say! *I* know! Why don't you try out your talk on *me*?" Hammer looked at him. "We could have a dress rehearsal, sort of," Neeley exulted, " . . . right up here in your room . . . Wednesday or Thursday night. Ha-ha-ha-ha! You only got four nights left—we could knock all the rough edges off the speech."

"What makes you think it's got any rough edges?" Hammer gave his bass chuckle, then sipped the sherry.

"Well!" Neeley was affronted. "No rough edges, no bad grammar, no wrong facts, nothing . . . perfect."

"Perfect," grinned Hammer.

Neeley soon finished his sherry and got up. "Think maybe I'll go down to Grant Park tonight, to the band concert. . . . I may see you later on."

"No need to rush off." Hammer sought briefly to placate him. "Wish I had the time to go with you." But he seemed already preoccupied as Neeley left.

Hammer sat there with his door open. He was thinking of Letitia Dorsey and his speech—hoping she might pass in the hall; he would give her the speech for typing; for he was eager to have it back in time for study—for memorizing, if necessary—before his notable effort on Friday night. He felt the days and hours running out on him and for the first time the speech had him nervous. He wanted to lie across the bed and sleep for an hour, but instead he sat at his desk and read the newspaper, waiting, determined to be up and alert when Letitia came by. Soon he thought of his new suit—bought for the special occasion; he went to the closet and took it out. It was dark blue and dignified, and he liked it; finally he returned it to the closet and sat down again. His realization that he was nervous made him more nervous still—and just today he had learned that the lodge's women's auxiliary, "The Daughters of Ezra," would also attend Friday night. Lord Nelson Turner, who had told him, was overjoyed and assured him that, with the lodge members *and* the auxiliary present, only a few friends or relatives were needed to "pack the hall to the doors and windows." Hammer, who was at first elated, then sobered, had been tense the rest of the day; now he realized he was scared. Friday night meant much to him. It was a symbol, a fulfillment; for he had come up the long, hard way.

Born on a South Carolina peanut plantation, he was nineteen years old before he could write his name. A white family had taken him to Charleston and made possible his start on an education. Eight years of callous manual labor and voracious book study followed. At last, when twenty-seven, he had earned the credits to attend a small college in Memphis for two years, before coming to Chicago and the Post Office. Always the main fact of his life had been hard work. Over the years it had made him serious-minded and a trifle vain. His marriage failed only because at that time he had no sense of humor.

At thirty-one he had taken this Chicago bride nine years his junior, who was soon revealed to be as frivolous as he was solemn. But, unlike him, she had tried to change her ways to please him, yet met no sign of *his* willingness to bend. There were no children and after five years of stifled discord he agreed to her suit for divorce. But secretly the blow to his ego was great, and although in every way masculine he had not since let his thoughts as much as graze the bogy of marriage; thereafter his infrequent and only concern with women was physical.

Books were his passion. And the more abstruse the book the better he fancied he liked it; still, despite a rare memory for facts, his analysis of what he read in books was sometimes, though not always, faulty as a result of inadequate formal education in second-rate schools; his general, broad, solid, common sense, however, was unquestioned, authentic. Wherever he lived—in a drab hotel, a boarding house, the Y.M.C.A.—he hoarded the books he bought and carried around a tattered library card. Finally he had taken his present room in Clotilda's house. Here, for six years now, he had found an atmosphere conducive to his efforts, that made his work seem meaningful. Also here, three years before, he had first conceived his grand plan of stating the black man's case through what he considered the gospel of history. And it was a foretaste of this gospel that on Friday night he resolved to give the Sons—and Daughters—of Ezra. But now the prospect frightened him.

At seven o'clock—past Lester's dinner time—Clotilda came home. Earlier that afternoon she had bathed, dressed, and gone downtown to a movie, appeasing an urge, a compulsion, to get out of the house. She hoped in some darkened theatre to gain brief deliverance from her torments. Now home again, if not cheerful, she at least no longer moped.

Lester, ravenously eating an apple, greeted her in the entrance hall. "Grammaw, where you been?"

"Just listen, 'where you been'—and where're your manners, Lester?" Clotilda wore a summer dress and her white lace gloves. "You don't ask grown people where they been—it's not polite. I've been downtown—now're you satisfied?"

"I'm hungry," Lester said.

"I'd bet on that." Clotilda, followed by Lester, went into the kitchen. "Where's Addie?"

"In the bedroom—mad about somethin'."

"Mad about somethin'!" Clotilda stopped in the middle of the floor and stared at Lester. "Mad about what? . . . *Addie*!"—she called toward the rear. "Addie!" She put her purse down on a kitchen chair and removed her gloves.

Soon Addie, in a robe, came in the kitchen. Clotilda was reaching two cans of salmon off the cupboard shelf; she turned around and frowned at Addie. "Addie, honey, I'd'a thought you'd already started dinner by now. Ain't you hungry? Lester is."

Addie looked surprised, then contrite. "I thought you'd be home pretty soon—but I'll fix it—I'll go get a dress on." She started out.

"Never mind, never mind," Clotilda sighed. "But Lord in heaven, what'll you two do when I pass on? I ain't gonna be around here forever, you know—you better start learnin' to do a few things for yourself."

Addie and Lester stood looking at her.

Clotilda at last smiled briefly at Lester. "How 'bout a salmon salad?—it's too warm to be standin' over a hot stove."

Lester pondered a moment. " . . . Okay," he said reluctantly.

Clotilda grinned. "Well, there won't be any pot roast—*that's* for sure."

Addie, her robe held around her, still stood in the kitchen door.

Suddenly Clotilda said: "I want you kids to go with Letitia Friday evening to hear Mr. Hammer. I ain't going—because most likely it would be way over my head. But you two can learn somethin'. Somebody in the family ought to be there—to back him up. How 'bout it?—will you go, Lester?"

Lester gave her a dubious look. . . . "Yes'm."

Addie was already scowling and writhing. "Oh, Grandma!—do we *have* to? Gol-leee!—who wants to go sit up for two hours listening to some old long-winded speech?"

"Well, once won't kill you," Clotilda said, unmoved. "—And maybe you'll learn somethin' besides all that foolishness you pick up from them kids at school."

Suddenly Addie's eyes began darting back and forth, as if her private thoughts were flying. " . . . Okay . . . okay, then," she said, "and after we eat now can I go over to Thelma's awhile?— just a little while—I won't stay long."

Clotilda's knees went slack, but she steadied herself against the sink; then glanced at Lester—who was glaring at her. Now, as she strove for control, an inspiration hit her. "No, not by yourself, Addie."—her voice was flat, metallic. "Lester can take you, if he wants to—and wait there and bring you back. You can do that." It was an ultimatum.

Addie gasped. "*Lester* take me!—what do I need Lester for?"

Clotilda was ruthless. "Why, you need him to get you out of this house, that's why—and to get you back in. Or else you ain't going."

Addie's face plummeted. She retreated a step in the doorway. Suddenly she broke into a crying, bawling rage and ran for the bedroom—the slamming bedroom door wafted down white plaster dust. Later she refused all talk and food for the night. Now Clotilda was wretched again.

🌀　　🌀　　🌀　　🌀　　🌀　　🌀

Hammer's Friday arrived in sweltering July heat. Addie, on her office lunch hour, telephoned Dunreith Smith; it taxed her petulant, childish feelings to have to tell him their planned brief meeting that evening was off, that she must go to the Sons of Ezra Hall on 47th Street to hear what she called "a damn speech." She had adopted much of Dunreith's vernacular and often returned it to impress him. It only made him laugh. Dunreith on the telephone said he was sorry, but otherwise it seemed to her he took the news with indifference. She spent the afternoon in a sullen pout.

Hammer had twiddled away the whole hot morning in his room. He was jittery, nervous. At noon he turned off his little electric fan and went out for a sandwich. When he returned it was already threatening rain. He took out his speech, now neatly typed by Letitia, and tried once more to study it. But his mind would not focus. Finally he laid it aside and stood at his screened window looking out over the housetops. The skies were lowering; ominous clouds had rendez-voused to the northwest, and the wind, gathering force in the threshing trees, came in against the house in great silent shuddering rushes. Now a vein of lightning climbed a black cloud bank, and Hammer, knowing what would follow, stepped back from the win-dow as a blast-bursting thunder clap rattled the window panes. The storm that soon hit centered on Chicago's Southside. It ripped off the roof of a neighborhood theatre and hurled dead tree limbs through the windows of store fronts. Then the heavens opened up and dumped an ocean of rain water on the streets, turning them into swirling, dirty streams. Viaducts were flooded to four and five feet; cars were stalled in fender-deep water, and many telephone and power lines were down. It was general havoc. Hammer sat down on the side of his bed, fearfully waiting, awed by the savagery of the storm. And when the sheets of black rain came down, he turned his desk lamp on, for it was like night outside.

It was only then that he thought of his audience. Would there *be* any? he wondered. The flooded streets would keep some—or all!—away. His jitters left as worry came. He got up and laid out his fresh linen on the bed—shirt, socks, underwear—and made ready for his bath.

Then came the telephone call from Lord Nelson Turner. When Clotilda called up to him, Hammer, now in his robe, went to the extension phone in the hall outside his room.

Lord Nelson was very upset. "I sure am lucky just to get ahold'a you, Ambrose—many people's phones're out, you know. It was somethin', wasn't it?"

"Yeah," breathed Hammer, awaiting with dread the real pur-pose of the call.

"One of th' committee members, Jim Dudley, just got me," Lord Nelson said. "He's wondering whether we oughtn't to call the thing off—till the next regular meeting, maybe. That won't be till September now, though. I told him 'No.' I tried to get Henry Lorraine, the chairman, but his phone's out. What do *you* think, Ambrose?"

Hammer hesitated. "I don't know," he finally said. " . . . If they want to call it off, it's all right, I guess." His heart sank.

"Dudley thought th' people just wouldn't come out . . . with their basements flooded, and windows broke, and trees down, an' everything. The streets're a mess . . . water's up over the car bumpers."

Hammer sighed. "Yeah, that's right . . . maybe it'd be better to just go on and call it off."

"Well, Henry Lorraine's the chairman. He's the only one that can really call it off. The rain's let up now and I'm goin' to try and get a cab over to his house—I'll call you back soon as I find out somethin'."

" . . . Okay," Hammer said. He slowly, stoically hung up and went back to his room.

Thirty minutes later he was in the bathroom, in a tub of sudsy water, when he heard Neeley galloping up the stairs shouting and laughing something back down at Clotilda. Neeley rapped on his bedroom door. When he got no answer, he came down the hall and knocked on the bathroom door. "Ambrose!—you in there?"

"Yeah . . . Open th' door."

Little Neeley, still laughing his high, hollow laugh, cracked the door. "Don't you go off and leave me, now!" he said. "I'm goin' with you, hear? I'll carry your brief case. Ha-ha-ha-ha!"

"May not be any meetin'," Hammer said—his dark shanks were too long for the tub, causing his bent knees to break the surface of the water as he sat raking a long-handled bath brush up and down across his shoulder blades.

"Oh, for cripes sake!" Neeley said. "That don't make sense. What's a little rain?"

"*Little* rain!"

"Well, it's one devil of a note . . . after you've gone to all that trouble getting your speech together."

Hammer started to say something, but they heard the telephone ring. Soon Clotilda called up the stairs again for Hammer.

"Get it," he said to Neeley.

Little Neeley went and picked up the hall extension. "Hello," Hammer heard him say. "He's in the bath tub, right now. . . . Oh, hello, Lord Nelson . . . *Oh!* . . . Swell! swell! . . . You bet I'll tell him. Why, it would've been crazy to . . . crazy, sure.— Oh, of course—Swell! . . . It's still at eight-thirty?—Swell! You *bet* I'll tell him! . . . Yes, yes!" Neeley banged down the phone. "It's all set, Ambrose!" he cried, running to the bathroom door. "—it's all set, boy. The meeting's on. That was Lord Nelson—they want you, they want you!"

Hammer, water streaming off his dark, hulking body, was already climbing from the tub—"Well, then! Let's get this show on the road."

🌀 🌀 🌀 🌀 🌀 🌀

Lord Nelson Turner opened the lodge hall at five minutes to eight for the meeting at eight-thirty. The hall was fairly small, with folding chairs along three walls and in the center area. There was a middle aisle bisecting the center chairs from the rear up to the speaker's rostrum, where a plain table with four chairs behind it usually sufficed for speaker and guests. High on the wall over the rostrum stretched a giant white rectangular banner of silk, carrying gold, purple, and red letters and symbols: "BEAR YE ONE ANOTHER'S BURDENS." then the figure of a black man standing in what appeared to be a wheat field, extending a sheaf of grain to another black man, and the legend—"TOILERS AND GIVERS."

In the rear of the hall at the end of the middle aisle stood a six-foot, high-back chair attached to the wall. Despite its severe lines and straight, varnished arms, it called to mind a throne. During formal lodge meetings it was the seat of the "Benevolent Don," the lodge head, whom the ritual required sit in *back* of the members. His second-in-command, the "Acorn," presided from the speaker's platform up front. But tonight was a public meeting; there would be no ritual.

Lord Nelson, his trouser legs rolled up above his wet shoes, had entered through the main door near the rear of the hall. He flicked the ceiling lights on, and, carrying a furled umbrella, hustled up the aisle to the speaker's platform. There he took a rag from the table drawer and was dusting off the table and platform chairs, when Henry Lorraine, the program committee chairman, arrived with James Dudley, a committee member.

"How could we call it off on such short notice?" Lorraine, a heavy man, was saying to Dudley.

"But Good Lord," Dudley said, "people just ain't comin' out, that's all—with the street sewers stopped-up and water in the streets so high you can't see a hub cap." Dudley, a tall man, was toothless and talked over smooth, pink gums. "And we're supposed t'get more dad-bloom rain t'night," he gabbled.

"Well, all I can say is, we'll just have to wait an' see," Henry Lorraine said. They walked up the side aisle to Lord Nelson on the platform.

Dudley ignored Lord Nelson. "If it was some well-known speaker it might be different," he said to Henry Lorraine, "—but whoever heard of this fella?"

Lord Nelson spoke up. "Well, you *will* hear of him, Dudley—he's writin' a book. He's an awful smart man. I know. I've knowed him for years."

"I ain't sayin' he don't know his stuff," Dudley said. "I just say people ain't comin' out in the threat of another pourin'-down rain, an' after all that storm, to hear some fella talk they never heard'uv."

Lord Nelson and Henry Lorraine said nothing. Lorraine took

off his enormous raincoat, folded it up, and placed it under a chair on the platform. Then the three stood off to one side of the platform and rehashed the storm.

At eight-fifteen two women came, putting their heads in at the door to inquire if this was where the speaking was. When overwhelmingly reassured, they took seats near the middle and stared around at the vacant hall. Then a lone man came in, and with diffidence sat in the rear. In a little while two women and a man, a lodge member, appeared and stood in the doorway viewing the empty chairs and looking at each other. At last they walked down, greeted the committee members, and took seats near the front.

At eight-twenty Letitia Dorsey arrived, with Addie and Lester. She and Addie carried umbrellas. Tiptoeing and smiling, Letitia led the two down the side aisle to the front row, near center, where they took seats with Addie in the middle. Lester, in his good suit, with white shirt and blue tie, was large, strong for his age, and sat poker-faced. Addie looked strained, preoccupied. Letitia tried to thaw them out by leaning across and prattling to them, then tittering at her own remarks. Addie and Lester smiled briefly, but were soon busy rubbernecking at the huge, gaudy silk banner over the rostrum.

Next an elderly lodge member entered the hall with his crippled wife. With a firm grip on her elbow, he helped her down the side aisle. Lord Nelson, who had been smiling and waving to the people as they arrived, still talked to Henry Lorraine and Dudley near the platform. Now he watched the crippled woman pitching and lurching down the aisle. "You see there?" he whispered. "If old man Carter brought his wife, everybody ought to come out."

Dudley grinned, showing his pink gums. "Yeah—*ought* to."

"Where's the 'Benevolent Don?' " Henry Lorraine said.

Dudley grinned again. "If you expect *him*, you'll be disappointed."

Lord Nelson sighed; then looked out at the eleven people in the audience; and sighed again.

At eight-thirty sharp, Titus Neeley stuck his head in at the door, gawked around at the hall, and gave a low, startled whistle. Then he disappeared. But in seconds he was back, this time with Hammer. He immediately led tall Hammer down the side aisle toward Lord Nelson, Henry Lorraine, and Dudley. Hammer wore his pince-nez, and was grand in his new dark suit. He gazed straight ahead as he strode down the aisle with the quiet pomp of a prime minister. The three committee members came toward them in embarrassed greeting and they shook hands all around.

"Sorry, Ambrose," laughed Lord Nelson. "Son-of-a-gun if that storm didn't knock us for a loop—thinned the crowd so."

"Hummph—well, I'd say so," blurted little Neeley, still gaping around at the near-empty hall.

Hammer, smiling, interposed. "Well, that's more or less to be expected, gentlemen. But we can just be more informal tonight, that's all." He gave his soft, bass laugh.

Finally, Chairman Henry Lorraine led them toward the platform. Neeley hesitated, then reluctantly turned to take a seat in the audience. But Hammer noticed. "Come on, Neeley—up here," he beckoned with his head. Neeley wheeled to obey, and drew a humorous, mocking look from Dudley. They all mounted the platform, as three more lodge members arrived to swell the audience to fourteen. With Neeley on the platform, there was a shortage of one chair, and the harassed Dudley brought one up from the front row. The five men took seats, forming a long row—Henry Lorraine was to preside and Lord Nelson would introduce the speaker. They sat waiting for ten more minutes in hope of late comers; but at last Lorraine arose, stepped to the speaker's table, and smiled.

"Ladies and Gentlemen: The Sons an' Daughters of Ezra welcome you. Our Benevolent Don, Mr. Jesse Blatchford, could not be with us tonight, but I am sure he is with us in spirit an' in thought. It is too bad about the weather. Otherwise we would have a packed house—I am sure . . . because our speaker has a ringing message for us—I am sure. Still it is my pride and pleasure to present to you our Assistant-Acorn, Mr. Lord Nelson Turner, who will bring you in his own way—I am sure—our distinguished speaker of the evenin'. So hear now Brother Assistant-Acorn Lord Nelson Turner."

Lord Nelson stood up trembling. He stepped forward to the table as the light patter of hand clapping quickly petered out. " . . . Mr. Chairman," the words finally came, " . . . Distinguished Platform Guests . . . Ladies an' Gentlemen: I feel a mighty considerable degree of bafflement here this evenin' at our meetin' bein' spoiled so on account of the terrible storm that came down on us today an' made it so hard for people to come out." He took a breath. "But our speaker . . . he has not flagged or failed us, has not contracted the cold-feet, Ladies and Gentlemen. He is *here*! An' I am honored an' proud to be the one to present him." Lord Nelson, his voice rising as he warmed to his subject, now half-turned to Hammer. "Our speaker is a college man! Our speaker is a moral man! A man of proved ability—for thirty years employed by this great guv'ment of ours, the United States of America. But most outstandin' of all, he has been a hungry book-reader all of his life. He has read hundreds of books! . . . books on politics, books on science, books on philosophy, on guv'ment, on religion, on law, on civil rights; he is an authority on the life of the late Dr. Martin Luther King—an' last but not least, books on history. On black history he has read *all* the books! An' now, Ladies an' Gentlemen, he is writing his *own* book on black history, has pretty near finished it, after years of studyin' and writin'. When he has finished his message to us this evenin', we will throw the meeting open for any questions or discussion from the floor."

Hammer now uncrossed his long legs and cleared his throat. Lord Nelson reached in his own coat pocket, pulled out a scrap of note paper, and, head-bent studying it, said: "Our distinguished speaker's subject for the evenin' is . . . 'The Need . . . For Greater Emphasis On . . . Th' Contribution Of The Black Man To . . . The Early Struggle For American Independence.' " He looked up triumphantly. "Therefore, Ladies an' Gentlemen, without further to-do, it is my distinct honor, pride, an' privilege to present to you Mr. Ambrose Hammer—*Historian!*"

Neeley on the platform jumped up and led the applause. But quickly sat down again when none of the politely-applauding audience stood with him. Hammer, smiling through his nervous pince-nez, stepped forward to the table and, even though the applause soon stopped, stood through an impressive pause—gazing out over his fourteen listeners.

"Mr. Chairman;"—his voice was hollow—"my friend of many years, Mr. Turner, Gentlemen on the platform, Ladies and Gentlemen: . . . I am indeed honored tonight to be invited by your eminent program committee to come here and speak on a subject I have been interested in for, lo, these many years. Like the gentlemen on the committee here, I was disappointed about all the rain, too; but—who knows?—maybe I was saved from a great embarrassment; for the audience might not have been bigger even if the streets had been bone dry." The audience smiled. "I had prepared some rather extensive notes to refer to t'night,"—he took his speech from inside his coat and held it up—"but sitting here just now on the platform, I decided not to bore you with a long, set speech, but rather I am going to try to talk to you man to man, an' woman—informally, so to speak, off-the-cuff—and maybe that way our minds will have a better chance to meet and benefit from each other, especially if there are to be questions when I get through." He paused and cleared his throat again.

"My interest in the field of Negro history," he said, "has always had a theory behind it, a purpose—call it what you will. I don't claim that this theory is brand new. Or even that it is more important than any of the other approaches urged on us today in the struggle for our rights. The only thing I do say is that the theory is worthwhile—right along with all the others—and deserves something more than just the neglect it seems to be gettin' today."

Now Henry Lorraine's son came in with his pregnant young

wife. They took seats in the front row near Letitia, Addie, and Lester.

"So what *is* the theory?" continued Hammer. "It is not one bit complicated, Ladies an' Gentlemen—just this: Accentuate the positive. You have heard those words in a song, have you not?— 'Accentuate the positive.' In other words, tell the American people what we have *done* . . . the good things . . . the positive things. They have heard too much, for too long, about what we have not done; how we have fallen short. We must show them that there is another side. So I thought that tonight it might be a good thing if we looked into this theory a little, examined it among ourselves. Started out, for instance, with some of the contributions made by our race at a time when the country was young, strugglin' to gain its *own* freedom.

"There are millions of Americans today who think about us only as burdens on them—barnacles on their ship of progress, as it were—who consider us, throughout American history, only as liabilities, never as assets. Now, these people are not all bigots, not all—as some excited folk nowadays would have us believe. They just never had the chance to know the truth; the whole truth, that is—unless they happen to be historians or scholars. Up til about five or six years ago the subject of black history, you know, was only taught in a few of our secondary schools, and our colleges and universities got only a smattering of it; even most members of our own race were ignorant of the contributions their ancestors had made.

"This is regrettable, Ladies and Gentlemen—most regrettable. How can we expect white people to concern themselves with our history if *we* show no interest in it ourselves. By this, don't we give the impression that it is not worth knowing about? Now, what our ancestors did may not look so spectacular today, but if time permitted me to give you the background, and the oods they operated against, believe me, you would see them as heroes—as *heroes,* Ladies and Gentlemen! So, as I mention a few examples of their deeds—many of them, mind you, as chattel slaves—I ask you to keep these odds in mind. Consider who these people were, what education they had, what encouragement—what rights."

Now a pair of new arrivals appeared in the doorway—two young men. One was stoop-shouldered, and stood rubbing his knuckles against his short, kinky beard as he grinned up toward the platform. His companion, in his late twenties, was olive-complexioned and skinny and wore a thick, bushy mustache; he was unsteady and weaved as he stood in the doorway and scanned the hall as if searching for someone. When at last his groggy eyes landed on Addie, he beckoned to his bearded friend, and they entered, taking seats in the rear near the door. Letitia, Addie, and Lester, up front, had not seen them.

"We all know," Hammer now was saying, "how the black man got here in the first place." He laughed—"That much black history we *all* know. And it is a dreadful story, my friends. The African slave trade shows us the vast capacity one human being has for cruelty—yes, savagery—toward another; it was human nature at its worst, its ugliest. Ah, but Ladies and Gentlemen, on this—just as the case today—no *one* race had a monopoly. Some of the Africans, for a price, helped Europeans to enslave and exile not only their racial, but their tribal brothers. Many black chiefs directed bands of black kidnappers to furnish the white slave merchants with their terrible cargoes. And the long voyages themselves—what horror!—can only be likened to the Nazi torture camps at Dachau and Belsen—sometimes half the shipment perished. But, moneywise, it was profitable. So, some of the African chiefs were as put out as the Liverpool shipowners when, early in the nineteenth century, England and the United States at last outlawed the slave trade—the slave *trade*, mind you, not slavery itself. Slavery, where it existed, continued til much later. But does not this evil collaboration of chiefs and slave merchants show us—human nature being what it is—that *none* of us, white or black, is altogether free from some lurking wickedness or other? Ah, my friends, this is somethin' to ponder—indeed . . . indeed."

Neeley, behind Hammer, sat forward on the edge of his chair in rapt, breathless involvement.

Hammer was earnest. "Our best knowledge is that the first blacks were landed in North America in 1619—in Jamestown, Virginia. Almost at once the new institution of slavery found favor—thrived. Then in 1636, Blacks were brought to Massachusetts. And before long all the colonies had some slaves. Yet with the introduction of slavery came also its sure opposition—in the North *and* in the South. But somehow," Hammer smiled, "the opposition was greater in the sections of the country where, because of soil and climate, their particular crops were not so well suited to slave labor.

"On the other hand, in sections where this labor worked out all right, where it was profitable, the people there seemed more inclined to shut their eyes to the evil. So in the end it was the people living where slavery was not a sound business proposition that attacked it with so much bitterness on *moral* grounds." Hammer smiled again. "You see?—human nature again, my friends— the white people involved were in general the same, but different outside causes played on their same human natures, and, as we could expect, got different results—one side defended slavery, the other damned it." Hammer removed his pince-nez for a moment and chuckled—"Ladies and Gentlemen, just imagine this for a minute: maybe if the conditions of soil and climate had been different, had been reversed, we might have had the situation of a civil war in 1861 in which the South invaded the North to free the North's slaves." This again brought smiles from the audience. Hammer was heartened; he laughed again and forgot his careful diction. "An' today instead of you an' me railin' all the time at Alabama, South Carolina, and Mississippi, we might all now be awful mad at Massachusetts, Ohio, and New York."

This brought general laughter. Neeley shot up his chin, squealing in glee, and beat his palms together. The two fellows in the rear who had come in last were overly boisterous and derisive in their laughter and seemed to have had too much to drink. The skinny one with the bushy mustache howled; bent over laughing, he turned to his bearded, stoop-shouldered friend and pointed up at Hammer—"Is tha' sonofabitch a preacher, or what! Where'd they *get* that fuckin' Uncle Tom!" He let out a yelping, gravelly, whoop of a laugh.

Addie, down on the front row, froze. Then she spun around—she had recognized the obscene drunken laugh of Dunreith Smith. On proof, though fearful, astounded, she jerked back around and faced the platform again. Lester was looking sideways at her. Then he turned around to see what it was that had disturbed her. In the instant his nostrils flared, quivered. He stared at Dunreith, then stubbornly glared, mumbling street corner oaths to himself, before he finally, grudgingly, turned back around toward the front and sat like an angry effigy.

Hammer by then was finishing his sketchy background of the slave trade and of slavery in the colonies, and now approached the burden, the thesis, of his talk—"Ladies and Gentlemen, would you be at all surprised to learn that th' first—notice I did not say the second . . . or the fifth . . . or the twenty-fifth—the *first* man to die fighting the British for American independence was a black? Did you know that? Well, he was. A black man named Crispus Attucks." Hammer paused and studied his audience. "Did you ever hear of the 'Boston Massacre,' that took place in 1770? I am sure you have—it's in all the school books. Every kid in school knows about the 'Boston Massacre.' But did you ever hear of Crispus Attucks?" Hammer waited. " . . . I dare say you have not. The school history books are silent on *him*. Well, let me tell you a little about him." He paused again for a moment. "As a young man Crispus Attucks was a slave in Framingham, Massachusetts." Hammer smiled, "Yes, Massachusetts—not Mississippi." The audience laughed again. "He was a brown-skinned boy, over six feet tall, and well-proportioned. But he was not a willing slave; his

work was lackadaisical and most of the time his master was angry
with him. At last he had Attucks flogged, and Attucks ran away—
this was in 1750. He could not be found. The Boston *Gazette* carried an advertisement describing him and offering a reward for his
capture. But Attucks had hired out to sea in a trading ship. Then
some years later he turns up, living in Boston, married to an Indian
woman. His former master never located him, and we hear of him
no more till 1770.

"By that time British troops were quartered in Boston—to put
down any uprisings over the hated Taxation Act. The presence of
these troops infuriated the citizens. One evening—in March of
1770—some boys in the street, carrying sticks, shouted taunts at
some of the soldiers. At last one boy threw his stick at a soldier and
hit him, and the soldier struck the boy in the face with the butt of
his musket. The boy, all bloody, set up an awful cry and ran off
with his mates raising a great alarm. Pretty soon a crowd was on
the scene. One of its leaders was Crispus Attucks. Now the British
soldiers formed a skirmish line and tried to disperse the crowd, but
it would not budge and instead jeered at the soldiers. Then Attucks,
who was in the forefront, cursed the soldiers. They fired at once,
and Attucks fell dead. Two of his white comrades, James Caldwell
and Samuel Gray, also fell with mortal wounds and died that night.
Two more, Samuel Maverick and Patrick Carr, died next day."

Hammer paused. He looked out over his audience for a
moment and waited . . . "My friends, two days later the whole
city of Boston held a great public funeral, and four of the five
bodies were laid to rest in a single grave." Hammer reached inside
his coat now, pulled out his speech again, and folded back some
pages. "And over the grave they erected a stone with this inscrip-
tion—(he read):

      'As long as in Freedom's cause the wise contend,
      Dear to your country shall your fame extend,
      While to the world this lettered stone shall tell
      Where Attucks, Caldwell, Gray and Maverick fell.' "

He paused again, his face solemn. "My friends, this grave can still be seen today—I have seen it—in the 'Old Granary Burial Grounds' there in Boston—close by the graves of Sam Adams and John Hancock, signers of the Declaration of Independence, and the grave of Paul Revere, first freedom-rider. It is a moving sight, I want to tell you. Over a hundred years later, in 1888, the state of Massachusetts erected a monument on Boston Common in honor of Attucks and his comrades. The monument is magnificent, Ladies and Gentlemen—the beautiful figure of Liberty holds in her right hand a broken chain, and in her left the flag; while at her feet crouches, ready, the screaming American eagle. The scene of the shooting is represented on a bronze tablet—the smoking muskets of the British soldiers still raised, Attucks lying dead on the ground, and the wounded falling back into the arms of their comrades. Ah, what an inspiring sight, my friends—a *thrilling* sight."

Gleeful, drunken Dunreith Smith in the rear now leaned against his black, bearded friend—Alexis—and laughed. "Where'd they *get* this God-damn white folks' nigger, man? . . . Huh? . . . *Haw! Haw! Haw!*—Oh, Christ!" He slapped Alexis' knee.

"Sh-h-h-h-h!" More sober, Alexis tried to quiet him.

Yet Dunreith let out still another hilarious yelp, but the audience was only momentarily distracted; they were too engrossed in what Hammer had just said. And little Neeley, in a spasm of pride, leaned over and whispered something to Lord Nelson Turner; then got up, hurried off the platform, and, by a door near the platform, left the hall. Soon he was back with a glass of water, and placed it on the speaker's table at Hammer's right hand.

By then Hammer had gone on to his next hero. He was telling of the black Peter Salem and his valor at the battle of Bunker Hill. He told how Salem shot and killed Major Pitcairn, a British officer, at the moment Pitcairn was leading a charge and shouting to his Hessian troops—"The day is ours!" Then of how Salem, for his exploits, was later presented to General George Washington himself. And Trumbull, in his famous painting of the battle, said Hammer, had taken pains to make the figure of "the embattled Salem" conspicuous.

As Hammer paused now to take a sip of water, a blubbery-fat, short woman entered the hall. She stopped just inside the doorway to scan the audience as if she too were searching for someone. Then she saw Dunreith Smith and Alexis and, with a quick little waddle, went straight over to them. She appeared to be almost fifty, and her face was spotty, piebald from a skin disorder—the spreading baby-pink had left only islands, blotches, of black; her stubby arms and her hands were the same. Dunreith, laughing, half-stood up to greet her, pulled her into his row of chairs, and made her sit down between them.

"Rosie . . . what'n the hell you doin' here?" he said, and gave his gravelly laugh. "You musta heard the preachin' and come in here to get religion . . . haw!"

Rosie was out of breath. "You better clear outa here, botha you," she said with stern, but alarmed, eyes. "The bulls are after you agin—they been lookin' for you most of the evenin'. I just left Bernie's Tavern—where you opened your mouth, Dunreith, and did all that talkin'." She frowned at Dunreith.

Dunreith grinned at mention of police. "I told you why I was comin' here, Rosie. I gotta date—see?" and he looked up front toward Addie. "You're a sweetheart to tip us off—but I ain't leaving." He grimaced. "I ain't leaving, Rosie, baby—so quit worryin'. Alexis, here, can go if he wants to," Dunreith glanced at his bearded friend, "but *I* ain't goin' nowhere."

Alexis seemed uncertain and sat silent, observing them, as Dunreith and Rosie spoke in spirited, gesticulating whispers. Rosie was insistent, but Dunreith in his liquor laughed her off. So she soon jumped up to go, again making violent beckoning motions to them—her black and white splotched face showed her vexation. But when they still sat, she waved them off in disgust and waddled hurriedly out of the hall.

Ten minutes later Hammer was still detailing the exploits of his black heroes of the Revolution. Now he told of how Lemuel Haynes, a minuteman, "covered himself with glory" fighting the British at the battles of Lexington and Concord. Haynes, said Hammer, was the "super-patriot type" and exposed himself to enemy musket fire recklessly, disdaining the cover of the stone fences along the route of the advancing Britishers, and later as a regular soldier fought with "conspicuous gallantry" through to the end of the war.

Meantime, two uniformed black policemen had appeared in the doorway. For a moment they surveyed the hall, then quietly walked over to Dunreith and Alexis. One of the policemen, short and stocky, with scar tissue over his right eye, bent down to them. "We wanta ask you fellows a couple of questions," he whispered. "Will you come outside, please?"

Alexis looked warily at them. But Dunreith, whose hatred of policemen was psychotic, smiled. "We're listenin' to a speech, man," he said, his breath reeking of liquor; he laughed and pointed up at Hammer. "This Uncle Tom's really goin' to town—layin' it on the line. Sit down a minute and listen—you might surprise everybody and learn somethin'." He gave a low, bitter laugh.

The other policeman, tall and blue-black, let a smile hover on his face for a moment. "We wanta talk to you," he said to Dunreith. "We're working."

Instantly a wild, agonized expression came over Dunreith's face. He turned to Alexis—"Tell 'em something, Alexis! . . . tell 'em we don't *care* to leave right now!"

Alexis rubbed his knuckles against his short, kinky beard and studied first Dunreith, then the two policemen, and at last only grinned.

The short, stocky policeman with the scar tissue whispered to Dunreith through grinding teeth—"Listen, we ain't playin'. We'll take both of you outa here and muss you up a little."

Dunreith laughed and contemptuously waved him off—"Aw,

man, that shit's ole hat to me." Then his olive complexion went sallow, hostile. "I ain't goin' nowhere—*nowhere*."

The stocky policeman reached for him. Dunreith, jerking away, upset a chair. The audience spun around and gaped; Hammer stopped in the middle of a sentence. The stocky policeman now dove for Dunreith and hugged him, patting his pockets for weapons. Suddenly Dunreith kneed him in the testicles and the policeman, wide-eyed, choked and sat down on the floor. The tall, blue-black policeman then knocked Dunreith down with his fist. Alexis jumped aside as Dunreith got up fighting. The short, stocky policeman, snarling, groped to his knees and pulled his service revolver; then finally, staggering, stood up. He stepped to one side and swung the revolver at Dunreith's head. The trigger guard glanced off Dunreith's left eyebrow, opening a clean, two-inch incision. Blood flew five and six chairs away.

Addie, in the front row, gasped and jumped up. But Lester seized her and hurled her back across two chairs. She began crying and shrieking.

Dunreith was down—kneeling at his chair and shaking his gory head to clear his brain. Blood spattered the front and shoulders of his beige corduroy jacket. He opened his eyes wide and pursed out his lips, blowing bubbles of bloody foam. Then he obscenely cursed both policemen and called their mothers "nigger whores." The crazed, stocky policeman now threw back a chair for more room; then lunged and kicked Dunreith in the liver. Dunreith doubled over and groaned. The stocky policeman then stepped over him, turned, and raised his revolver hip high. But the other policeman intervened and dragged Dunreith by the jacket between the rows of chairs out toward the door. The stocky policeman now wheeled and put his gun in Alexis' belly and frisked him, then hurled him toward the door. Alexis did not resist.

Suddenly Addie sprang clear of Lester, around frightened Letitia, and tore up the center aisle toward Dunreith. Lester took out after her. She outran him most of the way, until they had almost reached the rear. Lester caught her around the waist, as she screamed at the black policeman dragging Dunreith to the door— "You stop that!—You stop that!—You leave him alone!—You *black son of a bitch,* you!" She lunged at the policeman, but Lester, grunting, held onto her and slammed her back against the wall. She screamed at Lester now, but he blocked her return. The two policemen threw Dunreith and Alexis down the front steps and into a waiting squad car.

Hammer did not resume speaking that night.

Chapter Six

CLOTILDA tramped through the cool, quiet woods. Palest sunlight filtered down through the trees—leafy, luxuriant, cathedral-tall—and dappled the squills, violets, and other flora growing out of the moist earth. A slip of a girl, she had just turned sixteen and walked head-bent examining the dress she wore. She was perplexed; it was an old-fashioned dress and so long it nearly dragged the ground. She could not recall where she got it, nor why she wore it. Had somebody given it to her? . . . had her Aunt Clem made it for her? . . . or had she herself filched it from some old attic trunk? She could not remember.

Holding the dress clear of the weeds and flowers, she paused and looked about her. She was tired and longed to drop down in the long, but sparse, grass and shrubs and rest awhile. Then she imagined all sorts of little snakes and lizards skittering about through the old dead leaves and fallen bark, and instead she straggled on—to a huge oak tree. She stopped and leaned against it. The woods were silent, hushed; and what could be seen of the sky through the trees was a bright, limpid blue. Then she thought she heard light rustling noises high in the leaves of the trees; there was no wind; could it be a squirrel? . . . a bird?

Strange, she had not seen a bird all morning; now it must be noon, for the sun was straight up; how eerie the woods seemed without one bird. She wondered how much farther she must go. . . . Would she make it there and back by dark? If not, Aunt Clem and Pearlie would be worried, upset. And she would return home another way—take the highway back this time but not through the woods again, alone; for now she was frightened by the woods. But where was she going? . . . who had sent her? . . . *why* was she going? She must have been sent for something . . . but what? . . . sent where?

She was not lost; still she knew the woods could be tricky, a snare; had they addled her?—yet if she didn't know where she was going, how had she managed to keep a straight route through the woods, as if by compass? . . . for there were many little paths in all directions. She lounged against the big oak tree and let her hand go deep in the pocket of the old dress. Oh! . . . money. She pulled out a one-dollar bill and a silver quarter; it was from her Aunt Clem, she now recalled, who with it that morning had sent her on some errand. But why?

She looked back along her path and saw the tracks made in soft ground by the iron tires of a farm wagon, then looked ahead, up the path where she must go. At last she straightened up from the tree and started wearily on. It was late May; in the fragmented sunshine the woods were a melee of tones and tints; and, although the higher air was chaste, the soft ground gave off a vernal, mossy smell. Now the woodland began to thin out, and soon she came upon a stream, rippling and gurgling its deep, narrow way through the trees; the wagon tracks went alongside the bank and she followed them; then almost at once she was out of the trees and faced a hilly meadow from which the stream had entered the woods; there the warming sunlight came down unhindered, and she felt relieved to have quit the sinister woods; and, too, a fourth of a mile beyond was a group of small farm buildings.

Then suddenly she saw a white woman sitting on the bank of

the stream in the open meadow; the woman was undressed down to her slip and brassiere, and her grey, lank hair fell just short of her shoulders. She was taking off her stockings now, as if preparing to go in the water. Clotilda looked at her in flustered embarrassment, then started a wide detour around her. But the woman saw her and twisted around to watch her, as a shoulder strap of her slip fell off her blue-white shoulder—her face, though pale, seemed somehow weatherbeaten. At last she called to Clotilda—"Hey! . . . Hey! Thataway!" She pointed up toward the farm buildings. "Thataway . . . you'd better hurry—there ain't many left—because somebody broke in our smokehouse." Clotilda looked puzzled. The woman soon seemed exasperated at no reply. "Ain't you up here after one of them little *hams*?—them dollar-and-a-quarter hams?"

(The jarring, swift shock of comprehension woke Clotilda with a start from the dream. For a moment she lay breathless, quiet, afraid to move. Now she tentatively shifted one leg—the bed seemed extra large. And it was night—dark; and so still. Then— oh!—the whole horrid world returned with a rush. Everything was grasped, re-experienced—Addie's disaster at the lodge hall two nights before—Lester's wild scene after bringing her home—and her own frenzied loss of control, her railing and screaming at Addie—Addie, bitterly sullen, had since slept on the living room sofa. Now Clotilda began pitching and tossing in the bed, as her calamities, her misery, her sense of early lapse, her fears, ground down her weakened will. Again she rolled over and faced the wall; it was invisible in the solid blackness; her fitful sleep had fatigued her even more; finally she lay still . . . for almost an hour . . . lulling, coaxing sleep. Only after another hour did it grudgingly come at last.)

Alone, Clotilda entered the hospital during visiting hours carrying a paper sack of oranges. She wore her heavy coat, which now was flecked with a sooty snow that matched her greying hair. The elevator was automatic; she pushed the button for the fourth floor; as she ascended she fumed at herself—going to see a man she in fact despised; taking him fruit. She left the elevator at the fourth floor and walked down the corridor to Ward 9; it was a large room with two long rows of beds and a wide aisle in the middle; the ward was full of patients—all men; almost half were blacks. Clotilda started down the aisle, looking right and left.

Halfway down, on the right, she suddenly saw him. She went over to his bed; he gave a quick, amused grin when he saw her— he resembled a cheerful cadaver propped up on the cranked up bed; his teeth were no longer pretty, but now long, yellow, and eroded at the roots like teeth in a museum skull, yet there were the same large, wide eyes. Standing at the bed, she sighed and smiled. "Hi," she said. He tried to move his emaciated arm to reach for her hand, but failed. "My shoulders an' elbow joints're just about cemented solid, Clo. Calcium. Hips an' knees getting the same way. But I don't hurt so much as I did, somehow." Clotilda stood over him—there was no chair. Her face was impassive now; she put the bag of oranges on his little table.

"How you getting along?" she said. "Oh, 'bout the same."— he tried to shift toward her as he talked. "Crank me up a little, will you?" he said. She stepped to the foot of the bed and cranked the pillows yet higher. "I'm the wonder of all th' doctors," he laughed like a crone. "—They call me the 'Egyptian mummy.' They'd sworn I'd'a been in the ground long 'fore now. But time *is* runnin' out. Yet, I ain't feelin' so bad—pain's practically gone. This time last year it was awful—a year of hell. Only thing bad right now is about Pearlie and the children. Now that Pearlie's gone, they put me down. Won't come near me—ain't been here once. They sure are a crazy bunch. Pearlie would turn over in her grave." He spread his bony fingers on the sheet and shook his head.

Clotilda was stolid. "I brought you some oranges, there," she said. "Oh, that's nice." He was shiny bald now, with his smooth brown skin stretched parchment-tight over his skull; the short, stubborn hair at his temples was grey. "Pearlie and the children never knew," Clotilda said, " . . . did they?" "Oh, no, no," he grinned, "but the children just didn't like me anyhow . . . somehow. It's strange . . . ain't it?" Clotilda stood mute. Soon a poking, blind black man came through the ward selling newspapers. . . .

(Clotilda stirred in the bed. Then in the dark she awoke again—later, same night. She lay still, hearing the late-night, summer sounds of the city coming in through the screened windows; now she tossed over on her back—wincing as she imagined she, too, had arthritis. Soon she got up, sat on the side of the bed in the dark, and lit a cigarette; then with the lighted match looked at the little alarm clock—it was 2:40. When she finished the cigarette she got back in bed, but lay there thinking until sleep came only beyond 3:30.)

"This world and the next!" laughed Zack, the prison librarian. At least it seemed to Clotilda he was laughing when he wrote it. The letter was eleven big pages long, written in his acquired, wee, cryptic hand; the ink was green and hurt her eyes as, bi-focaled, head down deciphering, she sat in the springtime sunshine of her back porch. " . . . if there *is* a next," the letter went on, at page eight—"But who cares? Why, the preachers do, of course—yea, brethren. And all the fallen women. The deep sea divers too, when they're in their bathyspheres—our wonderful library here has a book on oceanography, you see. But who else cares? Oh well, a few more maybe, like some of the oldtime darkies—'You kin have this ole world; jes gi' *me* Jesus.' But, of all, the fallen women are the true believers. Ruby proves that. *She was fallen.* What do I care about the judges, lawyers, witnesses? And she went to her reward for it, too. Some would call her a sinner. I don't. She was worse— she was fallen. Yes, your daughter—but fallen. And her curse is on us all—on Lester, on Addie, me—and on *you,* Mamacita. But my heart is a stone. I am so objective. I am buried here—for this world and the next. I will never die. My whole life before seems a paradise—I wonder, I marvel, at it. Was that life possible? I ask myself.

Yes—it happened. Then, what came after? What buried me alive? Will you, or someone, tell me? Now, I will never die . . . I will never die . . . Oh, Mama Clotilda, will I *never* die? . . ."

(Clotilda lurched up with a start—still later, same night. The neck and bosom of her nightgown were wet with sweat. For awhile she sat in the dark with her palm pressed hard to her forehead; at last she reached over and pulled the chain on the little bedstand lamp; in the yellow light the clock showed 4:20; then she saw herself in the dresser mirror, and at once put the light out, but soon she got up, groped in the dark for her kimono, and, trailing it behind her, went into the kitchen.)

🌀   🌀   🌀   🌀   🌀   🌀

A week later Clotilda's grey hair was a gentian violet. She had rinsed it herself. Afterwards she combed it down at both ears and forward so that the stiff blue fibers came out from under like a ram's horns. The new color made her dark skin seem darker still. Lester was stunned when he saw her. He had come home that afternoon and found her sitting at the old grand piano; the ash tray before her was half-full of cigarette butts, as she bent over the keyboard in a deep, musing study, idly picking out with one finger the tune "The Last Rose of Summer." She was chewing a great wad of gum, and her jaw moved up, down, and around in wide, bovine sweeps. Her gum-chewing was recent and only the day before Lester, concerned, had asked her about it. She said it helped keep down the rushing noises in her head. But now when he saw her hair he stopped short.

" . . . Grammaw! . . . what'd you do to your *hair*?"

Clotilda did not look up. Engrossed, she continued plunking one piano key at a time.

Lester came across the room and stood over her; he watched her, his coltish face perplexed; finally he nudged her shoulder. "Grammaw, what'd you do to your hair?—it's *blue*."

Clotilda finally looked up at him. "I livened it up some." Then her voice threatened. "Why?—what's wrong with it!"

Lester backed down. " . . . Nothin'—I just got to get used to it . . . that's all."

"Where you been, Lester?"—Clotilda sighed and dropped her hand from the keyboard into her lap.

"Over at the 'Y'."

"This ain't Saturday—what you doin' at the 'Y'?"

" . . . Mr. Hammer . . . he told me to meet him there, for lunch."

Clotilda turned on him. "What? . . . *did* you?"

" . . . Yes'm—Grammaw, I wanted to talk to him. I went up to his room last night . . . and talked to him about Addie."

"You did *what*?" Clotilda stood up from the piano.

"Well, *you* won't talk about it. I asked him last night if he'd try to help us."

"Lord, have mercy." Clotilda turned away. Finally she turned back to Lester—"What'd he say?"

"Said he'd have to think about it—then told me to meet him today at the 'Y'."

"Lester, honest t'God. . . ."

"He can help us, Grammaw—if you'll just help, too."

"If *I'll* help! Lester, you have disgraced the family."

"Naw—Addie's done that."

Clotilda stood staring out the window.

"Grammaw, Mr. Hammer said today you know things you won't talk about. That if he knew more about what's goin' on he might could go to the police, or to a lawyer, and maybe have Dunreith Smith arrested again. The police turned 'em loose the other night—Mr. Hammer said they know Dunreith's in a dope ring, all right, but they can't prove it on him yet. He'd have him arrested about Addie, though, if you'd just say so." Lester twisted and grimaced—"Grammaw, why don't you *talk* to Mr. Hammer!"

Clotilda wheeled on him. "Lester, you're as simple as the days are long! Honest t'God! Why, it ain't none of his affair. I oughta skin you alive for tellin' all our business! You're a pest!" Clotilda wildly plunged her hand through her stiff blue hair; now it was all awry.

"Grammaw, *do* you know things you don't tell anybody?— just worry about 'em yourself? That's what Mr. Hammer says. He wants to help us—he said so today—so we can help Addie. We can't just do nothin'."

Clotilda sat down in a chair against the wall and stared across the room at the opposite wall. Soon she turned again to Lester. "Look, Lester, we got to handle this thing ourselves—just you and me. *We* can handle it. When Addie gets straightened out, from the other night, I'll talk to her. She's still awful mad at the things you said to her—madder at them, actually, than she is at you hitting her. You acted somethin' awful, Lester—awful. Where'd you learn such awful talk?—not in this house. It made me feel terrible—why, you acted like you hate her."

Lester was glum, impassive.

"What else did Mr. Hammer say?"

Lester did not answer.

"Well, he must have said more'n you've just told me."

Lester backed up against the piano. " . . . Well . . . he said there was more to this than just we, him and I, see. He said you been to Mrs. Turner, to get your fortune told. Mr. Turner saw you leavin', and happened to mention it to him."

Clotilda started flinging her head from side to side and cursing under her breath—"I tell you, that man Hammer better watch his step!—He better not get me stirred up!" But almost at once her tantrum subsided; she sat gazing mournfully off into space again.

Soon Lester left the living room and went on down the hall toward the kitchen.

Clotilda sat for awhile; then got up and wandered over to the piano; she stood over the keyboard, and, staring ahead out the window, began again her absent, idle, feeling and plunking of the keys. She was frightened by Lester's maturity, his push, and began to wonder what kind of man he would be—because new, unsuspected traits were showing, especially his temper; she recalled how frantic, uncontrollable, and lashed with shame he had been the night he brought Addie and Letitia home from the lodge hall. She saw Zack in him; he had slapped Addie in the face as they waited on the front porch to be let in. Letitia had used her arms and body to defend Addie and entered hysterical. Lester, once inside, circled Addie in the middle of the floor, yelling at her, and bawling tears of rage and frustration, while Addie stood insolent and dry-eyed. Clotilda, then still uncomprehending, mouth agape, had finally rushed him, cuffing him like a bear; he spun around against a chair and half-sat down, before she bullied him back to his room; then, in Addie's presence, she grilled the facts from Letitia and instantly herself took up screaming at Addie. Considerate Hammer and Neeley stayed away till well past midnight.

Clotilda sat down at the piano again, absently running her hand over the keys as she hummed "The Last Rose of Summer." She had loved the song since girlhood; her Aunt Clem had taught it to them, and she remembered how she and Pearlie used to sing it while washing dishes, Pearlie singing "lead" and Clotilda, alto. Pearlie had a nice voice and was proud of it, and—she well recalled—would sing a "solo" at the slightest hint. She often wondered now if Pearlie had died reasonably satisfied with the life she had lived, with her big family, with Chester. For a moment her recent dream of Chester made her doubtful. But she passionately hoped Pearlie had known peace, for she deserved to. Clotilda still fingered the piano keys. "The Last Rose of Summer" now rose in her throat, but the sick ache of her memories, her despair, soon throttled it. She knew it was her own fear that made her avoid Addie now—Addie came home from work each evening, ate dinner, then read paperbacks or watched TV in the living room till bedtime when she made down the sofa. Addie and Lester no longer owned that each other lived. Each day Clotilda grappled with countless possible solutions; she too had thought of putting the police on Dunreith, but was convinced this would only draw more attention to Addie's terrible, wilful error; she considered sending Addie away somewhere to school, but there was no money for that; then at times she studied unburdening everything to Letitia, or to Hammer even, but quailed before what she feared could be sensed below the surface of things—her own involvement. She even sometimes fought a mania that somehow her history lay exhibited in a showcase, on display for all to see. Finally she weighed returning to Hyacinth Turner, this time for a "definitive" reading. But the thought of Hyacinth's hostile probing terrified her even more than before. She then did nothing.

☒   ☒   ☒   ☒   ☒   ☒

Near six o'clock that evening Letitia came home and, for the first time, summoned the daring to knock on Hammer's bedroom door—her typewriter and the manuscript for the speech had brought them in closer contact, founding a kind of shy, tentative bond between them which was beginning to work subtle changes in Letitia's personality; she was now less timid, more objectified, designing.

It was a hot evening and tall Hammer, hard at work, wore pajama pants and a white shirt. When he opened the door, Letitia tittered. "Oh, Mr. Hammer—I shouldn't've bothered you. . . ."

Hammer edged behind the door, his head out—"Ho! . . . that's all right."

" . . . I wanted to talk to you for a minute . . . Oh, I can see you some other time. . . ." Letitia beamed, simpered and backed away.

Hammer hesitated, then grinned uneasily. "Just give me a minute, will you? I'll get presentable—then come on back."

"Oh, thanks . . . all right, then." Letitia, stilt-tall in high heels, fired a shower of smiles at him, then went on down the hall to her room.

Hammer put on trousers and a necktie and hustled about tidying up his room; then he opened the door wide and sat down at his desk as if to resume work, but he was nervous, jumpy; he reflected how before whenever the two had conferred about his book or her typescript, it was downstairs in the living room; now she had come knocking on his door. It made him feel cramped, on edge. He sat and waited, but when after twenty minutes she had not returned, he became strangely more restless, anxious; he went to the door and peeped down toward her room at the end of the hall; her door was open; soon he strolled casually down the hall and glanced in. Letitia stood carefully inspecting herself before the mirror powdering her nose; she had changed into another dress and now wore long, dangling earrings. Then she saw him in the mirror.

"Oh!—Come *in*, Mr. Hammer!" She wheeled and faced him with a blazing smile, her pale, sad, long face dusty with white powder. "Sit down—sit down, there." She pointed to a tiny chintz-covered chair.

Hammer paused; then, arching his eyebrows, he entered and sat down warily in the little chair that looked as if it might collapse under his weight. The door remained wide open. Everything in the room was frilly and feminine, except the square, black TV; the bed was made up with an ivory lace spread, and a kewpie doll sat propped against the bolster; the dressing table was a row-on-row inventory of nail polishes, mascara brushes, lipsticks, facial creams, powders, and bleaches. Now Letitia hurried more powder onto her face and, still with her fixed, brilliant smile, turned again to Hammer, but soon she seemed flustered, lost for what to do next, and stood with her hands at her side. At last she sat down in the chair distantly opposite him—" . . . I was just thinking, Mr. Hammer . . . maybe you could send your speech to one of the black newspapers. They might publish it. It's a shame not to do something with it—after you worked so hard . . . and had it typed and everything."

Hammer seemed somehow relieved. With a quick smile he shook his head. "No—no, I've put it away. Maybe I'll give another talk someday—I might be able to use some of it then."

" . . . Well, it's a fine talk," Letitia said absently. "But, Mr. Hammer, even if you'd had a big audience, they might not've understood it—it was too meaty for them . . . still, we don't know, do we? . . . for you never got to finish." But she looked off as if her mind held other thoughts.

"Well, it *was* an unusual evenin', wasn't it?" Hammer chuckled. Letitia poked out her lips and intently studied the carpet.

"That's what I wanted to talk to you about, Mr. Hammer. Have you seen Clotilda's hair? Why, she's going from bad to worse." Letitia's face got even longer as she looked imploringly at Hammer.

"Yes, I know." He gazed away.

"It's pathetic, Mr. Hammer. I don't know what to do—to help her, I mean. What can we do? We've *got* to do something. Why, I've never seen anybody so morbid—Addie always was a worry to her." Letitia shook her head. "It's bad—I don't understand it at all. And poor Lester, he's pitiful. He loves his grandmother so—her misery is torture to him. He came to me and said he'd talked to you, but that you wouldn't promise to do anything." Letitia smiled knowingly—"Oh, of course, that's not the case, but Lester expects a remedy overnight—he's a kid; he doesn't understand. But I'll tell you, Mr. Hammer, I don't either." The loose white octoroon flesh on Letitia's face and neck had sagged, making her look old.

"Lester's right," Hammer finally said. "I didn't promise— because I didn't know what to do. And still don't." He paused. "You can't go rushing into things like this—you can do more harm, you know, than good."

"Oh, I know that—and even after that horrible night at the

lodge hall, I still wouldn't't've thought things were so bad if Lester hadn't told me all the rest . . . Why, he and Clotilda knew, even before that night, that Addie was seeing this rat . . . Dunreith Smith. Oh, Mr. Hammer, it's just too dreadful to think about . . . did you realize Clotilda knew it before?"

Hammer leaned back carefully in the fragile little chair. "No—I knew nothing, nothing concrete, before Lester talked to me. But I thought something was distressing Mrs. Pilgrim an awful lot—just seeing her from day to day. I tried to get her to talk one night, but she clammed up on me."

"What should we do, Mr. Hammer—really? I think Lester came to you because he admires you . . . he sort of looks up to you as the man of the house—he's never known a father, you know. He can't quite understand not getting some response from you." Letitia's sad, saucer eyes lingered on Hammer; she vainly touched her hair and, as a seeming afterthought, said, "It's *so* true—every house needs a man in it."

Hammer stirred uneasily in the tiny chair; his eyes shifted, and he almost at once bent over his wristwatch—"Well, I'll get on back to work now, I guess. But I've got a few things in mind. I'll have to think 'em through, though." He stood up. "It's quite a responsibility, you know, to go pokin' around in somebody else's business. You can make a mistake—a bad mistake; and the other fellow will suffer then, not you. I sure wouldn't want to make a blunder." His face was solemn, disturbed. " . . . Well, Miss Dorsey . . . we'll see . . . we'll see. . . ." Thus preoccupied, he returned to his room.

Three evenings later, near eight-thirty, Alexis—Dunreith Smith's black, bearded friend—stood, stoop-shouldered, at his little kitchen range; despite the warm night he was brewing a pot of coffee; daily Alexis, a bachelor living alone, drank quarts of black coffee. His real name was James, James Potts, and ever since he gave himself the name "Alexis" he had caught only ridicule from Dunreith; yet for no amount of mockery would he discard the affectation, the gewgaw. He would only smile and knead his knuckles into his short kinky beard; then maybe reach for his pipe or mug of coffee. Besides being a heroin addict, he was a strange, mostly gentle, young man—a college dropout—who would sit and muse, daydream, for hours. His little third-floor apartment, that so reflected himself, was dusty, cluttered with quality paperbacks, and reeked of acrid pipe tobacco. In the kitchen now he poured himself a mug of coffee and took it into the living room, where he sat down and resumed reading a paperback—Kierkegaard's "Attack on Christendom."

Fifteen minutes later his erratic doorbell rang. He casually got up, pressed the buzzer, and opened the door. Peering down into the murky stairwell, he waited. Soon he saw a dark-brown-skinned man, tall, stalwart, pensive, ascending with great dignity. It was not until the caller's pince-nez glinted in the second-floor landing's puny light that Alexis recognized the speaker he had heard at the lodge hall. When Hammer reached the third floor and saw Alexis, he paused. "Are you Mr. Potts?—Alexis Potts?" he said in his deep voice.

Alexis, holding his pipe in his hand, was courteous. "Yes, I am. You're Mr. Hammer. I remember you—we heard your talk the other night."

"Yes? Well, I thought I might find Mr. Dunreith Smith here. I took the liberty of comin' by." Hammer was out of breath. "I had hard enough time tracing *you,* though," he smiled.

'I haven't heard from Dunreith yet today," Alexis said. "I expect to, though—in fact, I thought you might be Dunreith. Would you like to come in? I expect him, all right."

Hammer hesitated. " . . . That's very accommodating of you, but . . . well, I will just step in a minute . . . you might hear from him." He entered and Alexis closed the door. Hammer's face was moist from the humidity; he put his soft straw hat down on the little end table, pulled out his handkerchief, and dabbed his forehead.

"Have a seat." Alexis smiled and pointed to the chair he had been sitting in. Hammer sat down and dabbed his brow again. "I was having some coffee," Alexis said. "Can I get you some?"

Hammer in the heat seemed surprised by the idea. " . . . Why, no, thank you—I don't believe so," he said. Soon his eyes began randomly examining the room, as he tried to sense the game he thought Alexis played.

Alexis still smiled. "Excuse me, then—while I get another cup." He stepped into the kitchen.

Alexis' gentility stumped Hammer. How could this fellow be a friend of Dunreith Smith's? he thought, and be so refined, so intelligent-acting; he hadn't hesitated a second about recognizing him as the lodge hall speaker, made no bones about it. How could he ever be willing to own up to *that* night? A strange young man, yet nice enough, but maybe with no suspicion of Hammer's connection with Addie's family—only knew him as the lodge hall speaker probably; otherwise, he might not be so polite. Hammer felt the situation required caution, pains.

Alexis, shoulders stooped, soon returned with another mug of black coffee. "We'll probably be hearing from Dunreith before long," he said and sat down on the sofa. He smiled—"Because a girl he knows, Florence, called earlier and said she was to meet him here." Alexis gave a little chortle and rubbed his knuckles against his beard again.

Hammer smiled gravely and was silent.

"Mr. Hammer, that was some talk you made the other night," Alexis suddenly smiled—"Or tried to make, that is. I didn't get to hear it all, you know—ha! Dunreith and I had to leave suddenly." He laughed with his darting eyes.

Hammer smiled uneasily, then chuckled. "Yes—you fellows broke up our meeting."

"It was really the cops. Oh, we'd had a few drinks, but the cops got it started. But before they came, Dunreith was on the verge of heckling *you*. I had to yank him down a couple of times, there."

"Me?"

"Yes—about all that guff you were talking." Alexis laughed again. "You'll pardon my saying so."

Hammer paused, then shrugged and smiled. "Well, you just didn't agree with me, that's all. That's your right."

"We sure didn't." Alexis was suddenly grim. "It serves no good purpose to keep telling our people, blacks, that if they keep on trying, keep on being decent, being patient, patriotic, they'll eventually be accepted."

Hammer looked at him.

"They'll *never* be, Mr. Hammer. How any intelligent person—please, I don't mean any offense—could possibly believe that, is beyond me." There was fanaticism in his eyes. "I can't understand it!"

Hammer now sat with open mouth.

"Well, I can't," Alexis said. "Blacks have got to split off from this country—go somewhere and get some land and build something of their own. Or else do it here."

Hammer shook his head and smiled. "Why, you sound like a . . . some kind of black nationalist, or something."

"Well," Alexis said, with a painful grin, "I guess I am. But labels are not important."

"I won't argue this vast subject with you," Hammer finally said. "But when you've lived a little longer—and read some more—you may get a different slant on things. Well . . . maybe you will, maybe you won't. The main trouble with our people now, though, is that they're so frustrated, so bitter—almost vicious. But a close reading of history will show that that's what happens just before the breakthrough. If they really knew history, they'd be happiest at this time, rather than so upset. We're on the threshold of great things."

Alexis began methodically filling his pipe, then grimly shook his head again. "It's kind of sad, I think," he said, "to hear statements like that—so sad to hear people preaching all this hope, when there is none, absolutely. We're on the threshold of nothing—except violence."

"Well, I didn't come here tonight to argue that subject," Hammer said. He tried to smile.

"Mr. Hammer, we'll never be accepted simply because of the way we *look*. We're black. And our hair, our lips, our noses, even our limbs, are different. It's just that simple. Ah, you never thought of that, did you?" Alexis was bitter now, though he finally lit his pipe. "Did you see a newspaper yesterday, only yesterday—any of the papers?"

"I get the 'Tribune'—yes."

"Did you see the story—and the pictures—about the big international beauty contest in Switzerland, in Lucerne?"

Hammer nodded. "I glanced at it."

Alexis scooted forward on the sofa with great energy, looking around. "Oh, I wish I had saved that paper," he said. "Well, it was all about picking Miss Universe. In the picture there were three long tiers of girls, in bathing suits. They were from all over the world—Ireland, Germany, Italy, Korea, U.S.A., England, Japan, Puerto Rica, France, Nationalist China, Brazil, South Africa—*Caucasian* South Africa, that is—and every other place on the face of the globe except places where the women have flat noses, woolly hair, and black skins. Oh, there *was* one girl—from Grenada, I think . . . in the West Indies. But she was almost as light-skinned, straight-haired, and Caucasian-featured as the rest. Now, Mr. Hammer, why do you suppose it was that the vast—*black*—segment of the world's population was unrepresented? *Why?*" Alexis avidly leaned forward, his eyes alight.

Hammer hesitated, crossed his legs once, looked at Alexis, and said nothing.

"*Why?* Can you tell me why, Mr. Hammer?"

Hammer's brow furrowed. "I think I did see a colored girl once maybe—in a local, or national, contest . . . I don't remember which. It was on television—just briefly."

"Oh, the rare exception only proves the rule, Mr. Hammer," Alexis laughed grimly. "Can a flat-nosed, woolly-haired, straight-and-thin-legged black girl, although in perfect health, *possibly* be beautiful to the great majority of whites? Of course not. The so-called 'civilized' world will never entertain the idea. It's their aesthetics—the average white man's sense of aesthetics says *no*. His concepts derive from ancient Greek statues. Therein lies the whole story, Mr. Hammer. There's nothing else. It's the way we *look*. We don't look to suit them. In fact—no matter how sound our bodies, and how much we scrub and groom them—white people are shocked, secretly abhor, are repelled, by the way we look. Even many of *us* are ourselves victims of this cruel, Godless canard. All this, despite the opinions of the world's great thinkers and philosophers, past and present, that there is *no such thing* as a universal standard of beauty. How about——"

Hammer put up a hand to interrupt.

Alex would not stop: "—How about it, Mr. Hammer? Yes, whites keep telling us to be good, be patient, work hard, persevere, and soon—presto!—we'll be accepted. Just like all the other ethnic groups—like the Italians were, the Polish, the Irish . . . who, they say, all pulled themselves up by their bootstraps. This of course is sheer fantasy—a sadistic hoax! . . . We'll *never* be accepted as long as we can still be discerned to be even a little bit black. Think about it, Mr. Hammer. Christ, think!"

Hammer wavered, said nothing. At last he only sighed.

Alexis curled his lip in scornful anger. "Why, they loathe and despise us. We revolt them. Every group of newcomers to this country has been taken in, absorbed—everyone of them—except us. And we will never be. Yet, despite all our mistreatment and suffering, we insist on praising God." Alexis laughed riotously. "We insist on it! Blacks are probably the most religious people on earth

—for what, I'll never know. Oh, we can be so stupid, Mr. Hammer —God this, God that, God the other . . . and listening to all those greasy, pompous, chicken-eating, traitorous preachers. At times, I'm very anti-black, Mr. Hammer. . . . Sometimes I actually hate them, all of them—even myself—just as the whites do. The whites simply can't swallow us—they gag, and up we come. So the result is it's made different human beings out of us. Our suffering has. Whites can't understand why we act the way we do—why we deliberately do the things we know will most displease them, harry them, infuriate, enrage them—why we're loud and contemptuous— why we yell, sometimes before we're hurt, and revile—why we burn, rob, rape, and kill. We're reacting to reactions. So they say we're different. And they add this to our blackness. Then Jensen and Schockley—those great investigators!—say we're genetically inferior. Well, we *are* different." Alexis was trembling. "Yes! Yes!—we're different. And I'm glad of it! Otherwise we'd only be dull, dumb clods. Our reactions show we're human. Far more human than they are. And more *sane.* We mystify them, and, yes, they end up gagging on us and up we come. Ah, Mr. Hammer——"

Hammer finally broke in. "—And I'm gagging on some of your opinions, Mr. Potts." Then he made a desperate effort to smile, but failed. He too was grim. "Your views are melodramatic," he said. "They——"

Alexis was oblivious. "Oh, Mr. Hammer, we must go some-where—if not physically, then spiritually, emotionally—away, away, away, anywhere to ourselves, and disentwine our frantic arms from around the white man's neck. Let him live in peace. He'll certainly be a whole lot happier—and, in the end, so will we. I wish we could emigrate to some other *planet,* and leave this one to him. Why *must* we have to suffer so? Blackness is a stinking curse."

Hammer gaped. "Do you think many of our people believe like you?" he finally said.

"I can't say. Probably not. But many of those who do are even stronger, more radical, in their beliefs than I. Like Dunreith—they say we'll never be accepted, and there's no place to go, so let's stay and *wreck* it here. Even if we die. They're not communists—like poor Angela Davis—nothing so futile, so misguided, as that. They hate *all* governments by whites, no matter what their form. If Soviet Russia persecutes Jews, what would it do to blacks? —ask African university students who've studied there, who've been beaten and nearly lynched in the streets for dating Russian girls. The Russians don't like the way we look, either—any more than American whites. But what Dunreith and his ilk hate most of all is a phony God. They say fuck God. They really yearn for anarchy."

Hammer, visibly shaken, removed his pince-nez and held them in his hand. " . . . Why, that's . . . that's so preposterous," he said at last. "—to want to destroy everything. You helped build it, didn't you? You have fought honorably in every war the country's fought. You've done most of the hard, back-breaking work—much of it as unpaid chattel slaves—that it took to build the country and make it what it is today. A greater knowledge of history, you see, would make us not only feel, but know, we belong here. I hope to show this in my book."

Alexis struck his forehead in frustration. "Oh, Christ!" he groaned.

"I grant that color has slowed us," Hammer said, "Slowed us a lot. But we're about to overcome that now. We'll be accepted, accepted as Americans—proud, *black*, Americans."

Sadly, Alexis shook his head. "And you believe this," he said. "You actually believe it." He looked at Hammer steadily, earnestly, without hostility. "You know, Mr. Hammer, you arouse my pity— really you do. And I'm not being patronizing. You miss my whole point. *Of course* we fought in all those wars. . . . *Sure* we toted all dem bars, lifted all dem bales—for centuries. That's why we're such fools today to think this has won us an everlasting place in

Whitey's heart. Rather, in return, he's shit on us. And lynched nine thousand of us, outright—not even counting the 'legal' lynchings in the courts. But the day is past now when we thank him for it. You were speaking for a past generation the other night, Mr. Hammer—you did it well, sure, but it was all spurious, invalid— though not a little poignant too, because of the sincerity of your views. Oh, would that the world were like you see it. But it is not, and blacks by now can't avoid seeing it. So a new day has arrived. Cleaver said it in Folsom Prison, and it's the wave of the future : 'We shall have our manhood. We shall have it or the earth will be leveled by our attempts to gain it'." Alexis' eyes were afire now and he was breathing hard.

Hammer could only emit another heavy sigh. Gazing at the floor, he was silent, dejected.

But Alexis, ever the gentleman, now tried to smile. "Oh, well," he said, "there's no point in our going at each other's throats like this. We could argue it all night. But believe me, Mr. Hammer, we're poles apart. And I wouldn't want us to be on this subject when that maniac Dunreith comes. No, sir. Dunreith is crazy."

Hammer frowned. "What'n the world was wrong with him the other night? . . . He did act like a crazy man."

"Oh, as I said, we'd had a few drinks—I didn't want to go to the meeting. But Dunreith was to see a girl there. That settled it. And the gendarmes were looking for us, too, we found out later— and how ! They had gone by a tavern where a friend of ours, Rosie, heard them inquiring about Dunreith. And she came to the lodge hall to warn us. Oh, but that damn Dunreith—nobody can handle him."

Hammer studied Alexis.

"I suppose," Alexis said, "you're after him about something, too. Perhaps you're going to sue him for breaking up your meeting !" He laughed again with his darting eyes.

"Do you know Dunreith Smith very well?" Hammer said.

"Ha, we grew up in the same block—over on Calumet Avenue.

He's a couple of years older than I am but we've been friends all our lives."

Hammer pondered this.

"What's Dunreith done *now*, Mr. Hammer?"

Hammer uncrossed his legs. "I ought to wait and see *him*, I guess," he finally said.

Alexis shook his head. "I guarantee you won't get a second's cooperation out of Dunreith—whatever it is. Who sent you here, Mr. Hammer?" Alexis put his empty coffee mug aside.

"His wife and his mother both said he might be here—I just left his house."

"Listen, Mr. Hammer, stay away from Dunreith. You're not used to his type. You can't cope with him. If it's about his breaking up your meeting, well, just forget it. Dunreith is really kind of crazy—I've told you. He can be dangerous." Alexis gave an uneasy grin.

Hammer was stubborn, solemn. "I didn't come here on anything that trivial. I want to see him about . . . that girl—the girl you spoke of."

Alexis' lips parted.

"—The girl he came to see that night at the meetin'," Hammer said.

" . . . Addie? Do you——"

"That's right."

Alexis' eyes got big. "Do you know *Addie*?" But his look of shock soon vanished. "I see, I see—you're related to her."

"Well, in a way." Hammer uncomfortably poked his feet out. "I live at her grandmother's house—room there."

The telephone at Alexis' elbow rang. He looked at Hammer and let it ring again; then picked it up and said hello. "Florence!" he smiled. "Where are you, baby? No, I thought *you* were Dunreith—where is that crazy galoot? He'll come running in here any minute, now. Sure, come on. I've got a distinguished visitor here, incidentally. That's all right—you'll get to meet him. Okay, baby—

Dunreith'll probably be here by then." Alexis hung up and smiled. "That's Florence I mentioned, one of Dunreith's girls."

"I think I ought to go," Hammer said, but he made no move.

"Anyhow, Mr. Hammer, I certainly wouldn't say anything to Dunreith about Addie if I were you—at any time. He's very fond of the child."

Hammer bridled; his stubbornness returned. "Child is right—sure, she's only a child, and he should let her alone. He's a grown man—married."

Alexis shook his head again. "Yes, but you don't know Dunreith."

"No, I don't. I know he's doin' this girl and her family a great wrong, though. She hasn't got any father or mother—only her grandmother and little brother. Your friend's not only violatin' the law, he's taking advantage of the girl. It's not right." Hammer frowned, then looked over at his hat and got up.

Alexis also stood up. "Addie's got a mind of her own, though, Mr. Hammer—a strong mind, too. Nobody's going to take advantage of Addie—if she doesn't want it."

Hammer picked up his hat but controlled his voice. "How can anyone that age know what she wants, Mr. Potts? She's dealing with a *man* . . . an experienced man, too, I understand."

The erratic doorbell rang.

Alexis looked at Hammer. "If that's Dunreith, I just wouldn't mention Addie at all," he said. "Let this thing ride for awhile . . . we'll work out something—you and I will. We'll get together and see what can be done. But don't bring her up now."

There was a long, impatient ring.

Alexis went over and pushed the buzzer, then opened the door to the stairway and looked down. Already someone was floundering up the stairs.

"Hi, Smitty!" cried down Alexis, and after a short wait stepped aside to let Dunreith in.

Dunreith was a garish wreck. Bareheaded, his bushy mustache now somehow drooping, he wore a gaudy dashiki and really looked insane. The still-inflamed stitches over his left eye were a lurid red against his olive complexion as he squinted at Hammer and suddenly roared a laugh—"*Prof!*" He put out his damp, limp hand. "You don't know me, but I know *you!*" He wilted in another gravelly laugh. "You made that dog-ass speech the other night! Right?—*Hey!*" His eyes were wild one moment, glazed the next, as Hammer took the limber hand. "Hey! Yeah, the Professor!"

Alexis was nervously, falsely, hilarious. "Mr. Hammer, meet my convalescent friend, Mr. Dunreith Smith!"

"Yeah! Glad t'meet'ya, Prof!—damn glad t'meet'ya!" cried Dunreith, somehow tightening his hold on Hammer's hand now. "We're honored, ain't we, Alexis! Hey!" His face was pinched, ravaged, manic, behind the thicket of mustache.

"Thank you," Hammer said, finally extricating his hand from Dunreith's and glancing toward the exit door.

Unsteady, but blissful, Dunreith now tried to screw up one eye. "Where you goin', Prof? Sit down, sit down! Where you rushin' off to?" Though Dunreith seemed absolutely loose-jointed, Hammer smelled no whiskey on his breath. Uneasy Alexis only stood by and grinned.

At last Hammer gave a weak smile. "Thank you," he said, "but I should be goin'."

"Aw, Prof, sit down!" Dunreith, scowling, waved his scarecrow arms. "Sit down a minute . . . I wanta tell you how Goddamn sorry I am about the fuckin' cops breakin' up your meeting the other night—just a couple of black-ass, ignorant bulls. Alexis and I were just sittin' there listening to that simple, that dumb, speech of yours—Oh, Prof, it was awful—when these two ignorant niggers-in-blue come in and break up the meeting. Sit down, Prof! —I wanta apologize. Really, I want—" Dunreith's face was livid now, and he began to weave.

Alexis, stepping behind Dunreith, quickly nodded at Hammer

to obey. At last Hammer backed up to his chair and sat down again.

Once more Dunreith feebly cocked one eye. "Prof, my man, what're you doin' here?"

Hammer looked at him.

Alexis spoke up, laughing nervously at Dunreith. "Does everybody that comes to my house have to make a report to *you*?"

Dunreith finally flopped down on the sofa. Then he gave Alexis a drowsy stare. "Aw, dry up, you hump-back junkie. And give Prof here some refreshments or somethin'—where's your manners?"

Alexis did not smile. "Watch *your* manners, Dunreith. You're getting ugly, now. Remember, we have a guest."

Dunreith, laughing, slapped his thigh and yelped. *"Haw-haw-haw!* Yeah, you God-damn right we have! I know it! I know it, man!—great speaker—brilliant—national authority on spook history—grand guy! . . . yeah, really grand guy. Oh, I know more 'bout him than you think I do!" He collapsed in laughter again. Suddenly then he sat up, staring suspiciously at Hammer. "But what's he doin' *here*?"

Hammer sat observing him. "I came to see you, Dunreith."

Alexis' mouth fell open.

"*Me?*" Dunreith said. "Well, you see me, Prof—roll the dice."

"I came to ask you to leave Addie alone."

At first Dunreith's lips separated as if he hadn't quite heard. Then he gaped. Alexis quickly, deftly, stepped between them on the pretext of retrieving his coffee mug. But Dunreith's squeezed-up face twisted into a kind of crazed, bitter torment. His eyes dilated. "Oh, *Prof!*" he said, almost tearfully now—"Prof! . . . but I oughta known . . . why would you come sneakin' in here to meddle in somethin' that ain't nona your God-damn business? *Why?* . . . " At last he stared malevolently.

Hammer said nothing.

The soft, stitched scar over Dunreith's eye grew bulbous now, kidney-red, from his distraught rage. He squinted again at Hammer. "Why, God-damn your lousy fuckin' soul, Prof! . . . if it was anybody else I'd cut your ears off and throw 'em in your face— right now!"

"Dunreith, Dunreith!" Alexis said.

Hammer sat with a stubborn frown and said nothing.

Dunreith lurched forward on the sofa. "Prof!—why, why? Why'n the hell would you come in here messin' with me—and in my condition—about somethin' you don't even know me well enough in the first place to be talkin' about? Like I ain't got troubles enough already. *Huh?*" He scrambled to his feet, almost falling.

"I didn't come here to interfere with *you*," Hammer said. "You're interferin' with other people. . . . I only came to ask you to give Addie back to her family . . . to her grandmother, and her little brother. She can't mean that much to you—she's a child."

Dunreith stood gaping incredulously at Hammer. Then he finally backed up and sank on the sofa again. He sat shaking his head, then bent his head down in his hands. But soon he raised up. "Honest to God, Prof, that girl's saved your life. I mean it—saved your life, by tellin' me all the time what a nice, kind, good man you are. Otherwise, you'd never come meddlin' in anybody's else's business, *I'll tell you that!*" He was glaring, trembling.

Alexis tried to catch Hammer's eye, and jerked his head toward the door. Hammer saw, but ignored him.

Dunreith started muttering, half to himself—" . . . Tellin' me she can't mean that much to me. . . . Well, I'll——Prof, I don't understand you. Honest to God, I don't. I—I . . . " He was on the verge of tears.

Alexis went now and stood over him. "Dunreith, you're not feeling very well—why don't you go in the bedroom and lie down awhile? Come on."

Dunreith bent his head in his hands again. " . . . Says she

can't mean that much to me. I oughta fix him up? I oughta fix that Uncle Tom motherfucker up." He suddenly raised his head and glared again at Hammer.

Alexis turned to Hammer. "It'd be better, I think, Mr. Hammer, if you'd excuse us for tonight, and let Dunreith go lie down—he's not feeling well at all. You can talk to him some other time, maybe."

Hammer again ignored Alexis and looked at Dunreith. "Well, maybe I *am* wrong," he said to him, "—about her not meanin' that much to you. That shows, then, that you're a man of some feeling —and character——"

"Oh, will'ya cut it out? . . . will'ya please cut it out?" Dunreith grimaced and waved Hammer off. "I can't take any more of this sanctimonious shit of yours. It's sickening! . . . "

Hammer and Alexis were silent.

Dunreith spoke solely to Alexis now. "That girl is the only good thing that ever happened to me—*in my whole life!* You know that, Alexis! You *know* it!—why'n the hell don't you speak up!"

"Yes, Dunreith, I know it's true," Alexis said.

Weakly this time, the erratic doorbell rang.

Alexis sighed and went over and pushed the buzzer again. As he opened the door and waited, Dunreith and Hammer sat staring at opposite walls. Soon they heard a woman's heels on the stairs. "Florence, I think," Alexis said over his shoulder.

"Oh, Ch-r-r-r-ist!" groaned Dunreith. He struggled up from the sofa and looked around the room as if to escape.

"Hi, Florence," they heard Alexis say.

Florence entered. She was a buxom, brown-skinned woman of thirty, with big, scarlet, licentious lips. "Hello!" she smiled to them. Alexis introduced her to Hammer. Then she looked at Dunreith. "I came for you, Smitty boy. I figured you'd be stoned, all right —and you are, I see. I gotta cab waiting downstairs. Come on, now, sweetie—come on."

Dunreith stood sulking.

"Nice to meet you, Mr. Hammer," Florence said. "Take it easy, Alexis. Come on, Smitty—I told the cabby I'd be right down." She stepped backwards into the doorway.

Finally Dunreith, head down, muttering to himself, followed her out, and down the stairs.

Alexis closed the door and turned to Hammer, who, standing disconsolate, had picked up his hat again. "Whew," Alexis said, "I'm glad Florence came. Dunreith was getting nasty."

"I'll be goin' now, Mr. Potts," Hammer said, sternness in his voice.

Alexis spoke eagerly, seriously. "Listen, Mr. Hammer, I'm going to help you. Really, I am. Let me have your phone number— I'll call you. We'll work on Dunreith when he's feeling better. He knows you're right—that's the reason he acted up like he did. Maybe we can talk some sense in his head—and maybe we can't. We can only try. But you got him where it hurt when you said he had feeling, character. He's not used to hearing that—everybody's always saying what a bastard he is. That's something to remember. Appeal, then, to his 'feeling,' his 'character.' There's nothing to lose by it. You'll hear from me—I mean it."

Soon Hammer gave Alexis his telephone number, shook hands solemnly, and left.

🔳 🔳 🔳 🔳 🔳 🔳

Out at O'Hare International Airport, four evenings later, it was just getting dark. And the threat of still more rain had thinned out the few clusters of spectators up on the observation decks. In talkative groups—families, friends—they continued wandering toward the exits. But Clotilda stayed. She leaned forward against the breast-high steel railing, peering out toward the west, where parts of the desolate sky were streaked blood-red; the sun had long since settled out of sight far beyond the western runways. Now the thin warm rain began again. What an awful time for planes, Clotilda imagined, as she hoisted the shoulders of her raincoat over her damp blue hair. Soon a huge 747 jetliner went thundering down a distant diagonal runway, wet fuselage gleaming, tail and wing lights blinking like a Christmas tree, before it finally lifted its tons of weight off the asphalt like a giant tern.

Clotilda watched in awe, fearful, captivated; it was the third evening in one week these sights had fascinated her, for she had never flown. Sightseeing out here at O'Hare beat going to the movies, she thought, even if coming out did require a twenty-mile airporter ride from the Loop.

The movies had staled for her; they no longer took her out of herself, so she had sought this new distraction. As the slow rain came down on the observation decks, still more people scurried for the exits and shelter below. And as darkness slowly closed in, the great air field seemed all around like a lake of myriad lights, a vast, wet city within itself. Clotilda felt solitary, puny, in it.

After awhile she stepped back from the railing. Only a man and two little boys, apparently his sons, stood near her now, watching another big plane begin its ponderous taxiing out toward its assigned runway; the high, shrill whine of the jet engines was deafening to her. Darkness was complete at last. The rain had stopped again, although down on the asphalt tiny puddles of water shimmered under the lights of the field.

Soon a tall, ungainly, blond woman, after inserting her dime, pushed through the turnstile and walked onto the observation deck. She was thirty-five or more and wore a sharkskin suit tailored to her figure; her little umbrella was furled, and swung at her wrist, as she walked past Clotilda, stopping only fifteen feet down the railing to watch the plane like the others. But soon the man and two little boys wandered off and went downstairs. Clotilda held her raincoat on her arm now; although the deck lights were dim, her blue hair looked wild, cranky, odd. The woman took no notice of her, and stood at the railing watching activity down around a

DC-8 jet. A luggage vehicle had scooted up to the plane's nose compartment, attendants were loading food into the galley, and three rain-coated stewardesses boarded. Clotilda shot furtive glances at the woman now—but the woman seemed engrossed. Was she in trouble too? Clotilda wondered; no, just killing time, probably; didn't necessarily look unhappy; maybe waiting for her husband's plane; not sole and solitary like herself. But other people did have worries, she knew; she was not alone in this; although most did have someone to talk to; they could get advice; this woman had a husband, or mother, sister, or friends to talk to; besides she looked intelligent, probably didn't need advice, or maybe had the sense to stay out of trouble in the first place. Did smart people get into trouble? she wondered—or rich people? . . . This woman did not look poor, seemed respectable. Well, she was just another individual you saw in passing, like someone on a downtown street—one among a thousand, a person you'd never see again in life. The possibility slowly nudged in on Clotilda's awareness; this woman, after five or ten minutes, would leave, disappear; she was a total stranger and would soon be gone, too, forever. Why not ask her?—get her advice. But that would be so silly, and how could one get help without telling secrets, spilling one's guts; yet otherwise the advice would be no good, wouldn't fit the case; then why not talk to her? —tell her what was wrong—and *everything*; what if later she did blab it?—what difference would it make; they'd never once again glimpse each other.

Out of the corner of her eye Clotilda studied the woman, who was oblivious. Clotilda stalled; fear made her breathing change; she gazed the other way. Then suddenly she turned on the woman. "The rain's 'bout stopped, looks like," she heard herself saying— her smile was set, stricken.

The woman looked around, saw Clotilda's blue hair, and gaped. Finally, nodding, she murmured something inaudible and looked out onto the field again.

Clotilda paused, disappointed, but watched her, then suddenly smiled again. "I was just lookin' at you," she said. "That's th' loveliest suit you're wearing. I know. I'm a dressmaker."

The woman looked at her again. "Thennk you," she finally said; the speech sounded foreign.

Clotilda persisted. "I like to watch the planes," she laughed. " . . . this's my third trip out here this week. Got rained on today, though." She ran her hand through her damp blue hair.

The woman gave a weak smile and said nothing.

"I was just tellin' myself you was probably waiting on your husband's plane," Clotilda said.

" . . . No—my huspant's down in zeh passengers' lounge." The woman pointed below. "Vee're vaiting to meet his *bruder* . . . brother? . . . "

"Oh—why, you're from the old country," Clotilda beamed.

"Vee are from Germany, Vest Germany." The woman spoke earnestly and turned away.

Clotilda saw the opportunity; the woman even lived in a different part of the world; here was rare, special, security; yet she could not drag herself to the confessional; she felt her story too sad, ancient, wicked. From a close runway now a big 707 had just taken off; soon, nose up and engines thundering, it came low over the shuddering observation deck and headed out toward Lake Michigan. But when the din had cleared, Clotilda found herself again looking at the woman.

"Maybe you could help me . . . " she suddenly blurted, then faltered.

The woman looked confused, disturbed. "Halp you? . . ."

" . . . explain somethin' to me, maybe . . . I can't seem . . . "

"I'm sorry . . . I must go down to my huspant now. . . ." The woman began sidling away.

"—My little granddaughter's gone to the dogs," Clotilda said quickly, her eyes going after her. "Now I feel like I'm chokin' to death all the time—suffocatin' . . . and got rushing noises in my head so bad . . . "

The woman turned her back now and walked toward the exit.

Clotilda's voice got louder; she still called after her—"I brought Addie up in a good, clean home. But she's finished now— and only sixteen. Why, her mother—my daughter—was a good woman. It don't make sense. Now I'm just chokin' to death— can't get air, seems like . . . and all these noises in my head . . . ." Her eyes were distraught as she fiercely plunged her hand through her garish hair. But soon the woman had disappeared through the turnstile and gone below.

But Clotilda, though now alone, kept talking: "Now, I went wrong a time or two, myself," she called, "—when I was young, that is. Took advantage of my sister Pearlie once. It was a low-down trick, but I pulled it and been mortally sorry ever since—God in heaven knows I have. I had Ruby. But she was mine, and I loved her. She got Addie. Addie was hers, and, oh, how she loved Addie. I loved them both. But love was not enough. The hand of misery was already on them—*both*." Clotilda's voice was loud now—ringing, as if delivering an oration. "And who was the cause of that?—me or God? I caused them to exist in the world, so *I* must be the one. Yes, I am the one—oh, if only somebody could show me I'm wrong in that . . . wouldn't it be wonderful? . . . would I be tickled. I sure would indeed. Living would be a whole lot different; the few years left would be easier, I'll tell you. My life wouldn't be so rough." Soon she was waving her arms and shouting in gasps—"But now I got these rushing noises in my head . . . and I'm almost chokin' to death!—I can't hardly breathe, seems like! It's a fact! It's—"

An elderly man and wife had come through the turnstile onto the observation deck. They stood staring at Clotilda, and kept their distance. When she was aware of them, her voice died to a mumble; only her lips moved as she glowered at them. What were they gawking at? she exploded to herself. Defiant, she wheeled and faced them. The couple averted their gaze now and stood briefly looking down on the field, but soon they hurried to the exit and went below.

Clotilda was suddenly, strangely, wrought up, furious; her weeks of burden seemed now to set off a steeping rage against the world akin to paranoia. Snorting, she took two sticks of chewing gum from her purse and jerked off their wrappers. Then with her raincoat over her arm, and wildly chewing the wad of gum, she left the observation deck and went downstairs to the spacious lounge for passengers. She sat down for a moment but soon got up and went to the rest room. Other women, passing in and out of the rest room, stared at her hair. Her resentment mounted. She took up a stubborn position before a mirror and, preening forward, combed and manipulated her stiff blue hair until the women watching smiled. Leaving the rest room, she jostled a woman, then turned and glared.

She left the air terminal building, walked to the airporter stop, and boarded a bus that would take her back downtown. It had begun to drizzle again. But now as she sat in the waiting bus, gazing in a dudgeon out her window, she soon discovered her tensions slowly dissipating. In her fury she had seemed to experience a mirage, a sudden illumination, and at once her evolving sense of relief brought quickened pulse strokes as her crumbling mind now saw visions she construed as hope. She stared out again through the wet pane of glass at the strange night's blackness; daring to trust it had brought sweet blessings after all and at last. Soon the bus driver came down the aisle to collect the fares; when he had returned to his seat, he started the motor and headed out toward the Kennedy Expressway and downtown Chicago. Clotilda's mind sped ahead home; she felt a strange inner wrath at that household, and, excepting Lester, everyone in it; they had betrayed, rejected, her, she thought; now she would pay them back—leave, desert, them. Maybe by leaving she would blot out all relics, reminders, of what was; what is. Could it really be that hope lay only in this?

—yes, it must be so. *True* friends, *loved* ones, were the only salvation. Her escaped, broken mind commanded her. She would go—yes—yes . . . she would go . . . to Cleveland . . . Pearlie . . .

Chapter Seven

IT WAS August now—a Saturday noon—and Ambrose Hammer and Letitia Dorsey had just finished a full morning's work at the downtown public library. They came out of the big stone building and stood waiting with other pedestrians at a traffic light. It was hot, and Hammer wore his white suit and lugged his swollen brief case, while Letitia carried her purse and a brown envelope containing shorthand notes just dictated by Hammer. They had stopped work because Letitia said she was tired, and were headed to lunch now, then home. Letitia was smiling, but Hammer was grave.

"Oh, isn't it a beautiful day!" Letitia exulted, "—even if it is hot." She looked east out over Lake Michigan. "Just look at the lake—isn't it gorgeous?"

Hammer looked; then the traffic light went green; his finger tips touched her elbow as they started across the street. The white suit looked tight on him, and also made his skin seem darker still.

"I always call this 'resort weather'," Letitia laughed. "It makes me think of some lovely resort." She was wistful. " . . . a swimming pool, a pretty dining room, music . . . nice people for a hand or two of bridge, maybe." Walking in brown and white pumps she was as tall as Hammer.

"This is great weather." Hammer was laconic.

"Oh, it is! Have you ever been up to Barnhart's Cove—in Michigan?"

"I don't think so."

"I was up there three summers ago—with a bunch of women." Letitia giggled. "Four women!—Can you imagine? It was dull."

Hammer, steering her through the pedestrians, grinned.

They entered an air conditioned cafeteria on Randolph Street. Hammer bought them two chicken *a la king* lunches and iced tea, and they sat along the wall at a table for two. Hammer stowed his brief case under the table, where it constantly bumped their feet, and launched into talk about his book—that morning from his copious notes he had dictated the last section of his chapter on the Negro church.

Breaking off the talk about summer resorts had dampened Letitia's gaiety; although polite, she now forked her food in silence. Hammer soon too was silent.

Suddenly Letitia gave him a brazen smile. "Mr. Hammer, how would you like to go up to Barnhart's Cove—over Labor Day week end? . . . We could take the bus up."

Hammer looked in his plate, then gave her a furtive glance, before he went on solemnly chewing a piece of hard roll. Finally he took out his pince-nez and adjusted them on his nose to consult his little black note-book and glanced away.

Letitia squealed out a tittering laugh. "Oh, it would be all right!—we'd have separate rooms and everything. People our age don't need chaperons, do they?"

Hammer smiled. "Oh, no, no—I wasn't thinkin' about that. I was just checkin' . . . I was just checkin' to see if those dates are clear. I'm not sure—I can't tell yet." He nervously pocketed the notebook and removed his pince-nez.

"Okay . . . " Letitia smiled. "Okay, Mr. Hammer."

Hammer sipped his iced tea. "Maybe we could," he finally said. "But that's some few days away yet, is it not? We'll see."

"Oh, Mr. Hammer, it would be so relaxing for you—you need some time off." She tittered again—"I'd pay my own way, you know."

Hammer chuckled. "That's no problem."

Now a score of out-of-town teen-agers on a bus tour filed inside the cafeteria rail, followed by a deeply-tanned man and woman in charge.

Suddenly, on seeing the young people, Letitia's face went absent, glum ; soon she spoke with a nervous anger. "Did you ever see that Dunreith Smith any more . . . after that night at his friend Alexis' ?"

Hammer was casual. "Yes—oh, yes. Saw him day before yesterday."

"You *did* ?"

"I've seen him twice since that night."

"You didn't tell me . . . "

"Well, I've been working on the case, Miss Dorsey . . . by that I mean tryin' to talk some sense in his head. He's a hard kind of fella to figure out—sometimes I feel he's not quite as bad as they picture him."

"Oh, Mr. Hammer !—"

"—Well, I'm not sure, of course. He's unusual, though. He's awful warped—seems to hate the world and everything in it."

"He's a rat—Oh, Mr. Hammer !"

"He thinks he likes Addie."

Letitia balled up her pale fists. "Oh ! . . . that . . . that *dog*."

Hammer frowned. "It's more complicated than that. He's twisted—but so is Addie."

"Mr. Hammer, we ought to put the police on that man ; that's what we ought to do. Can there be any question in your mind—whatever ?"

Hammer broke off a piece of hard roll and munched it, then shook his head. "That would only make things worse," he said.

"What I've tried to do is appeal to his professed love for Addie—"

"Oh, my God!—"

"—Well, that's the only thing I can see that's got any chance of workin'. He's finally promised he'll start pullin' back from her. Whether he actually will or not, I don't know—but I really believe he was sincere when he made the promise. I'm convinced of it, Miss Dorsey."

"Oh, I *do* hope he'll leave that child alone." Letitia dabbed at her eyes with her handkerchief. "It's dreadful . . . just dreadful. And Clotilda—oh, my goodness, Clotilda—have you noticed her, Mr. Hammer?"

Hammer was glum, also. "Yes, I have."

"And she's out of the house now most of the time—I don't know where she goes. And is neglecting her work, too—her sewing. Mr. Hammer, I don't think she's taking in much money, do you? There sure are a lot of bills in the mail. I think her money's running low. I really do."

Hammer sat thinking. "Yes," he said, "it could be."

"And, oh, is she cross and snappy. That's not Clotilda—you know that; she's never been that way, never—we've been the closest of friends. And lately she just sits and glares at Addie—Lester's the only one she's halfway civil to. She loves that kid. And he loves her. But she won't even get *his* meals sometimes now. And the house is getting so untidy. It's sad . . . sad."

Hammer pulled his iced tea toward him and spoke with authority. "Our object is to restore Addie to her. If there *is* a solution, that's it. But Addie herself's driven by the very devil, it seems like. She's the one, as much as Dunreith, that's made it so bad."

"She's never got over her mother," Letitia said, shaking her head. "And those nightmares—they're about her mother too, I'm almost certain. But, we've been over all that before." She sighed and finished her fruit-jello dessert, then took out her compact and lipstick. Hammer leaned back from the table to let the bus boy take off some dishes.

"Clotilda used to want to talk to me about Addie," Letitia said, "—before that awful Dunreith came in the picture. But now she's so tight-lipped."

"Well, sometimes I kinda doubt if she's ever told *any*body all she knows," Hammer said. "Somethin's eatin' her. The answer's in somethin' she knows that we don't—and never will, probably. It's an unusual case, Miss Dorsey, most unusual—a case for psychiatry, maybe."

"It's all so awful. The house's not the nice place it used to be. I wish sometimes I could leave it . . . for a better life. . . ."

Hammer nudged the salt and pepper shakers back and forth like chessmen. "Well, you wouldn't want to leave just now," he said, " . . . under present circumstances. There're things we can probably do to help."

Letitia put out her hand on his forearm. "Oh, I didn't mean it that way, Mr. Hammer—of course I wouldn't want to leave now. I just mean, I guess, I'm looking for . . . well, a better life for myself someday, that's all." Now her elongated, pale face showed impatience, hurt. "Is there anything wrong in *that*?" She gave Hammer a peevish, scolding, look.

"Oh, no, no—not at all, not at all." Hammer got out his pince-nez again, reached for the luncheon check, and studied it; then took a ten-dollar bill from his wallet. "I just mean we've all got to try to keep a cool head now—that's all I meant." He pushed his chair back and reached his brief case off the floor. Letitia, dramatically batting her long eyelashes, pouted as they walked toward the cashier. Then unobtrusively Hammer turned to her— "Why don't you find out about that Barnhart's Cove? . . . They might still have some reservations left—for Labor Day weekend, maybe."

Startled Letitia was still looking at him as he paid the check and they left. At last she smiled to herself, feeling no need to make him the superfluous answer. He did not expect it, she knew, and in her heart she thanked him. Nervous all the way home, she left off her simpering now, and grateful, subdued, hardly talking at all, gazed out the bus window and congratulated herself. It was a beginning . . . and, strangely, she had already, for the first time in her life, begun to feel the very, very tiniest tinge of power.

〽 〽 〽 〽 〽 〽

That same day—and about noon—the hot glare of the sun on the windshield half-blinded Dunreith Smith as he sent the old Dodge flying east out the East-West Tollway. Addie rode beside him, and Rosie—of the roly-poly body and piebald face—sat alone in the back, as the heat ranged up through the floor boards and baked their feet. On both sides of the expressway the terrain was flat and tree-less; an occasional huge signboard was the only distraction.

Dunreith pointed at the glove compartment. "See if there're some sun glasses in there," he said to Addie.

Addie found the sun glasses and, refusing to look at him, handed them over.

"My God!—slow down, Dunreith," Rosie said, blinking her big eyes in her black and pink splotched face. "We'll git picked up." She turned and peered fearfully out the rear window.

Dunreith scooted lower behind the wheel and kept his speed.

Next to Rosie on the back seat were a thermos jug of lemonade and a cardboard box containing sandwiches and half a cake. Rosie laughed—"You're th' last one in the world that oughta want to git arrested."

Dunreith was sullen, edgy. He scratched his bushy mustache. "This wagon'll outrun any God-damned Indiana mounty on the road." His eye had healed, but there was a scar.

"Are you kiddin'?" Rosie said. "Mosta their cars are new— and souped up to boot." Her dumpy body sat on the seat like a sack of wheat, and her feet hardly reached the floor.

Dunreith said nothing.

For miles Addie had sat silent, staring ahead through the windshield.

"For cryin'-out-loud," Rosie said, "—this sure is some happy bunch, to be goin' to spend a day in the country." She leaned forward and poked her spotted face between them. "What's the matter with you two?—sittin' up there like two old hoot owls."

Dunreith gave her an insolent glance—"And what's the matter with you?—great speckled bird."

Addie turned on him—"Dunreith!"

"Don't pay him no mind, honey," Rosie said. "He's an evil bastard. What you see in him I'll never know."

"The great, *old,* speckled bird," soliloquized Dunreith.

Rosie sat back on the seat. "Dunreith, I don't pay any 'tention to you. I know you. You're just as crazy as a bed bug. If you don't quit smokin' all that pot you're gonna be cuttin' out paper dolls in the nuthouse."

"Old speckled bird," Dunreith mused aloud.

Addie turned on him. "You stop that, Dunreith!"

"Let him alone, honey," Rosie said. "Don't let him get you upset. I'm gonna tell him again how I got to *be* a speckled bird—"

Dunreith groaned. "For Chrissake, spare us, will you?" He gave his bitter, gravelly laugh. "Do we have to go through that routine again—'my little kids all got burnt up in a fire'—but you generally have to be drunk t'tell it."

Addie glared at him.

"I ain't drunk. And I'm gonna tell it," Rosie said. "—how I got to be a speckled bird, you looney hophead. It'll be twenty-three years, come this winter—Oh, God, is it really that long? I was young and good-lookin' then—"

"Haw," Dunreith said.

"Well, I was." Rosie turned to Addie—"Honey, I had three of the loveliest kids—"

"—each one by a different nigger," Dunreith said.

"Will you let me tell it, Dunreith? Jasper was six—he had a

long, scared-like, sweet face. *Little* Rosie was five—suckin' her thumb all the time, and big eyes watchin' me. Swerzie, she was three and a half—Swerzie could talk just as good as Rosie or Jasper, either one."

Dunreith was driving eighty miles an hour in a sixty mile zone. The straining old motor made a noisy thrumming vibration.

Rosie leaned forward to be heard. "It was the cold winter of 1948," she shouted—"February . . . me and the kids were livin' down on 43rd Street, in a building that had over thirty kitchenettes in it. Well, one evenin', around seven—it was snowin' to beat hell —I had to go out—"

"—to get some more wine," Dunreith said.

"No, Dunreith—to git some milk for my babies. You know that—you've heard me tell it before."

"You God-damn right I have."

Rosie turned to Addie. "Y'see, honey, he can't take it—he's got two little kids himself. So any time he gits uppity-flip and evil with me, like today, I know how to git him—I know, all right. Aw, he goes for tough, but the truth is he's as chicken-hearted a sonofa-bitch as ever lived—regardin' children. Oh, does it kill him when I tell about my kids." She turned again to Dunreith. "Yeah—suffer. Suffer! Yeah, when I'm tellin' it, just think it was *your* little kids, will'ya. Will'ya do that for me, Dunreith—huh?"

"Rosie's crazy," Dunreith whispered, shaking his head.

"Ah, Mr. Dunreith, just listen to this—as I said, I had gone out to git some milk for my babies. In the kitchenette next to mine a bunch of winoes had been partyin' all day long—makin' a lot of racket and just raisin' hell all that afternoon. By evenin' all of 'em was drunk, and some of 'em asleep. But one of 'em staggered, or fell, against their stove—and upset it. At the time, I was out to the store to get my babies some milk, Dunreith—hear, Dunreith? Well, comin' back I heard first, then I saw, the fire trucks. When I got to my building, smoke was just pourin' out the third floor where I lived—just pourin' out. I tried to run up the stairs, but somebody grabbed me. Then the flames started shootin' out all the third floor windows. I was screamin' and hollerin', but the people wouldn't turn me loose. . . . Aw, what the hell's the use of goin' into it. 'Bout an hour later the firemen carried my kids down, covered in a tarpaulin. I was still screamin' and hollerin', and run over and jerked the tarp back. They looked like three little barbecued possums."

"Oh!" Addie covered her face with her hands.

"An' that, Mr. Dunreith, was how I got to be a speckled bird."

Dunreith scowled behind his sun glasses.

"—*that's* how, Mr. Dunreith. It wasn't a month before the skin all over my body in places started turnin' white. I went to two or three doctors, but they couldn't stop it or make it turn back. They couldn't do nothin', nobody could. Finally I went to a spiritual advisor—remember old Madame Valentine? . . . she musta been eighty by then. She said my skin turnin' was a sign I wanted to be white. Maybe she was right. Who wouldn't?"

"Shit," Dunreith said.

"I *still* say—who wouldn't?"

Dunreith muttered something in his teeth and kept driving fast. Soon they approached a toll pay-station. He slowed and drove with one hand while he leaned sideways to fish forty cents from his pocket. "Why, God-damn it," he said, loud enough for the red-headed toll attendant to hear, "I'd sooner be in hell with my back broke than be white."

They had left Chicago a half-hour before and, heading east, had crossed over into Indiana on their way to Monday Williams' "farm"—Monday, a relative of Dunreith's friend Alexis, raised chickens and grew marijuana. Dunreith drove on out the tollway. The sun was high and the heat like a furnace.

Rosie turned to Addie. "How'n the world did you manage to get out, honey?"

Addie floundered, and finally sighed. "I just managed, that's all."

"Rosie, cut me a piece of that cake," Dunreith said.

"Well, ain't you got your nerve—askin' me for *any*thing. But you junkies always got a sweet tooth, ain't you? I thought we was goin' to wait and eat when we got out there—and have a little picnic like."

Dunreith was sinister. "That's right, but I'll take a piece of cake *now*—if you don't mind."

Rosie turned to Addie and laughed. "What d'you say?—should I, honey?"

Addie, still staring out through the windshield, was inattentive, irritable—"Oh, okay."

Rosie opened the cardboard box on the back seat beside her and used a table knife to slice out the wedge of cake. She handed it up to Dunreith on a paper napkin.

"Thanks," he said, and bit off half the piece. "Hmmm . . . pretty good."

"*I* didn't make it—it's a store-bought cake," Rosie laughed. "But *any* kind would taste pretty good to a junky right now, I bet —wouldn't it, Dunreith?"

Dunreith said nothing. He wolfed the cake, licked his fingers, and continued driving fast.

Rosie shook her head and turned and peered out the rear window again. "Dunreith, slow down! Your foot is just too dern heavy."

Dunreith kept his speed.

"Honey," Rosie said to Addie, "what's wrong with you? You sick, or somethin'—you feel bad?"

"Why don't you let her alone?" Dunreith said.

"*Me* let her alone—how d'you like that? For a change how 'bout *you* lettin' her alone? She'd be a damn sight better off, I'll tell you that."

Addie spun around, fury in her eyes. "Oh! . . . both of you —leave me alone!" She began crying and got out a kleenex.

Rosie leaned forward. "Sa-a-a-y, what's the matter with you?

What'n the world's got into you? Huh? Come on, now, honey—
tell Rosie."

Addie sniffled and stared ahead.

"Tell me, honey, is it that Dunreith Smith? *Is* it? Why, I'd
lynch him if he ever hurt you—that is, more'n he has already."

Addie clutched her wadded kleenex and said nothing.

"Is it him, honey? You just tell me."

Addie finally turned around; her freckles were wet, smudged.
"Dunreith wants to quit," she said. Her lower lip quivered. " . . .
says he's got too many 'chicks' already . . . can't afford them all."
She started crying again.

Rosie's big eyes dilated. "Why, that dirty dog!" she yelled
at Dunreith. "You lousy jerk you!" She began pummeling him on
the back and shoulders. The car swerved and the tires screeched,
but Dunreith rode the steering wheel and held the road.

Then he slowed to a crawl. "You hit me again," he breathed
through grating teeth, "and I'll pull off to the side of the road and
whip both you bitches' asses. Go on, hit me."

"I oughta kill you," Rosie said, panting, but she soon sat back
on the seat again.

They traveled the remaining forty miles in silence.

Monday Williams' "farm" resembled a gypsy camp. The
yard grass was tall and littered with old automobile tires, pieces
of picket fence, and blobs of chicken dung—there were as many
chickens in the yard as in the pen. A small lean-to barn and two
hen houses sat close behind the house. Monday, a little man, jet
black and Jamaican, sat on the porch shelling peas, as Dunreith—
the Dodge's radiator boiling—drove into the yard.

Little Monday grinned, showing decayed, green teeth—"You-
all better jump outa that thing quick, before it explodes," he called.

Dunreith crawled out and stretched, then came across the
yard and up onto the porch, extending both hands toward Monday
as if groping. "Monday—where are you, man?" he grinned. "—I
can't see you." He took out a pack of matches, lit one, and held it

in Monday's black face. "Oh, there you are—I couldn't make you out, man." He gave a wild, crazed laugh.

Monday grinned. "You're gettin' loonier by the minute, Dunreith."

Dunreith glanced toward the screen door—"Got any drinkin' whiskey 'round here?"

"You wouldn't get any if I did—drivin' an automobile. It's too hot to drink, anyhow."

Rosie and Addie approached the porch through the tall yard grass. Rosie lugged the thermos jug and Addie, her face inert, drawn, carried the cardboard box. Monday stood up and smiled— "Why, good-afternoon, ladies. Come right up. I'll go git some more chairs."

Rosie knew Monday and introduced Addie, before Monday went in and brought out two more chairs. Dunreith sat on the edge of the porch and, snapping his fingers and clucking, egged on a rooster chasing a hen across the yard. Finally sated, he turned to Monday—"Let's kill one of them gospel birds and fry him."

Indulgent Monday laughed.

Soon Rosie looked at Addie and got up. "Come on, honey," she said. "Let's go freshen up." She picked up the box and thermos jug and took Addie inside.

"Who's the girl?" Monday said to Dunreith.

" . . . Friend of Rosie's." Dunreith, restless, got up and stood on the edge of the porch.

"Why, she's just a kid, a school kid—ain't she?"

"Guess so," Dunreith shrugged.

Monday gave him a quizzical look. "How long have *you* knowed her?" he said.

Dunreith frowned. "Say, what'n th' hell's goin' on? You got nose trouble, man." He nodded toward the inside of the house. "Got any cold beer in there?"

Monday sighed, shook his head, and got up. "Yeah . . . come on in." He waved the flies off the screen door and they went in.

It was muggy hot inside. Rosie was sitting on the dilapidated sofa fanning herself with a man's handkerchief. Addie was in the bathroom. "How 'bout a can of beer, Rosie, gull?" Monday said, passing on through to the kitchen.

"Yeah, Monday—yeah, boy." Rosie laughed and pointed to her sandwich box and thermos jug on the floor. "But we brought provisions ourselves—we ain't gonna eat *you* outa house and home," she called after him.

Dunreith had flopped in a chair. Soon Monday returned with two opened cans of beer. After handing them out, he sat down and they talked.

Five . . . ten . . . fifteen minutes went by and Addie had not reappeared. Dunreith had downed his beer and now sat smoking a cigarette, fidgeting, and looking uneasily at Rosie. Finally he jerked his head toward the bathroom. "Go tell her to come on," he said to Rosie. "—Whut'n the hell did she do in there, fall in?"

Rosie cut withering eyes at him but soon got up and went in the rear to the bathroom door. She knocked—"Addie?" There was no answer. She knocked again—"Addie . . . Addie, honey." —then shook the door. It was hooked from inside. Dunreith suddenly stood beside her now. Rosie knocked, then shook the door again—"Addie, baby!" There was no response. Dunreith lunged against the door and sent it open as the hook inside flew off and hit the wall. Addie stood cringing in the corner by the water heater with her right hand behind her back. Her red Afro hair-do was mussed and her freckles smeared from crying. Rosie rushed in and grabbed her by the arm—"Come on, baby—Come on, now. We're gonna get somethin' to eat—you'll feel better when we get somethin' to eat."

Addie groaned and slumped to the floor. An empty iodine bottle left her hidden hand and skittered across the bathroom floor.

Rosie screamed. "Dunreith! — *Iodine!* — She's swallowed iodine! Oh, Jesus!"

Monday ran in as Dunreith grappled up Addie off the floor, carried her into the living room, and laid her out on the sofa. Addie was limp, and dark fluid oozed from the corners of her mouth.

Dunreith, his voice husky, turned on Monday—"Where's a hospital or doctor?"

"Gawd . . . I don't know," Monday said. "There ain't no hospital around here. There's a doctor in Marchfield—but, Gawd, that's miles away."

"Come on," Dunreith said to Rosie. Whispering oaths and obscenities, he caught up Addie off the sofa and ran with her through the front door out to the car. Rosie, her dress armpits dark from perspiration, ran heavily after him.

Rosie held Addie in her arms in the back seat as Dunreith jack-knifed the car back out of the driveway and onto the blacktop road. Addie was conscious and moaning—"Where're you taking me?—oh, my stomach hurts. I want to go to my grandmother. Take me to my grandmother. Oh, my stomach. Dunreith!—you take me to my grandmother!"

Dunreith whispered obscenities and, hunched low over the wheel, kept the accelerator to the floor on the straightaways and careened on the curves—the old Dodge shook and shuddered but exceeded eighty-five miles an hour.

Rosie pleaded with Addie. "We're takin' you to the doctor, baby—be quiet—be quiet, now." She hugged Addie to her.

"I want to go to my grandmother!" Addie struggled. "My stomach hurts—I want to go to my grandmother."

Rosie held her and with a kleenex tried to wipe the dark stains from her mouth. Finally Addie was quieter; but still groaned. "Oh, my stomach hurts. Take me home, will you, please—Dunreith, Rosie, please—take me home."

"God damn your soul to *hell*," Dunreith quivered.

Twenty minutes later they approached the little town of Marchfield. Farmers were coming into town on Saturday afternoon and the traffic was heavier. Dunreith had to slow down. When finally they came into the center of town, Rosie yelled to him. "Stop, Dunreith—stop and ask somebody where the doctor is." Just then Addie put her chin over the edge of Rosie's lap and was sick on the floor of the car. Rosie shouted—"Oh! that's good! that's good! that's right, honey—Oh, Jesus! Go ahead, honey, go ahead and spill your cookies. Oh, that's the best thing could ever happened—keep it up, honey, keep it up!" Addie finally lay limp over Rosie's knee.

Soon Rosie saw a cluster of men in shirt sleeves standing on the corner in front of a hardware and feed-grain store. She pointed —"Here, here, Dunreith! Here, stop here!" Dunreith slowed, pulled over, and stopped. Rosie put her piebald face out, and the men gaped. "Could any you please tell us where th' doctor lives?" she said. "—We gotta awful sick girl here—swallowed poison. We gotta git her to a doctor."

The men gawked at Rosie's face. Finally a young blond fellow wearing a T-shirt came two steps nearer the car. He pointed east. "Go two streeets over, to Franklin," he said, "and turn right. You go quite aways down Franklin—four or five blocks. Dr. Higglethorne's house is a big yellow stucco, on the corner of Bailey —his name's on the sign in the yard—you'll see it."

"Oh, thank you, mister—thank you ever so much," Rosie said, as Dunreith pulled off. Then she wailed—"Lord Jesus— Dunreith, suppose he ain't there—Oh, Lord." Addie's head was in Rosie's lap, eyes closed. Rosie leaned down—"Addie . . . Addie, how you feel, baby? . . . feel better?" Addie groaned and opened her eyes, but said nothing.

Dunreith found the Higglethorne house without difficulty. He stopped in front and jumped out of the car. Starting up the walk to the porch, he re-read the sign. It directed patients around to the side door—the entrance to the doctor's office. Dunreith turned and followed the cement walkway around, quickly rang the bell, and waited. No one came. His heart was lurching against his ribs. He rang again, hard. Finally he heard footsteps inside on the back stairs. A grey-haired woman, in her sixties, apparently the doctor's wife, opened the door.

"Could I see the doctor?" Dunreith said.

The woman studied him.

Dunreith, grimacing, began twisting and writhing. "We gotta sick girl in the car!" he said, extending helpless palms. "She drank iodine and's in a lotta pain."

"Bring her in," the woman said at once. "The doctor's asleep —I'll have to wake him."

"Thanks, thanks," Dunreith whispered, then turned and trotted back toward the car.

Soon he returned carrying Addie. Rosie ran alongside trying to smooth down Addie's wild hair. Addie was moaning—"I want to go home to my grandmother—Oh, please take me home."

"We're takin' you to the doctor, honey," Rosie panted. "Oh, thank God the doctor's here—thank God." Perspiration rolled off her piebald face in the muggy heat.

The doctor's wife admitted them to the waiting room, where they took seats. She left. The room was white and clean, and the magazines recent. Addie sat leaning against Rosie and began to cry as Rosie embraced her. Dunreith sat glaring at the opposite wall.

"What'll the doctor do to me?" whined Addie.

"He's gonna make your stummick quit hurtin', honey," Rosie said. "You got to be a brave girl, now, when he comes in."

Finally Dunreith looked at Addie. His eyes hovered, lingered, on her; then a look of tender anguished pain came over his wasted face before he stared at the wall again.

At last Dr. Higglethorne entered through a door leading from the front of the house. He was a pink, ponderous old man with a white clipped mustache; and wore a sports shirt and house shoes. He looked drowsily at the three and nodded a brief greeting, then told Dunreith he could return to the car. Dunreith left quickly. Higglethorne took Addie and Rosie into the inner office and examined Addie, and later pumped her stomach. When finally he had finished, and Addie's hysterics subsided, he wrote out two prescriptions and gave them to Rosie, then directed Addie to be taken home and put to bed. Rosie paid him, thanked him profusely, and soon led Addie out.

Returning to Chicago, Rosie rode up front with Dunreith. Addie lay curled on the back seat. Dunreith en route had tossed the unclean floor mat under a roadside culvert and now drove slowly.

Rosie turned to him—"I paid the doctor, y'know. Gimme my ten dollars."

"That'll be a pleasure," Dunreith muttered, reaching back for his wallet.

"I got two prescriptions here too."

"—And take enough for them." He handed Rosie the wallet.

Rosie turned around and observed prone Addie—"How d'you feel, baby? D'you feel better?"

"No . . . " Addie moaned.

"The doctor said you'll be all right in a couple days—Dunreith, we gotta stop somewhere and git these prescriptions filled."

An hour later as they entered Chicago Addie began to stir. Soon she sat up and, face harrowed, peered out mournfully at the street signs.

"You'll be home before long now, honey," Rosie said. "We ain't got much further."

Dunreith, though driving slowly, stubbornly ran a yellow light.

Four blocks later they stopped at a drug store. Rosie got out of the car and went in, as Dunreith lit a cigarette and arched his back in a twisting fatigued stretch. Then he sat slumped in the seat and smoked in silence. When he finally finished the cigarette he flicked it out the window. "That was a helluva thing you pulled today," he said to Addie. "You're lucky as hell—it coulda killed you. You're nuts—crazy."

Addie still gazed out the car window. "I hate you," she said. "All I know is, I hate you."

Dunreith said no more. A little later he sighed and lit another cigarette.

Soon Rosie, perspiring, returned with the medicine and they drove off. Addie sat limp with her head thrown back and eyes closed. Suddenly she lurched forward and retched, but nothing came up. She groaned and curled up on the seat again. "Aw, poor honey," Rosie said. "We'll be there d'reckly, now—won't be long. You can git in th' bed then, and you'll feel better quick. Here, put this medicine in your purse—the directions are on the bottles." Addie took the two vials but held them in her hand; and later left them on the seat.

About six blocks from home she sat up again. There was a yellow pallor on her face and her hair was wilder than ever. "Let me out here," she said. "I'll get a cab."

Rosie looked around at her; then at Dunreith. Dunreith kept driving.

"Let me out," Addie said, and started crying again.

"*You* might be crazy, but I ain't," Dunreith said.

Rosie turned around again to Addie. "Honey, we couldn't let you out here—you're sick."

"Let me out!" Addie wailed. "I don't want my grandmother to see."

"See what?" Dunreith said.

Addie's voice was cold—"See *you.*"

Dunreith said nothing.

"Aw, honey you're too weak," Rosie said. "Why, we couldn't put you out here in the street like that."

Addie, still crying, was soon dry-retching again.

Five minutes later they pulled up in front of Clotilda's house. Rosie got out of the car, went back, and helped Addie out; then led her up the front walk toward the porch. Lester was in the yard, with another boy. When he saw them his mouth fell open; he started running toward them, then suddenly stopped, wheeled, and raced back to the house. He ran up on the porch and yelled through the screen door—"Grammaw! Grammaw! Come here! Come here, quick!"

Rosie and Addie had reached the porch when Clotilda, wearing a housecoat and bedroom slippers, finally came to the door. Addie started screaming—"Grandma! Grandma!"—then collapsed to her knees on the porch. Rosie tugged her up and held her erect.

Clotilda seemed not to recognize Addie.

"It's Addie, Grammaw!" Lester shouted. "It's Addie! Somethin's wrong with her . . . That's Dunreith in the car—it's Dunreith, Grammaw! Let's call the police!"

"Oh, Grandma," Addie wailed, "I love you—I love you, Grandma."

Clotilda, ignoring both Addie and Lester, curled her lip and spoke to Rosie. "Don't bring her in here—this ain't her home. Take her on away from here. . . ."

"—Grammaw, Grammaw," Lester said, "that's Dunreith in the car! It's—"

"—Addie's awful sick," Rosie said, perspiration dripping ofl her chin. "We jist brought her here from the doctor. She needs t'go to bed right away—she's got medicine to take."

Finally Clotilda's eyes went bulging wide; she gaped at Rosie. Soon she started yelling—screaming and yelling—"Oh! . . . Oh! . . . Oh! . . . You've *aborted* that child. That's what you've done! You've aborted my grandbaby! Why, you low, dirty, stinkin' niggers! Call the police, Lester!—Hurry!—Go call the police quick! *Hurry!*"

Lester, transfixed, did not move.

"Oh, no—no, we didn't do that!" Rosie pleaded. "—She dranked a whole bottle of iodine."

Now Dunreith, glaring, scowling, put his head out of the car— "*Rosie*, come on!—what the fuck's wrong with you?"

"Honest to the Lord, we didn't," Rosie said to Clotilda. "Honest to—" Now she started backing down the walk toward the car. "Why, we wouldn't do a thing like that—we wouldn't think of—"

Clotilda screamed at her—"You lyin', spotted bitch, you!—You gutter niggers!—If I had a gun I'd kill you!—botha you! Call the police, Lester—*Hurry*!"

Rosie floundered backwards to the car, jumped in, and Dunreith sped off.

Addie dropped to her knees on the porch steps again and tried to clutch Clotilda's ankles—"Oh, Grandma! Oh, Grandma!—I love you! I love you, Grandma!"

Clotilda kicked her housecoat free and stepped back. "Get away from me—you little *slut*, you."

Lester led Addie into the house.

🌀 🌀 🌀 🌀 🌀 🌀

Addie was sick in bed for three days and ailed for another week. Letitia and Hammer had a doctor in for her twice during the first three days. Clotilda now was present in the house in body only; she had lost contact with surroundings, was no longer in charge, had isolated herself, and sat all day in the living room staring out at the street; at night she slept on the sofa. Addie had the first-floor bedroom alone, but the torments of the havoc she had worked beset her day and night; her grandmother's worsened, mind-bereft condition had panicked her and lacerated her conscience; this latter was a new emotion and made somehow gaining forgiveness her present sole hysterical goal; it was a need, a mania, comparable only to the frenzy of her self-reproach. Some days she would leave her bed, go in and face Clotilda in the living room, seize her hands and beg a hearing. But Clotilda, uncomprehending, would only sit and watch her maunderings, or move her lips as in some feverish, wistful prayer.

Addie's contrition impressed Lester. He had kept a steady vigil in or near her room during her bedfast days, and his seeming wild hatred had moderated the more he witnessed her distress, her remorse. The calamity visited on the house had awed, frightened, confused him, and help or hope from any quarter was grasped at.

One afternoon he saw Addie's bedroom door ajar, and knocked. "Addie," he said, his voice huskily soft and shy.

"You can come in, Lester."

He pushed the door and entered. Addie wore a robe and pajamas and lay propped in bed reading a magazine. "You feelin' better?" he said.

"Yes." She smiled at him; her face was thin and the pallor made her freckles stare.

"Grammaw ain't bought any groceries," Lester said.

Addie started up, then wanly smiled. "Oh, Lester—you're hungry, aren't you?" She lay back thoughtfully, then shook her head. " . . . No, Grandma's in no condition to buy groceries. . . . But do you want to go get some?—I've got some money." She swung weakly off the bed, went to the dresser and took out her purse.

"What's wrong with Grammaw?" Lester stood just inside the door.

Addie sat down on the bed and opened her purse; then, sighing, glanced up at Lester. "Lester, I don't know—I wish I did. She won't talk to me."

"Me neither."

"What groceries do we need? Make out a list. Here's ten dollars."

Lester came over, took the ten-dollar bill and stood holding it. "We oughta talk to Letitia and Mr. Hammer," he said. "Grammaw just sits up there in the living room and looks out the window; she won't say nothin'—the only thing she said to me yesterday was not to bring my sled up on the porch. Does she think it's wintertime?— in August? We oughta talk to Mr. Hammer."

"What could *he* do?"

Lester gazed off.

"Well, go talk to him if you want," Addie said. "I don't see what good it'll do, though."

"I've already talked to him—but both of us ought to."

"Oh . . . " Addie shook her head doubtfully. "I don't know—"

Lester frowned at her—"Grammaw got this way worryin' about *you*."

"Lester—please!" Addie's face got long. "Now, go make out your grocery list. Get some liver—I'll fix it for dinner and we'll make Grandma eat something."

After Lester left the house, Addie got out of bed again and went up to the living room. Her legs were weak, her stomach queasy. Clotilda was not in the living room. Addie turned around and went to the kitchen. Clotilda was not there. Next she went upstairs—Letitia and Neeley were at work, and Hammer out—and found Clotilda sitting at a window in Neeley's room vacantly staring out across the housetops.

Addie stood at the door. "Grandma—should you be in Mr. Neeley's room?"

Clotilda turned around—much of the grey had returned to her hair to mix in with the motley, fading blue; and her dress was not fresh, nor her fingernails clean. She gazed at Addie.

"You shouldn't be sitting in Mr. Neeley's room, should you, Grandma?" Addie said. "You know how he is."

Clotilda did not reply; but soon got up and, mistrustfully watching Addie, walked past her out of the room. Addie meekly followed her downstairs to the kitchen, where Clotilda opened the refrigerator as if looking for beer. When she found none she started out of the kitchen.

"Lester's gone out to get some groceries," Addie said. "I'm going to fix dinner. I know you don't feel well . . . why don't you go take a nice cool bath?—and I'll give you a manicure. You'll feel better—I'll go run the water now—okay?"

Clotilda paused in the kitchen door, flashed her eyes, and cocked her chin suspiciously.

Addie went into the little bathroom off the kitchen and started the water in the tub, then went in the bedroom and laid out fresh underclothing for Clotilda and brought back her robe. Clotilda frowned when taken by the arm to be ushered into the bathroom, but made no further remonstrance. Addie left her and closed the door.

When later Lester returned with two bags of groceries Clotilda had not yet reappeared. Addie sat in the kitchen with a glass of milk, as Lester put the groceries down on the kitchen table and wiped his forehead with the palm of his hand.

"You still hungry?" Addie smiled.

"Yeah . . . where's Grammaw?"

"Taking a bath."

"Let's talk to Letitia and Mr. Hammer tonight." Lester kept his voice low.

Addie went to the sink and rinsed the glass under the tap. "Oh, Lester . . . I still don't know—I haven't made up my mind yet. Should we?—do we have to?"

"The real estate office called this morning and said Grammaw ain't paid the rent this month."

"*Did* they?" Addie's eyes got big. "—What're they going to do?"

"I told 'em she wasn't in. They said she better call 'em right away."

Addie looked haggard, spent, and went over and sat on the tall kitchen stool, pressing finger tips to both temples.

"You oughta get back in bed," Lester said.

Addie sat gazing off in space. " . . . Maybe we *had* better talk to Letitia and Mr. Hammer," she finally said.

She glanced at Lester. He had just frozen on his feet staring bloat-eyed at the door. Addie looked. Clotilda, her body dripping water, was emerging from the bathroom—stark naked. Her breasts hung down like great dark loaves of dough, above pubic hair knotted into BB shot.

Addie sprang at Lester and spun him around. "Go out, go out," she breathed. "Hurry." Lester, averting his wide eyes, left the kitchen.

Clotilda seemed lost. Addie, near tears, ran to her. "Oh, Grandma!—you haven't got any *clothes* on!—don't you know that?" Clotilda stared at her. Addie started crying—"Oh, Grandma." She pushed Clotilda into their bedroom, jerked a sheet off the bed and swung it around her; then went over and closed the door. Clotilda still stood gazing at her. "Oh, Grandma—why would you do a thing like that? Lester saw you—didn't you know you didn't have any clothes on?" She pulled Clotilda down on the bed beside her. "Why, you don't even know who I am, do you?— *do* you, Grandma?"

Clotilda, her blue-grey hair awry and dripping wet, gave Addie another rude stare. "Do I know you—hummph!—do I know you. How could I forget you? Would to my Maker I could."

Addie grasped both Clotilda's hands. "Don't look at me like that, Grandma—please, please. . . ." She started crying again.

Clotilda was oblivious though stirring slightly on the bed. But suddenly she turned to Addie; then, smirking, looked away, nodding her head for positive emphasis—"I'm goin' to write to Pearlie in Cleveland—that's what I'm goin' to do. Made up my mind one night leavin' the airport. I'll just have her come on over here and get me. She'll come in a hurry too."

Addie, eyes wet, stared incredulously. "*Grandma!* . . . what did you say? . . . Oh, Grandma . . . Aunt Pearlie is . . . is . . . ." She could not bring herself to say it.

"You heard me—you'll find out—all of you. I'm gettin' outa here—I'm sick and tired of all of you. Pearlie'll take me home with her—see if she don't. She ain't never failed me yet."

Addie buried her face in her hands.

About seven o'clock that evening Titus Neeley came to Hammer's room. Hammer, in shirtsleeves, his long legs extended, sat in his armchair reading the evening paper in a cool cross-breeze, blowing between the open door and window, that billowed out the faded curtains. Little Neeley was unhappy—"Somebody's been foolin' around in my room today," he said, and sat down.

Hammer removed his pince-nez.

"—Turned my mother's picture around," Neeley said. "Even sat on my bed—and left a thimble on the window sill."

Hammer grinned. "You sound like the little bear."

"It was probably Mrs. Clotilda Pilgrim herself," Neeley said. "What's she doing in *my* room?"

"She's havin' her troubles, Neeley. She's not herself."

"Yeah. It's Addie—that's where her troubles are."

"There're a lot of things botherin' her, probably—she's had a hard life."

Neeley lowered his voice. "This place's going to the dogs, Ambrose—d'you know that? Saturday I had to ask her twice for some clean sheets. And my windows're filthy. It's gettin' on my nerves. I'm lookin' around."

Hammer methodically folded the newspaper and dropped it on the floor beside his chair. " . . . Well, I wouldn't. . . ." he began.

"—She's down there now," Neeley said, "just sitting at the front window staring out. Acts like she's stone crazy. She's mean, too."

Hammer shook his head. "You wouldn't want to leave right now, Neeley. The family needs our rent, bad."

Neeley thought on this. "Yeah, they probably do. She can't be taking in much sewing. But neither can we go on like this, can we?"

Hammer stood up and stretched. Finally Neeley got up too. Hammer smote him on the back and grinned. "My friend," he said, "don't do anything rash till you hear from me." Neeley left, shaking his head.

Hammer closed the door and sat down again; but soon got up

and went over to the window. He stood gazing out. The worsening situation in the house troubled, perplexed, him. The immediate problem seemed money. He knew it was Letitia who had paid the last telephone and light bills and that the rent was now past due. Moreover Clotilda needed medical—psychiatric—care. Yet he regarded money as insignificant alongside the human problem. How, for example, could two youngsters, already orphans, be brought to face the prospect of possible permanent derangement in their grandmother?—an enigma made thornier by Addie's change of heart, her tortured penitence.

But Hammer's greatest concern was Lester. The boy must not end up thrown into the seamy environment of the streets. He saw promise in Lester—the hopeful makings of a man of force, candor, intelligence—of education. Neglectful surroundings had been the curse of his own early life. All hope for Lester lay in elevating influences, in nurture, care. But Hammer knew at present Lester's life was centered on his grandmother, the only mother he had ever known; how now could he be expected to understand her silent, evil stare, when before he had known only a doting laugh or a playful massive hug? Hammer paced the bedroom. The only solution he could conjure up lay in an effort at calling, coaxing, back Clotilda's vanished mind—a solution requiring doctors.

Soon, at nearly eight o'clock—outside it was still twilight—Lester knocked on his door. Hammer still stood at the window. Thinking it was Neeley again, he only grunted. Then Lester opened the door. Hammer chuckled. "Well—Lester!"

Lester wore dungarees and a soiled sweater, and his hair needed to be cut. He seemed nervous, yet solemn—"Mr. Hammer . . . could Addie and I talk with you, and Miss Dorsey? . . . they're both downstairs." Hammer could feel his misery across the room.

He studied Lester. "I guess so, Lester—okay."

"Now?"

Hammer nodded. "Better bring 'em up here."

Lester left; and soon was back, trailed by Addie and Letitia. Hammer, who had put on a necktie, and now wore his pince-nez, gave them the three chairs and himself sat on the bed. Addie had been crying again and sat down and blew her nose into a kleenex, then held the kleenex wadded in her fist. Except for a constant twitching of the nose, Lester seemed calm.

"Hello," Letitia said, and gave Hammer her most brilliant, simpering smile. She sat glittering as if dressed for a fashion show; her short dress bared matchstick legs and bony knees, and costume jewelry clattered at her wrists and throat.

Hammer sent her a nervous glance and was grave. "How is Mrs. Pilgrim feeling this evening?" he said to them.

" . . . Well, she's . . . " Letitia hesitated. "She's in the bed-room right now . . . You can't really tell, Mr. Hammer."

"She's writin' something," Lester spoke up. "—a letter, I think. She told me to bring her some paper, and my pen."

"Well, we're goin' to have to have a doctor for her," Hammer announced. "I don't know what he'll say—but we've got to be adults enough to take whatever he tells us."

Letitia's avid eyes watched Hammer as he spoke; then she nodded and sighed. "Yes—I agree with you, Mr. Hammer."

"What'll he do?"—Addie, sniffling, looked up now.

"We don't know." Hammer showed slight impatience. "He'll examine her, of course. What he'll do, or prescribe, after that, we don't know."

There was silence, except for Neeley's loud little television in the next room. Hammer got up and closed the door. This made it warm in the room with the hot light bulbs and no more cross venti-lation.

Hammer spoke seriously to Addie and Lester now. "Has your grandmother got any money?"

Lester looked at Addie.

"I *think* she has," Addie finally said, clutching the damp kleenex. " . . . she had a bank book in her room."

"When was that?"

Addie hesitated.

"Addie, tomorrow you must find it," Hammer said. "—we must know. She's behind in her bills. Miss Dorsey, here, paid the light and telephone bills this month—and I'm payin' the rent tomorrow. There was a doctor twice for you too, Addie."

" . . . I'll try."

"You find it," Hammer said.

" . . . The doctor won't take her away, will he?"—Addie dabbed at her nose with the kleenex, but soon was crying again.

"Oh, Addie, stop that," Letitia said, but then softened her tone—"This is no time for tears, Addie."

Hammer waved silence as Lester clouded up at Letitia—"Well, we got to find a way out of this thing," Hammer said. "Everybody's got to pitch in." He smiled briefly—"In other words, we got to put on our thinkin' caps."

Addie, eyes flashing, turned on Lester. "The doctor'll take her away, I bet, if we let him, Lester. We won't let him." She was hard-faced and gaunt; and her neglected copper hair gave her a wild look.

No one spoke. But Letitia's white-powdered, long face showed added exasperation; she sniffed testily, tugged her dress down over her knees, and rattled her bracelets.

"I'm going to make her sleep in the bedroom from now on," Addie said to them. "I'll sleep on the sofa. And I'll talk to her more—I'll get her to start talking again. *I* can make her feel better—I know I can."

Letitia gave her a bored gaze.

"You'll be doin' a great thing, if you can," Hammer said. Lester's eyes went from face to face.

"*Don't* call the doctor," Addie pleaded. "Let me and Lester talk to her. Will you, Mr. Hammer?"

"I'm not averse to it at all," Hammer said. "You and Lester talk to her." He smiled—"Love, you know—just like faith—sometimes can move mountains." He got up—"We'll meet here again tomorrow night."

Addie and Lester soon went downstairs.

Letitia tarried in Hammer's doorway. " . . . You look tired around the eyes," she said to him. He said nothing. Suddenly she gave her brazen, brilliant smile—"I did what you told me to . . . remember?" Hammer looked blank. She laughed. "Barnhart's Cove, remember?—the reservations came today."

"Oh." Hammer swallowed.

"Well, you told me to find out about Labor Day weekend."

" . . . Yes—I'd forgotten. When is that?"

"Labor Day's a week from Monday."

Hammer sighed; then smiled. "Well, you've sent 'em some money, haven't you? So it's a deal. This is not a very good time to be leaving, though, is it?"

"Oh, think of yourself sometime, Mr. Hammer!—Goodness Gracious, do you ever?" Then Letitia finally laughed again.

"We're in a sad situation here," Hammer said.

"I know—and Addie tries my patience. She's the cause of everything."

" . . . Well." Hammer paused uncertainly. "But even if she is, I think she's repented now. Don't you think she's a different girl?—a new person? She's learned her lesson. I feel good about her . . . because she's solved somethin'—I don't know what it is. But I'm inclined to feel she's facing a brand new life now—a better life. Yes . . . she's solved somethin'."

"Well, Goodness, I hope so—but she's the cause of Clotilda's present condition—now, you can't argue that, Mr. Hammer."

Tall Hammer leaned back against his door jamb in thought— " . . . Well, it would seem that way, certainly—on the surface, at least." He studied for a moment, biting his lip. "But I'm not so sure all the time—my mind fluctuates on Clotilda—and I've thought about her a lot. Sometimes I get the notion there may be somethin' deeper—like the much bigger, the submerged part of the iceberg—

that we don't see. Oh, I may be wrong, of course. It's kind of a mystery. I hope, though, that someday it may be revealed to us."

"Poor Clotilda," Letitia said, shaking her head.

Hammer looked at her—"And poor Addie, Miss Dorsey. Think of her childhood—her mother. We can't forget that."

Letitia glanced at him and finally sighed. "No—no, we can't, Mr. Hammer."

Hammer yawned as he sidled back inside his doorway. "But we'll eventually have to have a doctor for the old lady," he said. "It can't be avoided. I didn't have the heart to insist tonight."

Letitia looked at him. "You're awfully tired," she said again. Suddenly she giggled—"Have you got any swimming trunks?"

Hammer gaped at her; then sheepishly shook his head. "No . . . nothin' like that."

Letitia laughed musically now—"And why don't you pick up a couple of loud sport shirts somewhere too?"

Hammer grinned. " . . . Very well."

Letitia laughed and feigned petulance and impatience. "Oh, you're so everlasting busy all the time!—when I'm downtown I'll pick up a few things for you. And you'll need some sun glasses."

Hammer chuckled and seemed resigned.

〽 〽 〽 〽 〽 〽

Meanwhile, down in the first-floor bedroom, Clotilda was writing. In a clean house dress, her hair combed and brushed, she had planted her bulk on a chair at the little night stand and, her glasses now mislaid, wrote in close, myopic concentration. Addie had peeped in on her after the upstairs conference, only to meet with a hostile stare. The ballpoint pen wormed laboriously across the ruled tablet in an oversize, eighth-grade script :

"Dear Pearlie,

Now don't get after me for not writing so long, Pearlie, sweetheart. I never was a writer, you know that.

But I have had a world of trouble since I wrote you last and everything has caved in on me, seems like. Addie has caused me an awful lot of trouble. She has gone down to nothing and is running around with a trifling nigger that is married and drinks and takes dope. He finally knocked her up, and the other day he and some awful looking woman brought her home. Pearlie, they had aborted her. She could hardly walk into the house. The doctor has been here twice and she is still weak as a cat. Pearlie, I took those children to raise and if they ever saw anything that was not right, it was not in this house. God being my Judge and Maker, this is true. But I have reached the end now. I can't take any more. That is why I am writing to you, to see if you could come and get me and let me stay with you in Cleveland. Maybe you could straighten me out. I know Chester is sick, but maybe he would let you come for me. Wouldn't he? I believe it would be such a big help to me. I'm catching it, Pearlie. Honest to God, I am. You have always been religious, most religious. I have not. Maybe I should have been, though, because I have had nothing but trouble all my life, seems like. It is mighty funny, Pearlie, me coming to you for help. I have not always been the sister to you that you was to me. It seems now I just live in the past all the time, just like I had a lot of happy memories, always thinking about what happened thirty and forty years ago. Sometimes when I go back too far, I get a loud rushing noise in my head and have to chew gum to hear myself think. Oh Pearlie, the big hopes I had for Addie. She was my one big chance. I had messed up my own life and I thought maybe if I could make something out of hers, I would wind up my days halfway happy. Lester is still a good boy, but Addie is ruined—and not out of high school yet. It is an awful calamity for me. Seems almost like a curse. And I have the dropsy and a bad ticker, you know. My days are running down, Pearlie—if I come there, you won't have me on your hands too long. Like a slow runner, in a way, I had hoped maybe to make a good finish. But Addie has blocked that. Every time I see her now, I see defeat. She is done for and so am I. She can't undo what's been done and neither can I now. Oh, does she rile me when she cries and goes on now, day and night, trying to beg back—so she can turn right around and crucify me to the cross all over again. But the truth is, she is evil—*Evil.* I see her and I see the devil. Oh, Pearlie, you must come and get me and take me out of this hell. Even Lester has turned his back on me and takes up for Addie. I never would have thought it—never. You see, it's her influence on him—she will have him pimping and smoking reefers before long, you watch. Oh, Pearlie, come and get me. Drop everything and come now before it's too late— please, please. You are my only hope for a little peace. Hurry, Pearlie. Come now, come—"

Someone knocked softly on the door.

Clotilda, in the frenzy of her pleading, started up—eyes wild, fanatical.

Again came the muffled knock.

She yelled. "Git away from that door!"

"Grammaw . . . Grammaw . . . can I come in?" Lester's voice was fearful, subdued.

"*No,* I tell you! Git away from that door!"

"Grammaw, please—I wanta come in." Lester opened the door.

Clotilda was already on her feet—"You git outa here!"

Lester stepped in, closed the door, and came toward her. Suddenly he dove for her neck, grappled with her, and hung on. "Oh, Grammaw," he sobbed. "Grammaw, what's the *matter* with you!—

what's wrong with you, Grammaw? Why're you acting like this—why're you treating me like this?" Lester shut his eyes, opened his mouth, and yammered like a calf. His big tears flew in Clotilda's face and his weight nearly choked her. She seemed hesitant now, confused, near relenting. Finally she pushed him off.

Lester stammered his words—"Grammaw, Addie's gonna be good—she promised me. Honest—she's gonna be good. She'll never see Dunreith again. She's tellin' the truth—she won't see him. Why don't you be nice to her? Be nice to her, Grammaw—she ain't feelin' well."

"Y'mighty right she ain't feelin' well," Clotilda flared. Finally she sat down. "Whose fault is that?"

Then Lester saw the letter. Quickly wiping his eyes with his fist, he glanced at Clotilda; then took a step toward the night stand. "What you writing?" he said.

"You git away from there." Clotilda scowled, threw up her big arm, and barred his way. "Git outa here and leave me alone."

Lester, thus restrained, now craned forward and cocked his head to read at a distance. "Come on, Grammaw—what is it? What you writing?"

Clotilda rolled her eyes straight up and sighed. "I'm writin' to my sister Pearlie in Cleveland—for her to come and get me—that's what I'm doing, Lester. I'll show you-all a thing or two." She leaned back in the chair to observe his reaction.

Lester's eyes went wide. "You goin' to *Cleveland?*—When you going? Can I go?—Can Addie?"

Clotilda set her lips and sadly shook her head.

"*We* can't go?" Lester said. "D'you mean we can't go? Aw, Grammaw, you wouldn't go off and leave *us*." He stood over her.

Clotilda dropped her chin on her chest. " . . . Well . . . Addie can't go, Lester."

"Aw, we couldn't leave Addie, Grammaw—we couldn't do that. Addie's changed—you see if she ain't. Don't leave *us*, Grammaw."

Clotilda sat with her hands in her lap and said nothing more. Lester could not make her talk. As she gazed across the room her mind seemed far away or blank. Lester, bewildered, stood for awhile watching her; finally he left the bedroom.

Addie had been sitting up front alone in the living room—waiting. It was dark outside and the tall floor lamp was lighted. When Lester joined her she saw his smeared face —"What's the matter, Lester? . . . is she worse?"

Lester went to the front window and stared out at the summer night. "She's leavin'," he said.

Addie stood up. "Leaving?"

"She's writin' for her sister in Cleveland to come and get her."

Addie, sighing, slowly shook her head. "Yes—this afternoon she told me that, too. But her sister's dead."

Lester turned around. "She got only the *one* sister?"

Addie nodded. "Only one sister—Pearl, Aunt Pearlie. She's been dead nearly five years. So's her husband, Uncle Chester—he died soon after she did."

Lester, mouth open, looked at her.

"Oh, Lester, we mustn't tell Letitia or Mr. Hammer. They'll call a doctor right away—he might send her away. And, Lester, you stop blabbing all our business to Mr. Hammer!—do you hear?"

"He's tryin' to help us—maybe a doctor could do her some good."

Addie's lip quivered. "Oh, Lester, can't you see?—the doctor would take her away. He *would*."

They were silent, and as they stood side by side gazing out the window, Addie felt for Lester's hand.

Chapter Eight

L ABOR DAY.

At noon Barnhart's Cove was all blazing sun, blue water, and white sand. Lake Michigan eddied in and lapped at the beach and the hilarious bathers' feet and, far out, gave a turquoise background for the few small boats under sail. Letitia and Hammer sat lounging in beach chairs, well back from the water, and, like jaded royalty at a spa, observed all the busy doings through sunglasses. Hammer felt naked—Letitia had bought him red swimming trunks and he now resembled a docile, white-heeled, Masai tribesman. Moreover, he eschewed the water.

They had just returned from a stroll. Letitia wore a daring lemon Bikini—her beanpole body and level chest notwithstanding—and puffed on cigarette after cigarette. She had not smoked before, and now constantly rubbed her eyes and swatted at flying sparks. So they sat bemused—as black children chased each other across the beach or knelt to mold fresh-made mounds of sand, and some of their parents, laughing and talking, played gin rummy for orange pop "treats." Letitia and Hammer occupied adjacent, but separate, rooms at the motel-like resort house that sat half hidden, two hundred yards inland, among some birch trees atop a sandy knoll. Letitia at some apt time or other—Hammer first noticed it the second night at dinner—had managed to dispense with his last name in order to call him "Ambrose." Now she sat up in her beach chair and, feigning petulance, turned to him. "Oh, Ambrose, won't you *ever* finish that book—so you can take a real vacation?"

"It *is* about finished." Hammer chuckled behind his dark glasses. "But my main worry is ever findin' somebody that'll publish it."

A big brown-skinned woman in a yellow bathing suit trudged by, convoyed by her all-sized brood of children. One little girl straggler paused in awe to study tall Hammer in his red swimming trunks, then ran on to catch up. "You ladies' man, you," Letitia giggled.

Hammer was oblivious. "I might have t'publish the darn book myself—that is, pay to have it published. Ha, they call that the 'Vanity Press.' I've already submitted most of the manuscript around . . . to a number of different places. They all seem to think it's not academic enough—not 'documented,' as they call it. Well, I never claimed to be any great scholar."

"Ambrose, I'd like to see just one so-called 'scholar' that works half as hard as you do—just one."

"Oh, my—there're plenty."

Soon Letitia smiled. "I haven't heard Mr. Neeley ribbing you about the book lately—has he stopped?"

"Oh, Neeley wasn't serious."

"Poor Mr. Neeley—I feel sorry for him sometimes . . . he's lonely, Ambrose. That's probably why he's so restless and fidgety most of the time. All those years, you know, he'd been tied tight to his mother's apron strings. Her death left his life empty, very empty, I think."

"Yes," Hammer said.

Letitia sighed. "Loneliness can be an awful thing."

Hammer smiled at her. "Not for busy people."

"Oh, yes?—and sometimes the loneliest people are the ones

that stay busiest, just to kid themselves they're not lonely." Letitia gave a tense laugh. "Ever think of that?"

Hammer grinned and shrugged.

"Ambrose, in school did you ever have to read any of Bulwer-Lytton's poetry?—'The Last Days of Pompeii?' Remember the lines that went—

      ' . . . I am as one left alone at the banquet.

      Lights dead, and flowers faded . . . ' "

Letitia lifted her face and closed her eyes to recall more, but finally said, " . . . I can't remember the rest of it."

"No," Hammer said, "I don't think I had that."

Letitia said, "Or Coleridge's 'Ancient Mariner?'—

      ' . . . Alone, alone, all, all alone.

      Alone on a wide, wide sea . . . ' "

Hammer, bare long legs extended, and idly flicking up sand with his big toe, laughed. "Say, you're quite a poet."

"No, but I do love poetry—don't you?"

Hammer was reflective. "Yes . . . I like poetry."

"What, Ambrose?—what, for instance? Recite some."

"Oh, I don't have anything particular in mind. . . ."

But Letitia looked eagerly at him—waiting.

Hammer touched his ten finger tips together like a consulting lawyer. " . . . Well . . . I like Shakespeare, of course. I like Keats. And Thomas Gray . . . when he speculates on what could have been made of a life, but wasn't, and so forth. . . ."

"Do I know that? . . ."

"Oh, sure—'Gray's Elegy Written in a Country Churchyard.' "

"How does it go, Ambrose—recite some of it . . . come on."

Hammer sat musing. Finally his deep, cadenced voice began :

      " 'Some village Hampden that with dauntless breast

      The little tyrant of his fields withstood,

      Some mute inglorious Milton here may rest,

      Some Cromwell guiltless of his country's blood.' "

He stopped and smiled self-consciously.

"Oh, Ambrose, it's so grand the way you say it . . . I see what it means, all right—that some of the people buried there could have been much greater than they were."

"Oh, some of 'em, maybe—under other circumstances."

Letitia looked at Hammer. "Do you know why you like that poem, Ambrose?"

Hammer smiled again, then shook his head. "You never know why you like a great poem. That kind of knowledge has not been entrusted to us yet—may never be."

"Those lines make you think of yourself, Ambrose."

Hammer paused. Finally he shrugged again. "Oh, it could be applied to me, maybe . . . and others."

"You even said once you'd liked to have been a judge—or a senator."

"Ho, ho!—now, wait a minute. . . ."

"Well, you said it."

"Maybe I would liked to have been something more . . . well . . . but, you see, I couldn't write my name till I was nineteen."

"That's what I mean!—that's just what I mean. You'd have been a great man, Ambrose—I know you would have."

"Oh, we can't be sure about things like that . . . life's too tricky." Hammer grinned. "But we all might handle things different if we had another chance. You, too—maybe," he laughed.

Letitia did not laugh.

"Oh, I was only kiddin'."

"Well . . . it's true," Letitia finally smiled. "—and would you like to know what I'd really liked to have been?" she laughed.

Hammer looked at her.

"I'd have been a housewife with six or seven kids," Letitia cried out, laughing a little hysterically.

"Hey!" Hammer slapped his bare thigh.

Letitia threw up both hands—"My poor mother had *nine*!

I'm the oldest. Oops!—I shouldn't't've said that." She put her hand to her lips and laughed. " . . . Well, Ambrose, I *am* no spring chicken."

"*I'm* fightin' off sixty," Hammer chortled.

Letitia fired up another cigarette. "Oh, Sabrina—that's what we all called our mother—just had such a hard time raising our family that she wanted me to be a career girl—said my life would be more interesting that way—not having the drudgery of a house full of kids, and all. Well, I'd never let on to her, of course, if she was living today, but I think she gave me the wrong advice . . . I know she did."

Hammer soon scooted forward in his beach chair. "Say, how 'bout some lunch, Miss . . . Miss Letitia?"

"Well, Stars Above! What's come over you? Did you say '*Letitia?*' I've wondered if you'd *ever* stop being so formal . . . you are the most formal man, Ambrose!" Letitia gave her high, simpering laugh, and boldly patted Hammer's hand.

"Why, I don't think so . . . Letitia." He stood up, furtively tugging his brief swimming trunks down.

Soon Letitia got up too, and they started leisurely across the sand toward the resort club house. The sun, though not hot, was warm and bright, but the dank heavy smell of the lake water came in over the beach and drifted inland. "Wonder how things are at home?" Letitia said ruefully—she looked near naked in the Bikini bathing suit and, though walking slightly bent forward, was nearly as tall as Hammer. "One thing I've noticed the past week," she said, "Clotilda's not so sulky. I don't mean she's cheerful by any means," Letitia laughed, " . . . far from it—but she's not so downright hostile. And she's sewing and ironing like mad. But it's all her own clothes. You'd think she was getting ready to go to Europe or some place."

At the moment, as he walked, cautiously, barefooted Hammer seemed determined to avoid any sharp stones or broken glass in the sand.

"Well, there's one thing—she's not flat broke," Letitia snickered. "Her bank book showed that, didn't it? Did you keep it?"

"Oh, no."—Hammer looked surprised. "I gave it back to Addie."

"But twelve hundred dollars won't go very far . . . unless some money starts coming in there pretty soon."

Hammer nodded, still picking his way across the deep white sand.

"Well, shouldn't you ask her for *your* money?" Letitia said. "—for her rent you paid and the money you paid me back with?"

"No, not yet. I want her to show some improvement first. And she might, at that . . . now that Addie's changed so."

"Oh, that Addie!—I sure hope you're right about her."

"Time will tell—but I think I am."

Letitia frowned. "It's her conscience, I guess, that makes her follow Clotilda around day and night like she does. . . ."

Hammer said nothing, and they walked in silence.

"What time's the bus go back to Chicago tonight?" he finally said.

Letitia stopped. Her pale, long face crimpled up in distress. "Oh, Ambrose, I hate to leave *so*! Don't you? . . . Have you had a good time? *Have* you?"

"Why, sure. I enjoyed it."

They stood facing each other.

"Do you like my company?" Letitia fluttered her eyelashes and gave her wilting, wheedling laugh.

Hammer was serious. "Of course. I enjoy your company."

They started walking again, and she caught and held his hand. "I didn't like the way you said that," she tittered, " . . . like I had to drag it out of you . . . you were so glum."

"I don't think I was glum."

"Serious, then."

Hammer looked at her. "Don't you want me t'be serious?"

"Oh, Ambrose"—fading Letitia caught her breath—"that's the only thing in this world I *do* want."

They walked along together toward the club house.

Labor Day—Chicago.

At noon the living room and little sunroom adjoining smelled of wet flower pots and dripping plants as Addie, using a pitcher, watered Clotilda's philodendrons, rose trees, ferns, and rubber plants. The house was closed up and cool, with the window blinds halfway down. Clotilda had brought the ironing board up in the sunroom and now sat on a high stool ironing her slips and underwear. With a tight-lipped intentness, she had been busy with departure preparations since the day she mailed her letter.

Lester, whom Addie had just served lunch, was ready to go play baseball, and stood near the piano wearing a catcher's mask. Addie stopped watering the plants and looked at him, then smiled. "Why don't you go tell Grandma where you're going," she said, "—and when you'll be back."

Lester took off the catcher's mask and went in the sunroom. "Grammaw, we gotta ball game today," he said. "I'll be back around five."

Clotilda, meditative, calm, turned around on the high stool and looked at him. "Mail man didn't come yet, did he?" she said, and resumed ironing.

Lester's eyes got big; he looked at Addie. "There's no mail today, Grammaw—this is Labor Day."

"Oh," Clotilda nodded, " . . . yes."

"What're we gonna have for dinner, Grammaw?" Lester said.

Clotilda carefully folded a finished slip and placed it on a stack of underwear. "How would *I* know," she said. "I may be gone anyhow when you get back."

"Gone—gone where?" Lester looked again at Addie.

"Oh, that's all right—you'll find out." Clotilda frowned. "Don't be so nosey."

Lester stood looking at her as she went on ironing.

"I'm goin' to Cleveland, Lester," she finally said. "But I told you. And I told you-all I'd show you what's what. Didn't I?"

Lester swallowed, then started to speak, but said nothing.

Addie, watering a fern, cut in—"We're going to have meat balls and spaghetti for dinner," she said brightly.

Clotilda looked at her. "Lester and I was talkin'," she said. "Would you let us finish, please?"

"Excuse me, Grandma," Addie sighed and soon withdrew to the other side of the living room.

Clotilda reached a cigarette from her pack on the window sill, lit it, and turned again to Lester. "Don't you wanta go with me?" she said. "I tell you, I might be gone when you get back."

Lester hung his head and twiddled with the catcher's mask.

"So you don't wanta go with your grandma, eh?" Clotilda said.

" . . . Sure . . . only I didn't know you'd be goin' today," Lester parried.

"I just might. Pearlie might drive on over here without even writin' . . . because this's a holiday . . . yeah, that's right—she might be drivin'."

Addie, in the living room, listened.

Clotilda slowed her iron and looked at Lester again. "I didn't think you'd ever want to be separated from your grandma," she said.

Lester finally looked up. " . . . I don't."

"Well, you better stay here, then—and forget about any ball game."

Addie came to the sunroom door. "Grandma, Lester won't be gone long—he'll be back by dinnertime."

Clotilda looked at her. "You *will* butt in, won't you," she said calmly. "Well, it don't make any difference—I may be gone by dinnertime, anyhow."

"Addie could come over to Washington Park and get me," Lester said.

"There won't be time enough for that." Clotilda continued ironing. Soon she sighed. "And just think, Lester—a few days ago you was around here blubberin' and carryin' on about me leaving you. Now you gotta go play ball. Well, go ahead, then—go on and play ball."

Lester and Addie stook looking at her.

Finally Clotilda pulled the electric-iron cord from the wall socket, gathered up her finished underclothing, and went back to the bedroom.

"Hurry up," Addie whispered to Lester, "—hurry up and go, before she comes back."

"I ain't got any money," Lester said.

"Oh . . . just a minute." Addie turned and went to the kitchen; and soon came back with fifty cents. "Here," she said, and gave him the two quarters. "Now, hurry."

Lester, swinging the catcher's mask, left through the front door. Addie went to the window and watched him; he seemed to lope as he walked down the street; she saw how he had grown, how strapping his arms and shoulders were, yet how babyish his face. She sighed, and her eyes somehow clung to him till he passed beyond a scraggly hedge, then under some trees, and at long last out of sight.

A half-hour later Addie was still doing housework, when Titus Neeley came home. Little Neeley entered the front door wearing a tan summer suit and a floppy straw hat that sat down on his ears. He closed the door and stood before Addie holding in the crook of his arm a dozen red apples in a clear plastic bag.

"Why, hi, Addie!" He gave his quick, high laugh, then looked down at the apples. "I was passing by a fruit and vegetable market and their apples looked so dog-gone nice, thought I'd bring a bag home. Here, take 'em and put 'em in the kitchen—maybe later on, you, or Lester . . . or Mrs. Pilgrim . . . might like some."

"Oh, thanks, Mr. Neeley." Addie leaned her dust mop against the wall and took the apples. "I'll tell Grandma you brought them."

Neeley looked around. "Where is your grandma?"

"Back in the bedroom."

"Whew." Neeley took off his straw hat, pulled out a handkerchief, and wiped his forehead, then glanced over at a chair. "I had *some* walk this morning—all the way across the Midway and back through Washington Park."

"My, that's a long ways." Addie stood holding the red apples.

Neeley gave his high laugh again. "Oh, you don't notice it so much, really—you're just sorta walking along and thinking, and the first thing you know you're where you were going and ready to start back. Ha-ha-ha." He glanced at the chair again, but remained standing. "I like to walk and think sometimes—and it's *so* beautiful out today. I came home to put on another pair of shoes— then I'm going to catch the bus out to the cemetery and take some flowers out to my mother's grave."

"Oh—that's nice," Addie said.

"I used to miss Mom so much," Neeley laughed. "—I'm getting kinda used to it now, though, I think. But Lord, it's about time. Ha, ha."

Addie put the plastic bag of apples down in a chair and reached for her dust mop.

Neeley grinned. "Walking this morning, I thought about a lotta things . . . and didn't feel nowhere near as bad about my mother as I used to." He cocked his head to one side, then nodded dubiously. "You . . . you can kinda get used to it after awhile, I think . . . if you try hard enough . . . try real hard."

Addie had sternly, forbiddingly, turned her back and was poking the dust mop under a chair, then along the wall.

"Aw, Mom was such a little-bittie woman," Neeley laughed. "You should've seen her—maybe that's the reason *I'm* such a runt.

Ha-ha-ha-ha! Listen to this. She used to love to pitch horseshoes.
Addie, it's a fact—honest to Goodness! . . . can you imagine?
Ha-ha-ha-ha! She was dog-gone good at it, too—she taught *me*
how. She'd always grab the horseshoe right at the middle, and toss
the open end dead at the stake—the shoe never turned once. She
could ring that stake something fantastic. At church picnics, down
in North Carolina when I was a kid, she and I used to play the
menfolks. We'd beat 'em most of the time, too."

Addie managed a faint smile. " . . . That was fun, I bet."

"Oh, yeah. It was for her too. She didn't get much recreation.
Down in North Carolina she worked in a canning factory . . . my
father, you know, took a run-out powder when I was just a baby."
Neeley laughed. "So that left just the two of us—her and me. But
Mom she was tough as a pine knot and, between you and me, was
probably glad to get rid of him. Oh, you should've seen her,
Addie—a wiry little pint-sized woman . . . with straight, iron-
grey hair that she wore with a little ball at the back—they say she
was part Cherokee. And a sense of humor!—Lord, was she sharp.
Some kidder! But she could be serious too, of course. You see, she
wanted me to be a doctor. But, oh, I wasn't cut out for that—it
just wasn't in me. She was probably disappointed in me, after she'd
spent her money putting me through the little college down there—
but if she was, she never let on . . . not the least bit. Well, when I
came up here to Chicago and got in the Post Office, I sent for her—
right away. And after that we were never apart for even one single
day—together all the time, Addie—why, it was ridiculous! Ha-ha-
ha-ha!"

Addie wore a strained, drawn, expression on her face and
used her dust mop now with desperate little jabs.

Neeley stood thinking for a moment. " . . . No," he finally
said, "if she was disappointed in me, she sure never showed it—not
one time. I always wanted to ask her—I almost did once—but she
never would've said so, even if she had been. Having a mother
around means a lot, I'll tell you . . . ah, little old Mom," Neeley

mused aloud. "She was something. Four years ago this October 17th she passed away in a coma at Provident Hospital. I had held her hand for two days and three nights—but she didn't even know I was there."

Addie, her lip quivering, clutched up the apples and hurried back to the kitchen. Neeley went upstairs and changed his shoes, then came down and soon left the house again. The moment Addie in the kitchen heard the front door close, she threw her head on her arms at the table in harsh, gasping sobs.

Clotilda was still back in the first-floor bedroom with the door closed. She had stacked her underclothing in two dresser drawers and now sat in a chair at the mouth of the deep clothes closet taking an inventory of her shoes again; she was placid, methodical, as she lined up shoes along the closet wall. Soon she leaned in and pulled out a big tan suitcase from the back wall of the closet. It had belonged to Eugene, her husband. She dragged it out and dusted it off, then opened it—his blue serge Sunday vest fell part way out. Clotilda could not identify it; her withered mind could not recall Eugene's burial in his blue serge suit, nor the undertaker's polite refusal to use the vest. Under the vest lay two little shirts of Lester's, worn when he was four or five and quickly outgrown. Next she leafed through two of Addie's old coloring books, vaporously wondering why the crayoned skies were never clear blue, but always black, a motley mahogany, or sometimes beet red.

There also, squashed into a corner of the suitcase, was Addie's little straw hat, with its tiny spray of wire-stemmed violets and the elastic cord that went under the chin. Clotilda's mind groped back; though straining, it could no longer discern Addie at that bygone Eastertime, nor the little flared coat, the patent leather flats, white anklets, nor the wary, serious face. She tossed the hat aside and picked up a book, Addie's *Ivanhoe*, opening it at a strange bulge in its pages. There, brownish-lavender with time and now stuck to the page, was a pressed, white carnation. For a brief moment Clotilda's memory seemed partially to clear as if through the mists she envisioned how Addie, with one arm in a cast, had managed to twist the flower off a wreath at Ruby's coffin and crush it in her hand throughout the day till bedtime. Clotilda shuddered and closed the book. She dumped the contents of the suitcase out into a big cardboard box and shoved the box to the back of the closet, then got up and set the suitcase out at the foot of the bed.

Soon there was a knock at the door. Clotilda stood looking, but did not answer. The door opened and Addie, hesitant and timorous, entered carrying the plastic bag of apples. She was haggard and her eyes were red. "Grandma, Mr. Neeley brought these." She put the apples up on the dresser. Clotilda stood staring at her—then turned her back, walked to the closet, and took down some coat hangers. Addie with both hands reached up on the dresser and opened the bag of apples. "Here, Grandma, take one," she said and held out a big red apple to Clotilda—"You should eat some fruit sometime."

Clotilda, turning around, looked at the apple, now at Addie, then gave a vacant sneer. "An' now comes the serpent—with an apple," she said, and turned her back again.

Addie stood with the apple in her hand. She put it back in the plastic bag, as Clotilda sat down in the chair again at the mouth of the closet. Addie watched her. "Grandma, will you tell me something? . . . look at me. Please, Grandma—will you look at me? I want to talk to you."

Clotilda did not move.

"Okay, then." Addie sat down on the bed. "But will you tell me what I can do to make you feel toward me like you used to? Grandma, listen—whatever it is, I'll do it. Honest, I'll do it."

Clotilda batted her eyes blankly and picked up a shoe to inspect it.

"I know I did some awful things," Addie said, "—some awful things to you. But that's all over—Grandma, it's all over. It was no use—it didn't solve anything—I was trying to wreck myself. I didn't care."

"Ummph," Clotilda grunted scornfully.

"Things'll be different from now on, Grandma—you'll see."

Clotilda shot a glance over her shoulder—"No, I won't see, either." Her voice had a sinister, exultant ring. " 'Cause I won't be in this house."

Addie looked at her. "Oh, Grandma. . . ." she at last said despairingly, and stood up. "Grandma, don't you remember. . . ." But again the words trailed off.

Clotilda began re-counting shoes.

"Grandma, Lester and I worry about you—all the time."

"Don't bring Lester into it."

"Well, don't you believe we do?—that *I* do?"

"Why don't you go on an' quit botherin' me—can't you see I'm busy? What you're talking about's all history—oh, yes—history. I'm lookin' out for number one now." Clotilda got up, left the bedroom, and lumbered up front toward the living room.

Addie followed her.

"Grandma, if you'd only listen to me—if you'd only give me another chance—I could help you—honest, I could. I would, Grandma. I'd help you here in the house, and keep my job and help out with expenses. Things would be different if you'd only try me out—this whole house would be different."

Clotilda now stood before the living room's big window and gazed out at the street. Addie stood behind her. Outside the afternoon was mild and sunny with a few white clouds overhead. Clotilda slowly weaved her head from side to side as if in a daze— "All that's behind me," she finally said. "I'm goin' to have a new life now—a little peace at last before I cross over Jordan." She leaned toward the window pane and peered anxiously up the street. Once a car pulled to the curb in front of the house. She craned forward, avid to see. A man and woman got out—but soon went down the street and into another house. Clotilda, breathing heavily, sank into the chair at the window and continued her vigil.

Addie stood looking at her and soon began wringing her

hands and writhing—"Grandma, can't you see why Lester and I worry about you. Your memory's failing—it *is*."

Clotilda kept her face toward the street, but sighed—"Ah, why are you so evil? Evil . . . evil—evil."

Addie stepped up behind her chair. "Grandma, don't you remember? . . . Aunt Pearlie's *dead*."

Clotilda still stared out at the sidewalk and began slowly weaving her head again. " . . . Evil," she whispered.

"She's not in Cleveland, Grandma—she's not any place. She's dead."

Clotilda shook her head sadly. "I swear before God—with that lie you surely musta reached the end of your tether."

"Grandma—why, Aunt Pearlie died five years ago. Don't you remember? Remember how mad you got because Uncle Chester didn't notify you? One of their neighbors got our address someway and sent you a telegram—remember? You said Uncle Chester didn't want you to come. You were so broken up about Aunt Pearlie and so mad at Uncle Chester that you got sick. The doctor put you to bed and wouldn't let you go to the funeral because of your heart. Don't you remember?"

Now Clotilda turned slowly around to Addie with a vague questioning stare.

"Our *green parrot,* Grandma—remember 'Pearlie,' our parrot?—you named it after Aunt Pearlie."

Clotilda's jaw slackened. Her quaking hand groped to the side of her face.

"Grandma, 'Pearlie' died only a week after *Aunt* Pearlie, remember?—You said it was the works of God."

Clotilda's eyes dilated and slowly, very slowly, her face began to bulge with horror. She began weaving her head from side to side again and rocking her whole body back and forth in the chair, whispering, murmuring, to herself. Then suddenly she uttered a terrifying scream—"*Oh, J-e-e-e-sus!*"—and dove her face into her hands.

Addie stood over her now and started to touch her, but drew back. But the suffering awed her. She continued standing for awhile beside the chair, watching Clotilda's crazed paroxysms in wonder. Yet she somehow felt no contrition—only relief, hope. Finally she tiptoed from the room. When she got back to the bedroom, she took fresh underclothing out of the dresser drawer and prepared for a bath. As she undressed, she planned how later she would go up front and try to soothe Clotilda, comfort her, plead with her again for forgiveness; only in this way could the family be restored— saved. She now sensed some hope.

Wearing her robe and carrying a bath towel over her arm, she went into the bathroom and ran a tub of water. Then she stood before the bathroom mirror examining her teeth, freckles, her red Afro hair. She remembered how during her time with Dunreith she had yearned for a pretty face. Now she didn't care; she was satisfied with her face, and with her looks generally. The only thing she craved now was a period of calm, a letdown free of crisis, when her pulse did not race, nor head throb from some new hurt. She took off her robe and got in the tub and, yawning from fatigue, relaxed in the soft, tepid water. For half an hour she lay in a conscious, straining effort to draw a curtain across her mind. Yet, though weak from illness, exhausted by housework, she could not curb her rampant thoughts—myriad images, impressions, flashbacks, afterthoughts, surmises, crowded in on her brain. True, her renunciation of the past was complete; yet daily, as now, she went on seeing Dunreith's scampish, scowling face. It was a curse, yes, still a tender memoir. They had been each other's confessor, exchanging curious hopes, bafflements, giddy yearnings and defeats. Addie remembered the afternoon when, caught up in carnal love and tearful frenzy, they had vowed a suicide pact. But three days later Dunreith laughed it off, calling them both "simple-ass squares." He was cruel and rotten, yet she pitied him. Still she would always wonder at his swift decision concerning her. So he had wanted to quit; that's what he said—had too many "chicks" already, couldn't afford them all. Well, he must also have had a heart of cement, after what they'd been to each other. It was so sudden, without warning—the day before their trip with Rosie out to Monday Williams' farm. They were alone, driving in the old Dodge out 55th Street, when he pulled to the curb and told her. Strangely, he would not look at her; yet, telling her, he became callous, crude—even laughed once. She had wanted to die, and the next day at Monday Williams' farm had tried.

But no more—for despite everything, there was now new hope; eventually the break-off had had to come, and it was good; she was glad. It was a decision—maybe she had always known it—that somehow, sometime, had to be reached; yet *she* had expected to be the one to have to reach it; not Dunreith. Why, why, why?— *how?*—had ever her months of trial, ordeal, with Dunreith got started? And why had they finally ended like this? She knew it was too late now for her ever to know; her break with the total past, including Dunreith, was final—absolute.

But she also knew her time with Dunreith had made her worldly-wise as well as worldly. She thought this good. Raw, gawky girlhood—its sad horrors—were forever over. So til her grandmother got well she, Addie, would be mistress of the house. This was no mere girl's job, but one for a woman, and she knew Dunreith had made her that—a woman. Yet it all had one aim only—her grandmother's recovery. Everything depended on that; for there must be a home for Lester and certainly provision for his education. As for herself, after high school she would go to work. This was not necessarily disappointing to her—especially if the family could be restored. She would be content, perhaps even happy.

And too there was the chance that someday she might marry; strange, she had never once daydreamed of herself as married—not even during the hectic months with Dunreith. Yet it was possible that later on she might meet a boy who could like her, want to marry her—she remembered how Clotilda used to laugh and tell Letitia there was somebody for everybody. What kind would he be?

she wondered. She didn't know; she didn't care: only she prayed he'd be nice to her; that was all—enough. And there might be children—there *would* be children. If only he was nice to her, she didn't care how many, but she did want a little girl—maybe one with chubby legs, who resembled a big-eyed, pretty, black doll.

Then almost at once Addie thought of her own mother. Through the sad grey dusks of memory she could see their home—the small, bright rooms, the modern furniture, the frou-frou lamps. And her father . . . ah, he too seemed dead—for she rarely thought of him, couldn't bring herself to feel he really lived, then or now. Clotilda, a few years ago, had mentioned him once, wondering, asking if they shouldn't try to be Christians and pray for him, write to him, maybe; Clotilda had said a person, a child, shouldn't begin life with such bitter, awful feelings toward another; it was not healthy, she said—especially toward a father, no matter what he had done. Addie's shock, her instant tears and cries of rage, had stopped and frightened Clotilda—who never broached the subject again. Since then, for Addie, her father was dead and buried.

Also now she thought of the baby, of little Lester in his crib, frowning and pawing hungrily at his mother; even then he was big for his age, with a large, bobbing head and a strong pair of lungs. Through the haze of time her life with that family seemed so long ago. Still her mother loomed always in the present. Was there ever, anywhere, another woman like her mother? There couldn't have been. Did any other such woman have to suffer what her mother had? Or come to such an end? It could not be. Addie's eyes began to sting, her throat to swell. At last she tried to shut her mother's image from her mind by concentrating on her present home, on Lester—on Clotilda.

She finished her bath, got into her robe, and left the bathroom. Entering the bedroom she saw on the dresser, where she had left them, the dozen red apples in the plastic bag. The room was cool and pleasant, the bed neatly made. She put on the under-clothes she had laid out, kicked off her mules and lay wearily on her back across the bed. Staring at the ceiling, she thought briefly of dinner and of how hungry Lester would be, but fixing meat balls and spaghetti was easy, so she needn't start till five; there was time for a rest and maybe too a nap. She closed her eyes.

Still, her crowded thoughts jostled each other. She was thinking of her grandmother—sometimes not without a tinge of remorse. Should she have done it? . . . made her remember Pearlie's death? She wasn't entirely sure now she had done the right thing. It had been so cruel. Yet maybe the shock of realization would somehow help her grandmother, make her more willing to face reality. Who knew?—it could be a turning point toward better days. Addie, however, still felt a great sorrow for her grandmother. Again she longed to return to the living room and try to talk to her, console, comfort her. Maybe, though, she should wait an hour or so, give her grandmother time to calm down some, to recover, to adjust to the harsh, brutal truth. Still somehow Addie's feeling of remorse lingered, would not entirely disappear.

Yet shortly her mind, numbed by entanglements, drowsy from fatigue, began to decelerate, drift away; only faintly now did she hear the cries of children playing in the street, or the neighbors' puppy yelping; she lay listless, attention slackening, losing hold, not half hearing; they were the sounds of the city streets; she had heard them all her life and found them not unpleasant; then there was added the revving noise of buses two blocks off, and overhead the drone of a plane headed out to O'Hare; but at last in her weary brain all these sensations began to merge and commingle until but one fading, distant, jumble remained; then soon came cool . . . . unhurried . . . sleep.

All the house was quiet now, upstairs and down. The westering sun had left the living room in quiet shade, the sunroom plants a darker green and spiritless. Clotilda, her hands limp in her lap, now sat far back in the shadows, near the piano—remote from the front window. The incoherent wildness of grief in her eyes had gone and her pulse had slowed; she was lethargic, stuporous; her eyes, moving along the wallpaper, were obtuse and dull; she had sat like a stone for an hour; only once she mumbled something inaudible, forming spittle on her lips but making no other sound.

Then at last she stirred; she stared around her; now slowly, laboriously, she got to her feet. She stood in the middle of the floor, hands clasped behind her back, dark dropsied legs apart, and yawned like a hippopotamus, then sucked air through her teeth, making a hissing sound, as she gazed around the room as if uncertain where she was. Her arms were like hams—recent inactivity had sent her weight to two hundred pounds. Now in delicate disdain she raised her chin as if to sniff the air and, frowning absently, began to pace the floor. Finally she ranged from the living room and wandered toward the rear. Her steps were plodding, clumsy, lagging. She paused at the kitchen door—a fork in the road—then continued on past. She tarried at the bathroom door, but soon went on. The house was hushed.

The bedroom door was open. Addie lay across the bed in deep sleep, sprawled on her back in her robe. Clotilda, her face first curious, then impassive, stood at the door watching her. She entered the bedroom, went over and sat in the chair at the foot of the bed. Addie's young breasts rose and fell in quiet breathing as Clotilda sat, still curiously watching; at times her gaze strayed over the room as if studying it for the first time; there was the big old-fashioned bed, its pink spread under Addie, the lamp, the faded wallpaper with its moon-in-scimitar design, and over the bed the Kansas wheat field picture that had come as a gift with the grand piano.

Clotilda, now a stranger to all these objects, soon resumed her curious watch on Addie. Once she stood up and gazed at Addie over the foot of the bed, then sat back down as her attention wandered. Soon bored, she turned around to examine the half of the room behind her. She saw her four pairs of shoes neatly lined up along the closet wall; next, her dry-cleaned dresses hanging ready in their white paper bags. Only then was she aware of the futile suitcase beside her at the foot of the bed. She stiffened—and stared down at it, then suddenly lifted her eyes and glared at Addie. Finally, grudgingly, taking her eyes away, she turned around again to look behind her—and on the dresser saw the red apples in the clear plastic bag.

Her lips parted in wonder. She turned and faced the bed again, studying Addie anew, but soon twisted around once more, viewing the apples that now held her awed, magnetized. In her contorted posture her left houseshoe came off and lay on its side near the foot of the bed. She tried to get up, but the chair tilted, leaving her still to gape at the dresser over her shoulder. Soon her gaze slowly swept the room as if to verify her whereabouts; her nostrils flared with an occult hate. She seemed reluctant now to look at Addie. But after a moment she leaned forward in her chair over the foot of the bed and glowered at her, then turned again and viewed the dresser. Yet soon her face began to lose its anger, assuming again a more passive mien. Without floundering or faltering she got up and approached the dresser. Careful, quiet, she pulled open the top dresser drawer containing many of her laundered things; next she took the apples off the dresser and one by one silently slid them out of the plastic bag into the open drawer. Then she turned and stood with the empty bag in her hand. Addie slept.

Now Clotilda began to quake and tremble. Wavering and casting about her she saw her lost houseshoe, stepped over and stuck her foot in it. Still she trembled. But soon she ventured another glance at the bed; gradually her eyes thinned to malevolent slits. She went around to the head of the bed and stood over Addie. For a moment the malignity in her features gave way to maternal wonderment. Then, as if remembering, she brought up the plastic bag and thrust in an opening fist, as a manic anguish came in her face. She grasped the open mouth of the bag with both hands, leaned far forward, and held it out over Addie's head and paused, then with a stifled grunt lunged forward and captured Addie's head in the bag, and, twisting a massive wrist, wrenched the bag shut.

Addie gave a tiny, slumberous shriek in the bag and pitched

over on her side, then violently onto her back again. Clotilda, using her elbows, scooted forward and pinned Addie's shoulders down; the collar of the bag, wrenched airtight in one huge fist, cut into the flesh of Addie's neck as she fought suffocation and the sudden, unknown weight athwart her. Then through the clear bag she saw and recognized Clotilda; her eyes flew back in her head; she tried to speak, cry, plead, scream, but the bag held all sounds. As Clotilda's huge fist wrung tighter and tighter, Addie's face began to distend, engorge; she threw her arms wide, gasping, laboring for air, as the bag collapsed . . . billowed . . . collapsed . . . billowed. Then suddenly she began to fight. She flailed at Clotilda with arms and elbows, screeching, moaning, muffled exhortations. Clotilda, grinding teeth, jerked her up by the bag now and gave her a vicious shaking, then, still twisting the bag tighter, threw her back onto the bed and clambered on top of her; now crazed, animalistic, she tried to sever the head by a savage wringing of the bag. Addie's eyes bulged like a frog's; her swollen freckled face was first crimson, then crimson-black; she writhed, lurched, and fought, but finally her struggles began to lessen; there came a debility in her waving arms and soon a lazy lassitude; at last the bag violently collapsed, now billowed to almost bursting, then slowly, feebly, collapsed again. Addie lay still. Yet for a moment her muscles twitched, quivered. Heavy Clotilda, panting and sweating atop her like a rapist, gave the bag one final, vicious wrench. But there was no reaction. Addie was quiet. The plastic bag, a shriveled mask for the face, was quiet too, as the happy cries of children in the street came in through the bedroom windows.

At five o'clock Lester came home. Addie's body still lay on the bed. Clotilda sat in the chair at the foot of the bed. Her hands were folded in her lap, her face serene. "Lester," she said, "look at Addie . . . what's wrong with Addie?"

Two months later—early November.

The second-hand, but shining Chevrolet was returning to Chicago in a drab, chill rain. Mrs. Letitia Hammer craned her long, thin body forward over the steering wheel and drove with a beginner's determination. Hammer, his long legs cramped, rode beside her. Lester, alone in the back, stared disconsolately out the side of the car through the wet, foggy glass. All afternoon it had rained, and the gossipy receptionist at Elgin State Hospital had told them, as they sat waiting, that "long rainy spells" made the mental patients more restless.

The three in the car traveled in silence. On both sides of the highway the scraggly trees, bushes, and grass were yellowish-brown and wet; and the solid buildings—some frame, some brick—seemed provincial, archaic, under the heavy skies. Hammer had not spoken since they left the hospital. The meager talk came from Letitia. Despite the dreary greyness of the day, the small stone in her wedding ring glinted atop the steering wheel, as she would first look carefully at the road, then glance at the ring.

Lester, his face thoughtful, still gazed out the side window of the car. "Grammaw looks thin," he said.

Letitia sighed. "Yes, Lester—she does."

"She didn't know us," Lester said.

"Yes, it's so sad," Letitia winced. "We were like total strangers to her."

Lester was silent.

Hammer stared ahead through the windshield.

Letitia glanced at him, then crinkled up her pale, long face. "Ambrose, *please* let's not work this evening!—let's take the evening off. After today I just don't feel up to it. Besides, if we're going to pay *them* to publish the book, we oughtn't to have to worry so much about their deadline."

Hammer did not turn his head. "You don't have to work," he said gently.

"I mean you, too—if you work, so will I."

"Okay," Hammer droned, "we won't work."

"Grammaw looks thin," Lester said again. "She don't look like she gets any sleep."

Letitia slowed the car and carefully took a curve; then smiled. "Well, she's got a bed, Lester—that is, a nice cot."

"She's by herself, though," Lester said. "—they got her locked up—by herself."

Letitia sighed again. "Yes—they had to do that, Lester."

Lester flounced and twisted, wild anguish in his face. "She didn't know me," he said, appealing to the back of Letitia's head.

"No, honey—but you must be a young man, now . . . and try to make yourself get used to that. You can, if you try. And you *must try* . . . you just can't be forever moping in my house. You'll be our son, Lester. We want you to be happy. . . . We do, Lester . . . really happy."

Hammer sighed. He would not look at his wife.

Lester stared out and said nothing.

Letitia gave a strange, farcical smile. "You're going to have the nicest room you ever saw, when we move. Oh, you should see the hardwood floors—they're beautiful. You'll have a nice three-quarter bed and a rug and a desk to study at. The place is so light and cheerful. You can fix your room up just like you want it, if you're a nice, obedient boy—and don't mope. Mr. Neeley's room is nice too. I've already showed it to him, and is he tickled."

"No use in me goin' to see Grammaw if she don't know me," Lester said.

"Oh, Lester," Letitia cried. "What did I just *tell* you?"

"—I'll go anyhow. I *will*, I *will*." Lester was frantic, belligerent.

They were coming into the city now. Hammer sat silent and gazed at the passing factories, warehouses, and railroad tracks. The rain had stopped, but as the murky evening settled and a few lights came on, the looming city took on for him an aspect of inscrutability. The city held closely its secrets, he thought, the fates of its dwellers, more closely than ever he had reckoned before. He had thought himself wise; now he felt ludicrous.

Letitia stopped the car for a red light, and, waiting, smiled at him. He did not look at her. She patted his hand, and he smiled faintly, but when once more the car pulled off, he withdrew into himself again.

After awhile, when they had reached the thoroughfares and boulevards, all the phosphorescent lights were on. "We're coming into the lights!" Letitia cried. "Look, Ambrose . . . Lester! The lights! Oh, how they shine . . . they really glare . . . in the puddles on the street. It's so weird!—I must be careful."

Yet the slow rain began again and they somehow felt alone, bewildered.

"I *will*," Lester, soon oblivious, repeated.

Letitia glanced at him in the mirror and frowned.

Hammer felt so desperate, absurd, he had the bitter urge to laugh. Now the riddle would never be solved.

"Oh, well . . . all right, then, Lester," said Letitia, relenting, and shook her head and took a deep breath.

"I *will*," Lester said once more. His angry, tear-smeared nose was flattened against his window as, almost as if to soothe him, the rain fell gently.